DRAGON'S BLOOD

Denicalis Dragon Chronicles – Book One

By
MJ ALLAIRE

Bookateer Publishing
www.bookateerpublishing.com

Layout and design by Ryan Twomey

ISBN: 978-0-9819368-3-3
Library of Congress Control Number: 2010935109

Dedication

I would like to thank just a few of the many people in my life that have supported me during my travels down this long, winding road:

My Florida Family — I love you more than anything! Thank you for always loving me.

My three children, Nick, Mic, and Toni — Without you, my life would be dull and lifeless, and where would I have gotten the characters from?

Baze — You've brought so many changes to my life. Thank you for having confidence in me always, through thick and thin, and for loving me for who I am, faults and all.

Kate — Thank you for planting the seed of confidence that got me started.

Jess — The little sister that I never had. Learn from my trials and tribulations.

Diamonds and her family — I couldn't choose a better best friend or second family for Toni.

Ryan — Thank you for being a tireless reader and for answering all of my many questions without hesitation, always.

Thank you all,

MJ Allaire

Dragon's Blood

ONE

Tonia was sometimes saddened by the idea that she did not have a real sister. At other times, however, she did enjoy the quiet peace she had by herself, walking in the woods on a warm summer day. Those times she could be seen catching firebugs and telling them her secrets, then letting them fly off to ponder her dreams. In fact, she would sneak away to the overgrown trees, trickling streams, and colorful shrubbery, any chance she could get. She loved walking through the forest as she searched for some new, interesting creature she could find, large or small, fuzzy or smooth. Often she would pretend she lived long ago, when powerful wizards and mighty dragons were said to have ruled their world.

She grew up in the small village of Uncava, located on the edge of where the land meets the sea, and where the spring rain was quite a common occurrence. The frequent rains brought by the spring season led to the lush, green countryside of summer, and everyone in the tiny village knew of their importance. After the cold, hard winter months subsided, the rains brought new life to both plants and animals. Many of the villagers said major storms were very rare in the spring, and Tonia believed this since she had not seen one in her lifetime.

While growing up, she spent most of her time in the nearby forest and valley foraging for bugs and creatures. As she wandered, exploring new paths, turning over rocks, and poking the most tempting of holes in moss-covered stumps with any odd stick she picked up along the way, her mind would drift back to

1

dreams of earlier times.

In one of her most frequent and favorite fantasies, she found herself walking alone through the deep forest looking for chickleberries or tarza vines. Instinctively, she would slow as she approached the corner of a large mound of dirt just slightly taller than she. She would then peer around the mass of interwoven vines and long dead leaves as stealthily as a cellar cat hunting the pesky moles that would sneak in at night and devour the roots and seed stores collected from harvest time. All of a sudden her surprised heart would stop, and a huge smile would light her face. Frozen by awe, her pulse would quicken when she realized just what she was looking at – a mighty dragon, previously hidden by the hill as it lay lazily basking in the warmth of the sunshine!

A large, green and brown beast with strong muscular legs, the dragon would have wide, protective scales covering its entire body. Sleeping in the bright valley sun, she would hear it breathing, almost snoring, while it rested peacefully. She would imagine what was hidden behind those closed eyelids... two huge, glowing orbs!

Suddenly, the dragon would shift in its sleep, and as it did, large, yellowed teeth would glisten in the morning sun. Tonia's approach would be as silent as the wind, and she would watch as the dragon continued sunning itself as it slept, oblivious to her scent. In her mind's eye she could see the enormous feet that held the weight of its muscular body. Razor-sharp claws resting at the edge of those feet could easily slice through a large stone in the flash of a firebug! Wings would be tucked tightly against its shimmering body, but she knew in an instant it could thrust them open and take off into the air as effortlessly as a bird. Its long tail would stretch endlessly, down the lizards back to the far side of the valley, or so it would seem. Cautiously the child would watch the dragon as she tried to determine if it was good or evil.

"If the old ones could do it, then why shouldn't I be able to?" Tonia would ask herself as she thought of the stories she'd heard as a young girl.

In her fantasy, she would remain close to the hill as she closed her eyes in deep concentration. She tried to use her mind to see if she could sense what type of dragon she had discovered. At first she would sense nothing, only darkness, then out of nowhere it would feel as if a door head opened and brilliant light instantly filled her brain. She would reel back a bit, as if being blown by a gust of air, then immediately realize that she could sense the dragon in her mind, knowing in an instant that it sensed her as well. They would communicate through their thoughts, both curious to learn more about each other and their kind.

This particular dragon would be a good dragon, and female, of course, because females are generally much easier to communicate with than males (so her mother tells her). Her mother would explain further by saying that the male of the species was raised to be tough and strong, and a little stubborn, and the female of the species was raised to be soft, smart, and much better at good conversation.

After a moment, she would step out from her hiding place from behind hill and approach the dragon. It would all be wonderful, and soon they would be the best of friends!

At the village gatherings, she and her two brothers had often heard stories about dragons which they never tired of hearing. Other stories described how some of the ancient ones were able to communicate with the dragons through their thoughts. They had heard many, many stories of both good and evil dragons at these gatherings. Unfortunately, it had been generations since anyone in or around the village had last seen a dragon.

The ancient ones would talk of the days long, long ago when the flying beasts were plentiful, and how one would have to take great care when hunting and traveling through the Hampa Mountains. Although many of these dragons were massive in size, the elders described how they could fly through the air as effortlessly as a leaf falling from a giant oak tree before the winter snows, cascading downward on a warm fall breeze. The dragons were also omnivores, enjoying both the fresh fruit of the forest as well as the fresh meat of the forest animals, so all of the village hunters traveled with care.

One summer evening around the village campfire a few years ago, one of the ancient ones told a story that had been repeated from generation to generation. It was a tale of a long ago villager who had witnessed a dragon as it first surprised and then killed a young mountain bear. Tonia remembered this story well because it was one of her favorite tales.

The setting for the tale was the middle of the afternoon, late in the fall, where soon the nuts and berries of the forest would be gone. Enjoying one of the few remaining warm days, a lone villager was out walking through the forest near the valley when he spotted movement – a young mountain bear on the far side of the valley. It was wandering along the edge of the forest and had easily caught the scent of the fruit that had recently fallen from a nearby pia tree. The man watched as the curious bear left the shelter of the forest and headed swiftly toward the lone pia tree. The hungry omnivore was obviously out looking for a late afternoon snack.

Pia fruit are a fairly large, circular fruit, orange in color with purple splotches mottling its thick shell. This outer shell is very hard, but inside lay the juicy, white, hidden meat of the fruit. Hidden at the core of this white meat was a large pia seed. The pia trees, which grew these fruit, were enormous and could usually be found deep within the Hampa Mountains. It was rare to find one at the edge of the forest, and far more unusual to see one in the valley below the mountains. Villagers frequently dried out the seeds that grew inside these fruit then use them to store things like dried berries, nuts, and occasionally water. Forest creatures also enjoyed this moist delicacy, and to the mountain bears they were an absolute favorite.

This particular bear easily found the fallen pia at the base of the tree. Soon it was sitting up on its back end, savoring every bite of the delectable fruit, fully engrossed in its feast, while in the distance, a pair of large, dark eyes watched.

Dragons have superb eyesight, allowing them to see incredibly far, farther than any person or other forest creature could even wish to see.

Unfortunately, the bear's hunger was stronger than its instinct, and the poor thing was not as cautious as it should have been. It never noticed the dragon that was perched on top of a nearby mountain, waiting, listening, and watching hungrily for its next meal. In one quick motion, the dragon was up in the air and sailing silently down towards the bear, unseen just above the jagged tops of the forest trees that protruded angrily into the afternoon sky. As the bear finished one piece of fruit and began reaching for the next, it turned its head slightly as it noticed a hint of movement from the corner of its eye. No sooner had the bear caught a glimpse of the dragon's approach, the dragon was on it, sweeping it off the ground.

The bear cried out in excruciating pain as the strong jaws of the attacking beast clamped tightly around its brown body. In one rapid bite, those powerful jaws snapped together and broke the bear's back. The dragon did this in mid-flight, never once touching the ground. It then carried the bear over the top of the mountain and out of the man's view to dine on its own afternoon snack in peace.

Tonia loved the dragon stories most of all. Ever since she heard her first story while sitting around the village campfire as a tiny girl, she had longed to see one of these ancient, enormous beasts. She often dreamed of watching them fly gracefully through the skies, leaving shadows across the valley floor as they meandered beneath the afternoon sunshine.

She frowned, remembering how the ancient ones had warned that the dragons might be gone forever, but she refused to believe this! Instead she believed wholeheartedly that there were still real dragons… somewhere. The land was wide, with forests and mountains stretching as far as the eye could see! There were many places dragons could hide and if she explored enough nooks and crannies, perhaps someday she would find one!

Two

Diam and Tonia had been best friends for as long as they could remember. At least ever since Diam's family moved to Toni's village when the girls were very young. Diam was a year older than Tonia, but the only way to tell was that Diam was the taller of the two. Tonia would sometimes go to Diam's house to play for an afternoon, often staying over through the moonlight until the sun had traveled far across the sky the following day. To Tonia, Diam was the sister she never had, but Diam was not an only child. She had a much younger brother named Jole. Jole was two and followed Tonia and Diam around like a forest mud puppy every chance he got.

Mud puppies were forest creatures that some villagers brought into their homes to be family pets. They were similar to wolves, but smaller, and were known for their springtime frolicking in the mud, hence their name. They could be found here and there throughout the countryside and made wonderful pets because they had such good temperaments and were very patient with children.

Jole loved playing with Tonia, and although his antics were tiring, they were also usually quite entertaining. Oh, how he could make them laugh, laugh, laugh! He loved pretending to be a dragon, running through the yard "attacking" the girls. He had endless amounts of energy, and more often then not, the girls would tire before he did.

Diam and Tonia were constantly venturing into the nearby woods or through the valley. While they explored, they searched

6

for magical creatures, berries to eat, and things to do. Every chance they got, they would sneak off by themselves, leaving Jole behind. It wasn't that they didn't enjoy his company, but how much serious exploring could they do with a two-year-old on their heels? As it turned out, the only time they ever had to themselves was generally when he was napping.

One warm morning in the early spring after Diam had spent the previous day and night with her good friend, the girls were outside picking vegetables. They chatted as they wandered through the garden, catching up after Diam's recent visit to her grandmother's house in Wead, a village about half a days walk to the northeast. Once they finished gathering enough ripe vegetables, they brought them into the house to Tonia's mother, Jeane.

"Thank you, girls," Jeane said with a smile. "Now, would you mind doing me another favor?"

She added the last question knowing they probably wouldn't mind, in fact, they tended to be more than willing to help when there was an adventure to be had. Tonia was a good girl, always anxious to help anyone in need. Many people in the village loved her for this very reason.

"Sure," Tonia answered without looking at her friend. Diam nodded, always curious to know what new adventure awaited them.

"What can we do?" the older of the two girls asked.

"Well, I want to make something special with chickleberries for dessert tomorrow. Could you take a bag out into the forest and try to find me some?"

Jeane struggled to hide a smile when she saw their faces light up at the sound of "dessert" and "forest." She knew the girls loved her desserts, but she also knew they thoroughly enjoyed exploring the woods and valleys around Uncava. Most of the time, they were inseparable. Searching for berries would just give them another excuse to be together, doing something they loved.

Exploring!

Sometimes chickleberries could be difficult to find, but she asked them to try their best to fill the whole bag full of the succulent, sweet fruit. She cautioned them that several forest creatures also liked the berries, and warned they may have to go quite far into the forest to find them.

"Please, be careful."

"This sounds like fun," Diam said as she nudged Tonia's arm. "Come on, let's go get a bag and do it now. It could take all day for us to find what we need and we'll need to be back before dark."

Before they could leave, each of the girls diligently packed a bag with specific supplies for their excursion, which they would sling across their backs as they hiked. In each bag they would have at least one pia shell filled with water, some fruits and nuts, a torch, some rock sparkers, and a change of clothes. Rock sparkers were a special kind of rock and if you knew how to use them, you could start a fire quite easily. They also packed a pair of pants and a warm shirt, knowing when the sun fell behind the mountain, it could get rather chilly. Even during this time of year, depending on how dense the trees were, the forest itself could bring on its own chill, and in some places, the sun didn't shine through at all because the overhead branches were so thick. These areas could be as dark as they were cold.

Although they weren't planning on being out after dark, a recent near tragedy occurred which prompted proper preparations for daylong excursions into the forest.

On a beautiful spring morning a few years back, two children from Uncava, Jera and Cayce, ventured into the forest. They were completely unprepared and, ironically, were out in search of the same forest fruit, for almost the same reason. Everyone knew how much work it took to find the special berries, but nobody ever said it wasn't worth it. Everyone agreed that one taste of chickleberry porridge, chickleberry syrup, chickleberry pudding, or just about anything with chickleberries, was worth all the wandering through the forest it took to find them.

On that beautiful spring day not so long ago, the pair of youngsters traveled deep into the forest before losing their way. Although they thought they knew where they were, the path they had been traveling on seemed to simply disappear into the leaf litter. They spent the whole afternoon wandering around, desperately trying to find their way back to the village. Even though they were lost, the children managed to pick whatever berries and fruit they found along the way. This was a good thing, since by late afternoon they had still been unsuccessful at finding their way back to the path that would return them to Uncava.

Jera and Cayce ended up spending the night in the forest. They were cold, scared, and eventually found shelter beneath some brush they found in a secluded grove at the base of a small hill. Neither said anything, but they were both very frightened they might become the next meal for hungry mountain bears or growlie cats. The night grew colder as the dampness that accompanied the darkness settled into the forest as the moon slowly began its nightly journey across the deep blue sky. As the evening wore on, the slight fullness the children felt from the meager meal they had eaten earlier that afternoon wore off, leaving them both uncomfortably cold and hungry. For all the chickleberries they collected, they could not fill their bellies. Chickleberries were tasty, sweet, and delightful, but they would not keep a belly filled – just a mouth happy.

Since they had not planned on losing their sense of direction, the children didn't bring any other food or water with them and had no way to make a fire to keep warm. Neither had ever spent the night in the forest without an adult around. The night wore on and they huddled together in fear, neither of them sleeping a wink all night.

The next morning, men from the village flooded the forest in search of the children, calling out their names as they looked behind trees and within bushes. By early afternoon, the search party had found them – dirty, frightened, and very hungry, but safe and free from injury. Happily, they returned the weary children to the village for a warm bath and a generous meal.

As a result of this near tragedy, it was now mandatory that every villager venturing into the forest for more than an hour or two carry a bag containing the necessary emergency supplies with them.

"Just in case of trouble," the old ones would tell the children. "You never know what adventures lie in the forest!"

For Tonia and Diam, it was the adventure of simply being in the forest that excited them the most. It was comfortably warm outside on this day, which was about average for this time of year, and the girls were excited to be together. By the time they had properly prepared themselves for their berry hunt, the sun was shining brightly overhead and had recently cleared the tops of the surrounding forest. The dew covering the trees sparkled like miniature candles, glistening beautifully in the mid-morning sunlight.

Tonia took in a deep breath and smiled – she loved this time of year! There was something special about the arrival of spring. She appreciated it even more than when the warm winds of summer finally blew in, carrying the pollen from the valley flowers all the way to the river, like little fairies on their way to get a drink. In spring, the fresh rains would fall, washing away the final remnants of the previous cold and dreary winter. Soon after those rains, new life began to emerge in the surrounding woods as vibrant combinations of reds, greens, and yellows, sprouted up out of the browns of the slumbering valley. It truly was a beautiful time of year.

As they walked, the girls commented on the beautiful day, how good it was to be together again, and the recent trip that Diam had taken to her grandmother's.

"So, did you have a good time visiting your nana?" Tonia asked as she kicked a stone into a ragged cluster of thin, green grass.

"Sure did, but I missed you so much! I wish you could have come with me," Diam replied as she exhaled a partial sigh. "I love my brother, but sometimes his energy is just too much! Besides, you're like my sister and it's just not the same when you're not there with me."

"Yeah, I missed you, too… a lot!" Tonia's reply was like a kitten's cry for milk, starting out as a low murmur, but ending in a lion's roar. "I had to help Mom and the boys with a lot of the spring chores, but I sure wish that I could have gone with you. I love going to your nana's house! Besides, while you were gone, Micah drove me crazy! Do you know what he did?"

Diam shook her head no, knowing that there was no telling what kind of new antics Tonia's younger brother might have been involved in.

"He took Bandy, my new pet frog, out of his cage, claiming that he had gotten out by himself and was lost in the house somewhere. After searching through every room and under every rock, I was frantic and almost in tears! When he finally realized how upset I was, Micah called me into his room. He reached deep into the center of a large pia seed, where he usually puts his dirty clothes, and pulled out a much smaller pia seed. This one was cut in half then wrapped together again with a tarza vine. He opened the smaller pia seed and guess what? There was Bandy! I thought Mom was going to seriously hurt him when she found out."

Tonia's voice rose and fell as she explained the recent stressful event to her friend. Diam nodded as she recognized the irritation in Tonia's voice. She was obviously just as exasperated now as when it all happened.

"Aw, poor froggy!" the older girl said, reiterating her sympathy with a crinkle of her nose. "So, Micah was the one who took Bandy out of his cage and hid him from you?" When Tonia nodded her head, Diam added, "Well, that wasn't very nice!"

"Yeah, he did," Tonia, still excited, said with a frown. "Once I realized what he had done, it didn't really surprise me. Micah's just like that, you know? But I still thought I would just have to hurt him myself… after waiting in line behind Nicho and Mom, of course!"

As she said this, a mischievous smile tugged at the corners of her mouth.

The girls nodded, laughed and strolled lazily along the path in the forest, scouting the nearby shrubs for chickleberries. So far they hadn't found any. As they walked deeper into the woods, they continued to talk, still catching up on their time apart.

"So how is Jole doing?" Tonia asked.

"He's fine," Diam quipped sarcastically. "While we were at Nana's house, he was chasing one of their mud puppies and tripped over a stone in the yard. When he fell, he landed on a branch and got scratched up, but not too bad."

"Oh, man! I bet he cried!" Tonia said, half feeling sorry for him, half laughing at the fact that she could just picture how he had gotten himself into the situation in the first place.

"Well, he started getting teary-eyed, but just then the mud

11

puppy ran back over to him and started licking his face. Jole started laughing, and pretty soon he was back up and chasing it again like he had never fallen at all!" Diam smiled as she described her little brother's antics.

After nearly an hour of chitchat, the girls discovered they had ventured deep into the woods and arrived in a place they had rarely traveled to before. It was here where they finally came across their first signs of chickleberries. Although the fruit could be difficult to find, one could always tell when they were getting close to the berry bushes because some animals often left behind evidence on the ground – like little tufts of leaves and big red splotches of chickleberry juice.

They continued on and soon found themselves approaching the bottom of a hill. When they got there they stopped and looked around for a moment then quickly agreed it was time for a break. The walk had been long, and although to their minds it seemed like just minutes, their legs told them differently.

They slowed their pace and noticed a wide fallen tree next to a large mound of rocks and boulders, which jutted precariously from the side of the mountain. As they got closer, they could see the pinks and yellows of a large, flowery bush next to the rocky mound that had previously been hidden by the fallen plant life. The ancient, fallen giant had previously been one part of the forest that could be seen all the way from Uncava, rising above all the other trees and poking into the sky. Judging by its condition, the pair of friends guessed it had been lying on the leaf littered ground for quite some time. Thick clumps of gray moss grew in patches over the top of its trunk, and wiry vines intertwined lazily through some of its branches. A few smaller trees had sprouted up through the leaf litter here and there around the tree. The branches of the old giant were completely leafless, many of them decomposing on the forest floor around it. These were obvious signs that it had been there quite a while.

Although the tree was resting in a jagged, lifeless line across the edge of the forest floor, some of the branches were still extending upwards as if grasping for a second chance at life. In some of these extensions, near the top area of the oak, the girls could see a multitude of spider webs. Some had remnants of long dead meals while others appeared to be fresh and newly woven. One of the webs, high above their heads in the topmost branch, was covered with old cocoons, bug skeletons, and leaves from the trees which reached higher still. The spiders in these webs had been very busy, indeed.

The girls decided to rest and spotted a rock near the base of the fallen oak at almost the same time. This large, dark, stone was at the end of the tree farthest from the spider webs, which was just how Tonia liked it. She loved most forest creatures and bugs, but spiders were a serious exception. She just couldn't bring herself to get near enough to one to really look at them closely, much less to hold one.

She glanced back at the cluster of linked gossamer strands, stared at them for a few seconds, then carefully examined the base of the tree with a shiver. It was obvious she was nervous.

"Oh Diam, you know how I hate spiders!"

"Why, though? You like every other creature and bug you've ever laid your eyes on. What makes spiders so different?" her friend asked with a scowl of confusion.

"I think it's because when I was little, I was sleeping in my bed and one crawled up my arm. It didn't hurt me but it scared me so much that I had nightmares for a long time afterward."

As Tonia said this, her cheeks flushed the color of a pink rose as the memory of the tiny, harmless arachnid crawling up her arm came back like it had just happened. She shivered again as she looked up at Diam with embarrassment.

"I just don't like them."

The girls sat down on the rock and shrugged their bags off their backs. They enjoyed the warm sunshine for a few minutes then began groping inside their bags, mutually mindless of how carefully they had organized them that morning. They had thought it wise to put the food beneath the extra clothing so it would be protected, but now it seemed as if it was only being protected from their grasping hands. Finally, they each withdrew a snack, and Tonia immediately buried her hand back into the shadows of her bag as she searched for her pia shell filled with water. Soon they were sitting side by side, backs against the warm hillside, sharing their meal and enjoying the cool breeze blowing through the trees. It was as if the wind followed the base of the mountain all the way from the valley, just to find its way to them. After a few moments of uneventful silence, Tonia stood up to take a look around.

She first noticed it when they had been walking toward the fallen oak, but now she took a closer look at the beautiful bush on the right side of the rocky mound. It was covered with small, green leaves and bright yellow and pink flowers that had a strong, sweet smell, almost like honey. The bush itself was enormous! Tonia's mischievous smile returned as she realized that both of them could climb into the middle of it, be at least an arm's length apart from each other, and remain totally unseen from the outside of the bush. Turning her attention to the trees above, she immediately saw a break in the branches where the sun shone down brightly on the bush for a period of time every day. It was no wonder why there were so many flowers crawling across the leaves!

Turning her attention back to the rocky mound, something odd caught her eye, but she couldn't quite make out what it was.

"Doesn't this look strange?" she asked Diam as she pointed at a moss covered area on the nearby hill.

"Sure it does, if you say so," the older girl answered wryly, "although I'm not an expert on rocky mounds." Tonia always knew when her friend was joking and this time was no exception.

"Ha, ha," she returned as she crinkled her nose in defiance. "I think it just looks funny, that's all."

As she stared at the mound near the backside of the tree, her eyes detected a small crevice between the trunk and the mound, which began about two feet off the ground and crawled upward. The rocky mound itself had some brush and moss covering parts of it, especially over the edge of the rocks, near the trunk. Ever curious, Tonia moved the brush aside near the mysterious crevice and found herself quite surprised by her find.

"Diam, look at this!" she exclaimed.

THREE

Diam slid off the rock where she had been resting and joined Tonia next to the wall. "What did you find, my friend, the spider lover?" She asked sarcastically.

"I think I found an entrance to a cave!" her friend replied as her voice quivered with rising excitement.

Together, they moved the brush aside and indeed discovered an entrance to a cave hidden behind years of overgrowth and fallen leaves. The girls immediately felt the unmistakably cooler air dancing on their skin and caressing their faces as it poured over them from deep inside the hole. The temperature between the two environments was quite different and made them both realize how much the air outside the cave had warmed up since they embarked on their berry hunt.

The entrance itself was small and oddly shaped. Rocks of various sizes surrounded the base of it, littering the ground between the fallen tree and the stone wall. This was the perfect place for small critters to make a home. It would also be ideal for slithery snakes to go looking for the inhabitants of such hiding places.

"I wonder how long it's been here."

Diam's thoughts reached her lips and her inquisitive nature came out in whispered words.

"And I wonder why we've never found it before!" Tonia replied. Her eyes were wide with wonder and curiosity but her thoughts were already moving on to bigger and braver ideas. She and Diam had been up in the forest many times, occasionally

15

playing with some of the other village children, but mostly just exploring together. They knew these woods like they knew each other, and a secret in the woods would be like a secret one would try to keep from the other. But they never had been able to keep secrets from each other, and probably never would.

"I've never really been to this part of the forest before," Diam noted. "I guess we should make exploring fallen trees near rocky mounds much more of a priority."

"True," Tonia replied. She peered into the darkness and added, "Well, you know what I want to make *my* new priority?"

As the words left her lips, the corners of her mouth began inching upwards. When she smiled this smile, anyone could tell she was up to something. She grabbed her bag off the trunk of the tree and started digging inside it again. "I think we need to use one of our torches and check out this cave!"

"Are you crazy?" Diam's anxious retort was echoed by the surprise in her eyes. "I know you're a curious girl, and you love getting dirty and doing things that boys usually do, but isn't this a bit much?" Diam asked this half-knowing her concern would have little effect once Tonia put her mind to something. Her friend was just stubborn like that.

"Come on, chickleberry butt," Tonia teased. "Don't tell me you're scared of a little cool, dark cave!"

"Of course I'm scared," Diam answered defiantly. "I don't want my mom to find out I was eaten by a forest creature in a deep, dark, unknown cave just because you wanted to satisfy your curiosity." Diam's reply was defensive, almost pleading, although she knew she always enjoyed any adventures her friend convinced her to go on.

"You're not going to get eaten by a forest creature, silly," Tonia said bravely. "I'm here to protect you!" She smiled as Diam rolled her eyes. "Besides, we have torches, and from my years of experience, most creatures of the forest don't like fire."

She stared at Diam with a bright-eyed, adventurous look of total confidence.

"'Most don't like fire,' you say?" Diam questioned without hesitation. She paused as her brown eyes tried to penetrate the darkness just beyond the shadowy entrance. "Are you sure?"

Although she knew she was doing it, Diam found herself totally unable to hide the doubt in her voice.

"Of course I'm sure," Tonia confided with a smile. "Come on, let's get hot! Daylight's burning and so is my curiosity!"

Tonia was so excited at the prospect of exploring a new cave that she was practically jumping out of her skin with anticipation.

The friends worked together to wedge sticks they'd found on the ground nearby into the thickly packed dirt and surrounding rocks. After a few moments they had successfully secured the brush covering the opening with a line of tarza vines, which allowed a small amount of light to fall into the shallow entrance. Although it paved their way into the cave, the unblocked entrance didn't allow enough light in on what might lie ahead in the ominous shadows.

Next, they removed a pair of rock sparkers from Tonia's bag, which Diam then used to light one of the torches her friend anxiously held out for her. Diam had done this many times before, and it didn't take long for the torch to shine brightly with a crackling, orange flame of reassurance. Both girls felt the heat swirling around their faces, reminding them of the sun, which was no longer peeking through the canopy above.

Tonia thought it would be a good idea for them both to have a torch lit since they really didn't know what kind of mysterious cave dwelling creatures might be hiding inside the pool of blackness ahead. She quickly retrieved the other torch from her bag and they lit that one as well. Afterward, they pulled their bags back up onto their shoulders, ready to continue exploring.

Before entering the cave, Tonia scavenged around the area until she found a long stick lying close to the fallen oak. She couldn't see any spider webs inside the partially lit opening, but she definitely wanted to be prepared, just in case. With a stick in one hand and a torch in the other, she looked at her friend, nodded, and one at a time they climbed through the entrance.

"Okay, soooooo, how will we find our way back if we get lost while we're in here?" Diam asked her ever-so-daring friend.

They had stopped just inside the entrance, where the sunlight gave way to the torchlight, but neither was sufficient to truly see what they were doing. They could tell that the floor of the tunnel, at first scattered with small rocks and boulders and stuffed with fallen leaves, gave way to a mostly earthen floor, dusted with small pebbles. Although they couldn't see much beyond the entrance, there seemed to be some strange humming or buzzing noise coming from within. Tonia tried to look deeper into the cave from where she was kneeling on the ground as her hand dug into her bag, but it was no use. She couldn't see much, but the torches now emitted enough light to see her immediate surroundings fairly well, now that her eyes were better adjusted to the darkness. She extended her torch into the air in order to get a better view of things.

"Hmmm," thought Tonia as she waved her torch from side to side, creating an array of dancing shadows on the rocky walls within the cave. "Wait! I think I put the smaller bag I always carry around with me in my big sack. Let me look."

She was just about to hand Diam her torch to hold when suddenly, from the shadows over their heads, the girls heard a startling noise and an accompanying flutter of air. Birds, nesting in the rocks near the ceiling of the cave entrance took flight all at once, creating a small whirlwind in the small cavern. The winged creatures flew up to the upper area of the cave and exited through a small opening. It was one neither of the girls had noticed while exploring the outside of the cave.

Tonia, after getting over her initial surprise and fear, watched the flying shapes as they rose up in a spiral making their exodus. Having spent such a long time scanning the outer landscape, it occurred to her that she should have noticed something like a hole in the ground large enough for these birds to escape through. She made a mental note to see if she could find their escape route once they finished exploring the subterranean tunnel. It probably wasn't obvious, which would explain why she never realized the cave was here in the first place. She smiled to herself, slightly amused with the wanderings of her mind.

After settling down from the flurry of activity created by the frightened birds, Tonia propped her stick against the wall and down on her knees to resume her search in her bag. She handed Diam her torch then opened the bag in such a manner as to get the most of the light the torch provided. She shuffled, pulled, reached, and grasped, all with the most strenuous look on her face, crinkling her nose and closing one eye. Finally, with more of a sigh of relief than a stroke of genius, she proclaimed, "Aha! I found it!"

Diam said knowingly, "I've got a feeling I've figured out what you have in mind."

"Okay, smarty pants! Just what are you thinking I'm thinking?" teased Tonia with a smirk.

"Oh, that you are probably going to say we should fill the smaller bag with bread crumbs and leave a trail of them on the dirt floor as we walk deeper into the cave," Diam challenged. "This would be fine, of course, unless we happened to be followed by very hungry animals… like giant cave birds! Or how about bread crumb starved bats that end up eating our trail as they chase us, before wanting something more filling than crumbled bread to eat!" she continued.

Tonia couldn't help but chuckle at the dramatic expression and mannerisms her friend displayed in the torchlight.

"Well, if one of us would have thought to *bring* some bread crumbs, it would have been a splendid idea!" she said with enthusiasm. "But since no one thought of it – silly us – then I guess we have to go to plan B'"

"Oh, great," a flippant Diam replied. "I can't wait to hear plan B!"

"Remember that large, flowing bush I was enamored with right outside the entrance to the cave?" As Diam nodded, Tonia continued. "Well, I was thinking we could take this bag back out there and fill it with as many flowers as we can fit in it. Then we could drop a flower every few steps as we explore the tunnels without fear of the flowers being eaten by bread starved birds OR bats!"

Tonia was trying very hard to look seriously at her friend, but she was having a very difficult time of it. Holding back her oncoming laughter, she kept moving forward with her explanation of plan B. "I had also thought perhaps we could do the same thing with small rocks, but decided the flowers were probably better for two reasons.

"One, I definitely don't want to lug around a bag of rocks

19

through the cave, but if you're up to that kind of workout, then it just *might* be an option."

At this point, the smile was creeping across her face.

"Two, we could drop the rocks, but knowing our luck, they would blend in with all the other rocks on the cave floor. So leaving a trail of rocks might not be the greatest idea."

She stopped and looked at her friend, faking a frown at first, but it wasn't long at all before her face broke out with a giant grin. "I'm kind of siding with the flower idea," she finished.

"Good thinking," Diam agreed, again rolling her eyes. "My guess would be that less creatures eat rocks than flowers, though, so maybe you should empty your pack so we can load you up. I have a feeling that you should be in charge of the rocks, because it was your idea."

Both the girls laughed and retreated back through the cave entrance. Once there, they crouched beneath the flower-laden bush and began plucking as many of the multicolored confetti as they could possibly stuff in Tonia's smaller pack.

"This should be enough, and I must admit it's far lighter than a bag of rocks," Diam said giving both the girls a good laugh.

"Alrighty, then," Tonia said as she gave Diam a quick but loving hug. Her voice drooled with anticipation as it echoed back at her. With a decisive nod, she turned and prepared to crawl back through the cave entrance.

"Let's do this!"

FOUR

It was obvious that Tonia was thrilled about their find and couldn't wait to start exploring. Diam, who had been hesitant in the beginning, couldn't help but be more aroused about it now after watching Tonia's undeniable excitement.

Tonia took up the lead, her torch held out in front of her. While they were outside picking the flowers, Diam had found a large stick for herself and she carried it with her now as she followed her determined friend into the shadow-filled tunnel. The bag of flowers was slung diagonally over her shoulder and it rested slightly opened against her stomach. Every few feet or so, Diam would take one small flower from the bag and drop it behind her. She soon realized that dropping the flowers was actually a very good idea, because the deeper they went into the cave, the darker it seemed to get. Dropping the flowers every few feet provided them with a sense of security – the thought of getting lost never entered their minds.

After twenty steps or so, the path took a sudden turn to the left and they followed it. For now, they were following one main tunnel, adventurous blood coursing through their veins.

"This is a piece of cake," Diam thought out loud.

The air in the cave was cool and damp. There was a faint, far away, sound that could be dripping water, or something rocking back and forth, and they detected a slightly musky scent in the air. They weren't sure if this was from the cave being well hidden behind the fallen oak, making the interior air become stale, or if it was caused by something else.

"I'm surprised there aren't any spider webs across our path yet," Tonia commented to her friend with a brief shudder. "You'd think there would be an army of them in here, especially with all those webs clinging to the branches on the oak outside the entrance."

"Maybe, maybe not. There might not be any if something happened to pass through these tunnels recently."

Hearing Diam say this made the hair stand up on the back of Tonia's neck, but she remained silent and they continued on. Unable to bridle their curiosity, they made their way deeper and deeper into the cave. After a while they could feel an air of tension building and they were too busy watching where they were going to talk much. They also listened to an array of sounds – the noises all around them would have been hard to miss. The cave creaked, animals scurried in the distance, and there were other sounds – those they could not readily identify – many sounds added to the moment, which in turn added to the tension.

After about thirty minutes, they came to an area where the tunnel forked so they stopped to rest and consider which direction they should take. They pulled their bags off their backs, removed their pia shells and drank the water, which had been sloshing around in their packs as they walked.

"Well, captain," Diam whispered, "which way do you think we should go?"

"I don't know," Tonia whispered back. "Have you heard anything about what's on the other side of these mountains?"

Although her voice was light and friendly, Tonia's dark eyes were cautious as they surveyed the area around them. The torchlight only traveled so far into this unfamiliar, underground world, and from the corner of her eye she could see Diam shaking her head in response to her question. In all her life, everything she needed had been on their side of the mountains, so why would anyone ever go to the other side?

"No," Diam finally brought herself to say, not wanting to take her attention away from the darkness just beyond torch's reach. "I've listened to many of the villagers and ancient ones talk about dragons and mystical creatures around the campfires, but I've never heard mention of the other side of the mountains. I never really thought about it. What do you think is over there?"

"I don't know," Tonia answered. Much of the bravery once found in her voice subsided to a doubtful, nervous whisper. The girls sat in a hushed silence for a minute, each lost in their own thoughts.

"Listen!" Diam whispered. One of her arms shot out from her side like an attacking snake as she grabbed Tonia's hand.

"Huh?" Tonia's reply was short and to the point. She didn't want to speak; she didn't want to not speak. She wasn't even sure if she wanted to listen right now.

"Shhhhh! Do you hear that?" Diam asked. She squinted her eyes as she attempted to peer through the darkness of one of the adjacent tunnels. The girls listened intently and Tonia could barely hear the sound of trickling water in the distance, coming from somewhere down the path to the right.

"There's water in that direction," she whispered as she pointed to the right fork.

"Water?" Diam replied.

"Water."

This made Tonia feel better knowing it was only water that had their pulses rushing like the wing beats of a buzz fly. "Well, I guess that settles it! Let's go that way and see what it is. Maybe there's an underground stream or something flowing through these mountains. Wouldn't that be great to go back to the village with news of a hidden cave, where everyone could go hide during a storm?"

Tonia's words hit Diam like a rush of calm and she had a little chuckle at her own expense for getting so nervous over such a little thing.

"Absolutely!" she agreed, now getting more excited than scared. "Come on, let's check it out!"

The girls continued through the cave, following the tunnel to the right of the fork, with their newfound courage. Diam continued dropping a flower here and there, and as they walked, they listened to the sound of water grow increasingly louder. Soon, they notice a bend ahead, and the path was steadily going deeper into the unknown. The water sounded very close here and when they arrived at the bend, they instinctively slowed down.

Neither girl knew why they did this – it was just another feeling they had.

Tonia was funny like that sometimes. She often felt she could sense things that were about to happen. She had no explanation for it; it was almost like intuition.

The young girls slowly peered around the curve in the tunnel and saw a small stream a few feet in front of them. It was about four feet wide and flowed through a narrow entranceway in the rock wall on the right side of the room. It gently flowed to the left, following the tunnel further into the cave.

They peered into a fairly large cavern, where the ceiling stretched upwards, far above their heads, and many rocks, large and small, were strewn about the floor. Large patches of clingy, dark moss had grown across the rock wall where the water flowed into the room. There were small rocks and pebbles along the edges of the stream, and some of the larger ones sat firmly in the middle of the water, glistening with moisture. Much larger boulders lined the far end of the cavern on the other side of the stream.

The girls made their way over to the steam with slow, careful steps.

"It looks like this has been flowing through here for many years," Tonia whispered to Diam.

"Why do you say that?"

"See these smaller rocks and pebbles? My mom once told me that as rocks roll and bump into each other in a river or stream, it makes them break off into smaller pieces. They keep rubbing against each other and eventually become smooth. Look at those stones – they are small, round, and smooth. There are lots of small rocks and pebbles like that here."

As Tonia explained this, it was obvious she was proud to remember some of the things her mother thought important to teach her when she was younger.

"Makes sense," Diam agreed, timidly looking around, still unsure if they were really alone in the cavern. "So, what do we do now?" she whispered.

"What's that?" Tonia asked as she pointed to the edge of the opposite side of the stream, inadvertently ignoring her friend's

24

question.

Diam tried to see what Tonia was pointing at just as her impetuous friend began stepping across the rocks lying in the stream, bravely making her way towards something unknown which had obviously caught her eye.

"What is it?" Diam asked seeing Tonia risking getting soaked head to toe in order to get to whatever it was she saw. It must be worth the risk, because even if Tonia enjoyed getting covered in dirt like a mud puppy, she was seldom known to willingly drench herself in water. Jole knew this and often teased her by scooping up pia shells of water and hiding behind a tree or wall and jumping out just at the right moment to catch her off guard. This always drove Tonia crazy and she could frequently be overheard talking about how she would get him back one day.

Tonia knelt down next to an unseen object and looked at it carefully. She found a small stick on the ground near her then used it to pick up a somewhat wet, almost tiled, substance. She held it up for Diam to see, her eyes sparkling in the torchlight.

"What is it? Diam asked again, but this time her voice changed to an intrigued whisper.

"It looks like snake skin," Tonia answered, turning the stick this way and that as she prodded her newfound amusement. After a few seconds she added, "Yes, that's what it is, but it's different than any kind of snake skin I've ever seen before."

"Hmm," her friend replied quietly, but when she couldn't think of anything else to say, Diam fell silent again. Leave it to Tonia to go right over and pick up anything from any kind of creature… except spiders, of course! Diam smiled as she turned her face to the ground, not wanting to give away any indication of her thoughts about how silly her friend could be sometimes.

"I wonder where it came from."

Tonia voiced her thought quietly, most to herself, but spoke it loud enough so Diam overheard.

"It was probably washed here from some place upstream," Diam suggested as she watched her friend place the wide strip of reptile husk back where she found it. Smiling the entire way, Tonia stood up and carefully made her way back across the bubbling line of water. When she was halfway across, one of her

25

feet caught the wet, moss-covered cap of a brook stone and the younger of the two girls almost wound up on her bottom in the cool liquid.

"Well, as much as I hate to say it, I think we should head back. We didn't come across many berries for my mom, and we still have to walk back through the cave and the forest to get home." Tonia's word slipped through her lips before her adventurous spirit could catch and stow them away.

"Maybe I can stay over again tonight and we can come back tomorrow!" Diam's suggestion quickly changed Tonia's contemplative gaze to a glowing smile. "I'm sure my mom and dad won't care if I stay again. We don't have anything special happening tomorrow, and I can definitely use the break from Jole. He was my second skin the whole time we were at Nana's."

"That sounds like a plan," Tonia agreed. "I'm sure if we tell Nicho and Micah, they will want to come back with us, too. That way, we'll have the boys with us in case we run into any trouble." Tonia hesitated for a moment as her nose wrinkled with a thought. "Not that we *need* their protection or anything, of course, but Mom has told me many times that we're safer when there are more of us."

"You mean, 'there's safety in numbers'," Diam said, correcting her friend.

"Yeah, whatever," Tonia sighed. "You know what I mean."

The girls took another quick look around. Not seeing anything suspicious, they filled their pia shells with water from the stream. They then headed back the way they came in, following the flowers on the floor back to the entrance of the cave.

"Wow, this cave is awesome!" Tonia said excitedly when she caught sight of light breaking through the darkness near the exit ahead. "I still can't believe we found it!"

"*We* didn't find anything," Diam corrected her again. "YOU found it. It was you who noticed the crack in the wall, and you who thought to investigate further."

"True, but we were together when I found it, so WE found it!" Tonia hugged Diam, sharing all the joy of her discovery with her dearest friend. In fact, she would not have wanted to share such a grand discovery with anyone else.

"I'm so glad you were here to share this with me, and I can't wait to tell the boys!"

"I like exploring with you, too," Diam agreed. "Neat things always happen when you're around," she said as she smiled at Tonia.

At the entrance to the cave, Tonia suggested they leave their sticks just inside where they could find them easily when they returned.

"Here, hold this."

Diam handed her torch to Tonia then pulled her bag down her shoulder and dropped it directly to the dirty cave floor. Her hand disappeared into the shadowy interior for only a second before she removed her pia shell of water.

"Hold the torches so I can extinguish them."

Tonia silently followed Diam's suggestion and held the pair of flickering torches away from her body. As Diam poured water over each flame, both torches crackled and hissed their angry disagreement for a few seconds until the hiss of heat and parallel trails of steam had completely subsided. Diam returned her pia to her bag and without giving it another thought, slung the bag back over her shoulder. Tonia handed Diam her torch and, one at a time, the girls carefully climbed out of the cave.

When they were safely outside, Diam asked her friend to give her the torch again. Although unsure of the reason, Tonia complied. Then, almost as if Diam's thoughts were speaking directly to her own mind, Tonia reached up toward the rocky mound and carefully removed the tarza vine which held the dangling brush away from the entrance. The scraggly cluster of gray moss quickly fell back into place with a soft *swish*, hiding the entrance to the cave once more.

Diam carried both torches over to a nearby tree with large green leaves and set the two moistened sticks upon the ground. She again pulled her bag off of her back and set it down beside the torches, then broke some of the larger leaves off the tree. With the care similar to that of a mother bandaging a child's wound, she carefully wrapped the small, round blankets of green around the fire end of each of the torches. Once they were securely wrapped, she used a length of tarza vine to bind the leaves to each torch.

This done, she then put her torch, leaf end down, inside her bag. She slung the bag up onto her back again then quietly carried Tonia's torch over to her so she could do the same.

As she was putting her torch away in her own bag, Tonia glanced up at the treetops. She tried to determine how late it was and whether or not they still had time to look for chickleberries or the hidden hole in the top of the cave that the birds escaped through when they had first entered the cave.

"It looks like it's getting kind of late, but I think we're okay for now," she told Diam. "Let's go a little farther into the woods to see if we can find some fruit. If we go back home after being gone all day without any berries to show for our day of adventure, Mom will wonder what we've been up to."

"She'll probably wonder what we were up to even if we came back with a few bags!" Diam said with a big smile, always aware that mothers know when their children have been up to something. Tonia had known Diam so long that her mom could always tell if Diam was stretching the truth, even when she was unsure if her own daughter was.

The girls quickly made a circle around their new favorite area searching for berries before they turned and headed back the way they had come. Soon they noticed a barely visible, narrow path branching off the main path they were following. Neither girl remembered seeing this narrow path before, so they decided to take it, even though they both knew all too well that daylight was growing short.

They followed the leafy path further into the woods, quietly thinking about the cave they had found and wondering if they would be able to return to investigate it further tomorrow. As they walked, they looked carefully for chickleberries, with Tonia looking left and Diam looking right. Just when they thought they would have to give up their search and head back, they found what they were looking for – a cluster of chickleberry bushes lying just beyond the path.

"Oh, good! Am I glad we found these!" Diam exclaimed. The relief in her voice couldn't be any more conspicuous. "I sure wouldn't want your mom to be upset if we ended up going back empty-handed. She might not let me stay over, and if that happened, who knows when we could come back up here to explore the cave again?"

"Oh, I see," Tonia complained with an act of surprise. "So now you *want* to explore the cave." She tried to give Diam a serious look. "And I really thought you were scared earlier." She didn't realize that her teasing and taunting would cause a small amount of friction between them, but by the tone of Diam's response, it did.

"I was!" Diam told her sternly. "I didn't know what we would find in that cave!"

"Well, I'm glad you're okay with it now. If my brothers come back with us tomorrow, you definitely don't want to act scared. Micah will never leave you alone about it if you do!" Tonia warned her with a nod of understanding.

"Yeah, I know," Diam conceded.

She knew Micah and his personality quite well. He could be ruthless at times.

As they were talking, Diam turned the extra bag upside down. When the remaining flowers cascaded to the ground, she noticed they had already begun to turn brown. When the bag was empty, the girls worked together filling it with chickleberries.

After a few seconds of picking the plump, ruby red berries, Tonia suddenly froze and looked at her friend. One corner of her mouth twitched with a hidden grin.

"You know what?" she asked as she stared at Diam, but before her friend could answer, she added, "We never ate any lunch today!"

With a mischievous smile, she popped a handful of berries into her mouth.

"I was thinking the same thing," Diam replied as she glanced down at the berries in the palm of her hand. "We did eat some snacks from our bags, but it definitely wasn't a real meal."

Since there were plenty of berries on the bushes, the girls helped themselves to a few handfuls of the juicy, succulent fruit. They continued picking as they snacked and soon their bags were full to the brim and it was time to head back to the village. Diam helped Tonia gently lift the largest bag onto her back, then they switched places and Tonia helped Diam in a similar fashion.

They were careful not to squish the berries because they were both well aware of how it would take days to get the stains off their skin. Once this was done, they turned and began walking back through the forest toward the village.

Neither of the girls had realized how late it had gotten, but as they crunched their way through the shadowy forest and felt the cooler, early evening air brush gently across their skin, they passed nervous glances between them. They both knew if they didn't hurry, they would have to try to relight the torches in order to see since the trees were still dense enough in this part of the forest that moonlight alone would not be enough to tell where the path led. They both were well aware that the idea of lighting the torches now, after soaking them with water, could prove a difficult ordeal. The flammable part of both torches was still damp and the leaves housing them did nothing to dry them out.

They picked up their pace and before long were relieved to see the campfires of the village. A moment later, the familiar darkness accompanied by nightfall began to fall over the surrounding valley like a cool, charcoal-colored blanket.

"Boy that was close!" Diam said as they neared the security of the village. "I sure didn't want to be lost out there after dark."

"True, we definitely know the forest by day, but without a working torch at night, I'm glad we didn't have to find out if we really know the forest as well as we think we do," Tonia agreed. As she smiled at Diam in the darkness, she added confidently, "I don't know about you, but I was pretty sure we would make it back in time."

In the surrounding gloom of night, the girls caught sight of a dark figure approaching. They stopped to watch it but within a few seconds, they realized with relief that it was only Nicho.

"Where have you two been?" he questioned sternly as he met them in the yard. "Mom was beginning to worry about you. You know you shouldn't be out in the forest this late in the day! She doesn't need that kind of stress after what happened last year." Although his voice fell silent, his eyes continued to admonish them.

"We're sorry," Diam said as Tonia nodded. "We had a hard

30

time finding berries."

"But Nicho, wait until you hear about our day!" Tonia added excitedly, ignoring his irritation at their lateness. "Do you and Micah have anything planned for tomorrow?"

"I don't know," he said as his gaze ventured to the bag on his sister's back. "Did you manage to get enough chickleberries?" he asked, changing the subject. Both girls nodded.

"Good. Before you start telling me about your forest escapades, let's get them in to Mom, so at least she knows you're both safe."

They entered the house and brought the chickleberries into the kitchen.

"Sorry we're late, Mom, but we had the hardest time finding these!" Tonia explained.

"I figured you would," Jeane said. Although she didn't make a scene, the children couldn't help but hear the immediate relief in her voice. "But next time, would you please not stay out so late? I was really starting to worry about you girls!"

"I know, and we're sorry," Tonia said apologetically. Just a few inches away from her friend, Diam lowered her head in acquiescence.

The smells in the kitchen were wonderful and quickly changed the focus of the conversation from the girls' lateness to the thought of dinner. In the brief silence between words, the two girls' stomachs could be heard growling like fierce animals.

"What's for dinner? We're starving!" Tonia asked eagerly.

"We're just getting ready to eat," Jeane replied. "Why don't you girls wash up while the boys help set the table."

They girls did as Jeane suggested, and the boy helped, if not somewhat reluctantly, in the kitchen. Soon they were all sitting around the table, eating dinner and enjoying each other's company. After everyone had finished eating, they all worked together to clean up before relaxing for the night.

Five

A s they were cleaning up, Tonia pulled Nicho aside.
"I have to talk to you," she whispered.

"Let's get this done, then we can all go into my room and talk," he told her.

Soon the clean up was finished and Jeane went to work on the new jacket she was making for the coming winter. Outside, a soft breeze blew the warm spring air through the valley as countless, glittering stars twinkled their nightly conversation across the cloudless sky. Just beyond the windows they could hear the familiar chorus of crickets as they sang their endless melodies in the surrounding darkness.

Nicho, Tonia, Micah and Diam all headed into Nicho's room. In order of age and without any previous planning, they sat on separate boulders that served as chairs. Nicho, being the tallest, stepped over the heap of clothes to the stone seat in back. Micah followed close behind his brother and sat to his left. Diam took over an empty space next to him, and Tonia sat next to Nicho. The younger of the two girls leaned toward the huddled group as she prepared to whisper something of obvious importance.

"What's going on?" Micah asked in his typical, impatient voice. Although he tried to sound irritated at the interruption of his evening plans, it was obvious he was struggling to mask his curiosity.

"Diam and I want to talk to you boys about something, but you have to promise us a few things first," his sister answered softly.

She paused and glanced once over her shoulder toward the bristly, onyx-colored bear hide that conveniently served as a door. Knowing the long, thick pelt provided a great barrier to sight, but little to sound, she lowered her voice even more, suddenly sounding much older than her eleven years. She looked at her brothers with a stone, cold look of pure seriousness.

"First, Micah, you definitely have to promise that if we include you in this, you'll be on your best behavior and will not, absolutely will NOT, get on our nerves when we do what we plan to do. That's not too much to ask, is it?" She stared at her younger brother with doubt-filled eyes of milky, brown cream.

Micah tossed her a look of complete innocence and smiled.

"Well," he paused as he scratched his chin and stared up at the ceiling, "I guess it all depends on what this is about."

Tonia sighed and frowned as she continued to stare at him in silence. When he finally dropped his eyes to see her reaction, he realized she was serious. With a chuckle of surprise, Micah waved his hand with a "go on" gesture. Although she kept her mouth shut at his reaction, Tonia eventually scowled at Micah before turning to look at Nicho.

"Second, if we share what we found today with you, you have to promise you won't tell anyone in the village about it – not a single person!"

She waited for a moment for her words to sink in, looking from Nicho to Micah and back to Nicho again. She looked at Diam, who nodded, then Tonia lowered her voice even more and added, "Not even Mom."

The boys listened to her with interest as Diam nodded again.

"It's that important!"

As she waited for their answer, Tonia could see Micah's curiosity getting the better of him. She was almost certain that he would have no choice but to agree to the terms.

"Diam, is there anything else you want to add?" Tonia asked her friend.

"No, that about sums it up," Diam replied as her gaze drifted from her friend to the boys.

Nicho turned to look at his brother for a moment before he finally broke the line of masculine silence.

"Okay, okay, we agree." He could almost hear Micah's mind spinning as the younger boy nodded his ascension.

Tonia was briefly surprised that Micah didn't offer a sarcastic response, but he didn't disappoint her for long.

"Yeah, yeah, whatever. Now tell us what this is all about before I lose interest and decide to go kidnap Bandy again," the younger boy grumbled.

This was when Diam decided to take over.

"Well, you both know that Tonia and I went out into the forest this morning, looking for chickleberries for your mom, right?" she asked.

"And from the looks of it, you found plenty," Micah retorted with a tone of indifference. "So, again I ask you, what's this all about?"

Neither girl was surprised with his obvious impatience.

"While we were looking for the berries, we found a fallen oak tree," Tonia began.

Trying her best to ignore him, Diam couldn't help herself as the excitement built up to the point where she felt as if she might explode. In response, she blurted out, "Yeah, and tucked behind the downed oak tree, Tonia spotted the entrance to a hidden cave!"

Her voice was almost too loud and Tonia's darting look of seriousness shushed her friend. The last thing they needed was for Mom to come in wondering what they were doing.

Tonia had never been able to hide anything from her mother, and what with all four of them huddled in Nicho's room, she knew Mom would be sure to know something was up. All she would have to do was ask, and the look on her only daughter's face would have screamed, "Mom, we're doing something we're not supposed to."

"No way. A hidden cave?" Nicho asked. Although his surprise was genuine, he kept his voice low.

"I thought we knew all the caves in the area, especially with all the exploring you girls do."

"Yes way," Tonia said. "And we even went inside to check it out," she continued as her eyes sparkled with an adventurous sparkle. She looked right at Micah, knowing he would be jealous about this little tidbit of information. Although she expected him to comment on their find, his reaction surprised her.

"Cool!" exclaimed Micah excitedly. "What did you find? Did you see any creatures or secret rooms when you went in?"

"Yes!" Tonia replied, her own voice now growing loud with excitement.

"Shh!"

Diam scolded her friend as she put a single raised finger to her lips, then waved a hand in a repetitive motion as if she was pushing Tonia's voice down to the dirt floor beneath their feet. Tonia nodded and smiled sheepishly at her friend before she turned her attention back to Micah.

"There were big, green, hairy creatures, with fire coming out of their eyes and slimy drool dangling from a wide, gaping mouth filled with jagged, rotting teeth! Their breath smelled like rancid food that has sat out in the hot summer sun for a week – it nearly killed us both!"

"No way!" said Micah, taken by surprise. "Really?"

His eyes blazed with interest now but the girls could hear the unmistakable doubt lingering in his voice.

"No," Tonia admitted. "I'm just pulling your leg."

Micah playfully pushed her off the rock she was sitting on and Tonia couldn't help be chuckle. It tickled her each and every time she managed to trick Micah, which wasn't very often. He could invariably trick her, and everyone else, more often than anyone could ever dream of tricking him.

"No, we didn't find any creatures, but Tonia did find some snake skin," Diam offered in answer to Micah's question. After a few seconds, she looked at Tonia and winked.

"We were waiting for you boys to be with us before we got into anything too major. Then again, we didn't search the whole cave because we ran out of time. We had to go back out and look for chickleberries, because by the time we found the cave, we hadn't found that many berries yet," she explained.

"So, tomorrow, do you boys want to go back there with us? I really want to explore it more and see if we can find anything interesting," Tonia invited, pausing to wait for their answer. When they didn't reply as quickly as she had expected, she continued.

"Come on, guys. This could be something really important! It's right on the side of a mountain, and we think it might even go all the way through to the other side. I've never heard of anyone going to or coming from the other side. Maybe we'll meet other people!"

As her eyes sparkled, she whispered, "And maybe, just maybe, we'll find dragons!"

Six

"Okay, okay," Nicho said after Tonia's last statement. "I don't have anything planned for tomorrow. What about you, Micah?"

Micah simply shook his head in a negative manner, indicating he had no plans.

"Okay," Nicho continued. "Let's start thinking seriously about what supplies we would need to bring with us then."

"Definitely torches, food, and water," Diam stated. "Today all we had were nuts, chickleberries, and a little bit of water. The two torches we packed really came in handy, too," she added.

"And let's not forget our flower bags." Tonia said this with some pride. "We definitely need to have some extra bags, just in case. Maybe we could pick some chickleberries before we head into the cave." As she said this, she looked at Diam for approval. Not surprisingly, her friend didn't hesitate to nod her agreement.

"What in the world do you mean by 'flower bags'?" Micah asked.

The look on his face was one of confusion and surprise, indicating his belief that this MUST be a girl thing – flowers in the hair, flowers in the bags! If he had any say in it, there would be no way they would have him playing with flower bags! They could dress up mud puppies all they wanted to, with pretty clothes and flowers in their fur, but there was no way they would get him to play with flower bags... absolutely not!

Ignoring Micah's reaction, the girls explained how they picked the flowers from the bush just outside the cave, leaving the trail

37

of pink and yellow blossoms along the tunnel floor so they could find their way back to the entrance.

Nicho nodded his head with smiling approval as they explained their brief adventure in the cave.

"That was a pretty good idea, whichever of you two thought it up," he said.

"Tonia did," Diam admitted as she shrugged. "She's got more of an imagination than I do, that's for sure. It's probably because of all the critters and bugs she's always playing with. Well, it's either that or maybe dealing with her bothersome brothers."

Tonia snickered at her friend.

"No way! You're just a little more conservative with your imagination than I am, that's all. Well, except when there is a dangerous stream down an unknown passage!" Tonia said as she leaned over and gave her friend a reassuring hug.

"Yeah, yeah, yeah, so what else should we bring?" Micah asked with a huff of excitement mixed with. Monsters and dragons? Wizards and trolls! Yippee!!!

"I can't wait for tomorrow!" he young boy finally said as his own imagination began boiling over like a full pot of chickenbird soup over a campfire.

Nicho remained quiet, lost in thought, while the others gradually turned their focus back to him. After a moment, he spoke.

"Micah, I think you and I should definitely bring our short swords with us, just in case something comes up. I'd rather be safe than sorry."

"Now, wait a minute," Tonia began, clearly offended. "Why is it that only you and Micah get to bring short swords? Just because we're girls doesn't mean that we don't want to be safe, too! You never know, Nicho, Diam and I could have yours or Micah's lives in our hands one day!"

The group of curious young adults was completely unaware of just how realistic this statement would turn out to be in the not so distant future.

"We could be armed with just a wiggly worm or a hardened slice of chickleberry bread!" Diam added with an attempt at a look of concern.

"Oh, all right," Nicho relented with a sigh. "Micah, go over and see Uncle Andar. Ask him if he has a few short swords that we can borrow, but don't explain the real reason. Just tell him we're going hunting."

As Micah got up and turned to head out of the room, Nicho added, "Also, see if he has a couple of long bows and a few dozen arrows while you're there – we may need those, too. Wouldn't it be awesome if we brought home a cave boar for dinner?"

After Micah left the room, Nicho and the girls continued preparing their list of necessities for their adventure the following day. Diam decided she needed a change of clothes to spend the night again, so she quickly ran home, saying she'd be back in a flash. She wanted to be well prepared for their trip so she packed a second change of clothes, a few extra rock sparkers, some dried meat, and extra fruit. With this done, she kissed her mother and father goodnight and headed out the door.

Just as she was running down the path that led back to her friend's house, she spied Micah heading toward her. Criss-crossed across his back were one long bow and one short bow. Cradled in his arms were two quivers of arrows and two short swords, their blades protectively sheathed within shadowed pieces of thick, rustic leather. When Diam realized he was struggling to keep from dropping the cumbersome items, she quickly put down her bags and grabbed the quivers from him so he didn't spill any more arrows than he already had. Micah looked over at Diam as the corners of his mouth turned up. Just as you would think a 'thank you' was in order, the smile turned upside down and was quickly accompanied by a stern look of disapproval.

"Where were you when I spilled the arrows before?"

Diam eyes flashed as her immediate reply flew across her lips.

"If you're not up to carrying a few arrows, maybe you should stay home tomorrow. I wouldn't want you to strain your shoulder carrying our flower bags!"

At times, the sibling rivalry between this unrelated pair was quite similar to the tension found between Micah and Tonia. Although they frequently squabbled amongst themselves over the silliest things, this time neither Diam nor Micah was willing to risk their chance at exploring the cave the following day so they held their verbal snakes of sarcasm in check. Diam silently slung the quivers over her shoulder then bent to pick up one of her bags. In like fashion, Micah shifted the bows behind him until they rested comfortably against his back before reaching down to grab Diam's extra bag. Without so much as a glance at each other, they turned and made their way up to the house, each matching the other's silent steps.

By the time they reached the house, the tension between Micah and Diam seemed to have evaporated into thin air. Back in Nicho's room, the four explorers got comfortable again as they discussed who would carry which weapon. Once they had all the details worked out, Nicho made a final suggestion.

"Since I'm sure we'll be up very early, we should probably go to bed. I talked to Mom already and told her we're going to be hunting for valley pheasants tomorrow, probably for the entire day. If we can find a big one and kill it, she will be very pleased with us! You know how much Mom loves roasted pheasant."

Although all the children knew this, they also knew that she wasn't the only one who loved the taste of juicy, fire-cooked meat. Whenever any of them caught the savory, tantalizing scent of valley pheasant, gently rubbed with alia leaves and sour marsh grass, they would come running as fast as they could.

They told each other goodnight and with that, headed off to bed, each dreaming of adventure, dragons, wizards, caves, and of course, roasted pheasant.

Seven

Tonia woke up slowly, coming out of a dream long before the sun began traveling across the sky. In her dream it was the middle of the night and she was walking through the forest in an area that she didn't quite recognize. She wandered amongst the trees for a few minutes, and when she saw no one else, she decided she was alone. Around her, wide, gray patches of fog swirled lazily in the cool, damp air. A few moments after she decided to explore the area, she thought she heard a voice softly calling out to her.

"Toniaaaa…"

"Where are you?" she whispered in response to the soothing, gentle voice.

She suddenly had the sensation that she was falling. It was almost as if a magic spell was taking hold of her, drawing her toward something she could not see.

"Toniaaaa?"

The owner of the unseen voice was still soft but more questioning this time.

Feeling like a puppet at the end of an invisible tarza vine, Tonia followed the sound of the faceless voice. Before long she found herself at the edge of the forest where the ground abruptly dropped over the edge of a jagged, rocky cliff. She stood motionless as she looked around for the owner of the voice, but again saw no one. Just as she was about to take another step forward, she was quite surprised to find herself standing on the top of a mountain. She stopped where she stood and peered through patches of fog.

The surrounding valley was covered with intertwining, ghostly tendrils of the thick gray mist, which bled into the dark gray landscape after erupting from some unseen place far below her.

Her eyes eventually made their way over the edge of the cliff, drawing her focus toward a deep, nearby crevasse. At first she saw nothing of interest, but after a moment she found she began to make out a dark shape with a multitude of dark, jagged fingers jutting out all around it. She froze as she stared at the object, then chided herself for being afraid of an inanimate object. The shape was that of a dead tree which was extending outward from the side of the cliff, about fifty feet below her. She stared at it for a few seconds before she realized there was a cage of some sort hanging from one of the wider, gnarled branches. Her eyes moved from the eyelet atop the cage to the dying branch, and she quickly understood that the bridge between the two was a thick rope made from many braided tarza vines.

She stared at the cage, confused.

Why would someone hang a cage from the side of a cliff? Although the tree holding the cage was large, even in the dark she could tell it had no leaves and appeared to be quite dead.

As she thought this, another thought came to her. Not only why would someone hang a cage from the side of the mountain, but HOW?

She squinted her eyes in an attempt to see the barred enclosure more clearly. It looked as if something could be inside of it... some large, bulky heap, which took up most of the space inside of the cage. As she was trying to figure out what it was, she noticed the dark, undefined shape seemed to be shifting!

"What in the world?" she thought to her dream-self.

As she watched the indistinguishable shape, it moved once more. As it did, a pair of brilliant blue-green eyes turned and looked up at her. The first thing Tonia noticed was how bright the faceless eyes were. The second thing she noticed was how they were nearly overflowing with an incredible, overwhelming sadness.

Her own eyes widened in surprise. Was the shape in the cage what she thought it was?

She shook her head, unable to comprehend what she was

seeing. Although it was in her dream, the shock of the situation felt totally real.

"Toniaaaa?" the gentle, pleading voice called out again.

Although the voice was in her head, as she watched the creature in the cage, she had the oddest thought that the voice she was hearing was really coming from the shadowy, confined creature. It was staring at her now – looking up at her in hopeless desperation as she stood frozen with stunned disbelief.

A dragon. A caged dragon. A dragon that was trapped, needing her help. It was calling her, pulling her towards it somehow, begging for help, pleading for release.

Draco.

In the blink of an eye she was back in the cave they had been exploring earlier that day, wandering around in the dark tunnels with Diam. Small pink and yellow flowers were scattered on the dirt floor all around them. She could almost smell their sweet fragrance as they listened to the sounds of the stream flowing nearby.

As she briefly opened her eyes she realized what was happening. She was in her home. She was in her bed. It had only been a dream.

The young girl stayed where she was for a few moments, allowing the last remnants of sleep to leave both her eyes as well as her mind. She opened then closed her eyes, the earlier dream forgotten. Instead of a foggy, deep ravine, she was now picturing the cave in her mind, with nothing but the peaceful sounds of the bubbling, lazy stream flowing deep within it. As her imagination began to take control, she suddenly pictured herself standing near the stream as she listened intently for any other sounds. She looked up at the rock cluttered ceiling over the flowing water and there, peering at her in the torchlight, was a small pair of eyes. She stood frozen in silence, watching the mystical pair of eyes, unsure of what creature was hiding behind them as it watched her curiously in return. Without a sound, the eyes blinked rapidly when suddenly...

"Whaaa?!?!" Tonia squealed as she felt something brush against her arm.

"Shhhh!" Diam said nervously as she tried to quiet her friend.

43

"I'm sorry. I didn't mean to startle you."

Tonia's heart was racing and she took a few seconds to calm down.

"I was thinking about the cave and what we might find there today." Her words came out distorted and almost unintelligible as she continued to emerge from her dream state.

"Yeah, I thought I heard you wake up so I waited, but then you didn't move much, so I wasn't sure. I'm thinking about getting up and grabbing something to eat." Diam's words hovered in front of her friend before they materialized in her mind moments later.

"I suppose we *should* get up and get moving," Tonia agreed with a weary yawn.

With quiet steps, she made her way to the room that the boys shared, careful not to wake her mother. A good night's sleep had been tough to come by for all of them during the past year. This was especially true for their mother.

Tonia decided to wake the boys up one at a time. Nicho woke up easily, as usual. Tonia, lightly touching his arm, said, "Nicho, wake up," and stepped back as he opened his eyes. He looked at her, focused for a few seconds, then stretched and threw the covers back as he stood up. He was ready to go.

Micah, on the other hand, rolled over onto his other side and pulled his covers closer to his chin. This, also, was typical.

"Come on, Micah, wake your sleepy butt up," Tonia said as she poked him roughly in the arm. "If you don't get up, we're going to leave you here while we go hunt for dragons and wizards," she warned.

When he still didn't move, she added with an audible chuckle, "You'll be left here alone to do chores for Mom all day."

"Hmmmph," Micah muttered as one eye fluttered open briefly before he grunted and decidedly pulled the covers over his head in an effort to go back to sleep. "Darn you, Tonia. The chickenbirds aren't even up yet!"

"Yes, but the sooner we get moving, the more time we'll have to explore," she explained patiently. For Micah, however, her patience would not last long. This could be a very long day. She began pulling his covers off of him in an attempt at motivating him to get out of bed.

With another grunt of disapproval, Micah stretched, making indescribable noises as he did so. An unpleasant odor wafted from under the sheets as he shifted beneath them. He was known in the family as "Prince Palluda" for this very reason. He smiled proudly, took a deep breath, and opened his eyes.

"That skunk-rat stew for dinner last night sure was good," the younger boy stated matter-of-factly as he smiled innocently at his brother.

"Micah!" Tonia complained. She crinkled her nose, covered her mouth, and quickly turned on her heel, mumbling something behind her hand about how she and Diam were going to find something for breakfast.

The boys soon joined them and they ate together in silence, thoughts of the possibilities of the day's coming adventures dancing through each of their heads. After breakfast, they began gathering their gear.

Outside, the darkness was just beginning to surrender to the twilight of the coming day and the morning air was crisp and cool. In wouldn't be long before the dew on the forest trees would glisten and sparkle with the arriving sunlight.

The four explorers dressed appropriately with jackets and leggings, knowing they could remove the extra clothing as needed and carry it in their bags if the day warmed up enough, which it invariably would. They each had a short sword sheathed around their waists, along with a bag slung across their backs to carry their supplies. They packed all the necessities for an adventure – food, torches, extra bags, rock sparkers, and a few other miscellaneous items.

In addition, the boys each carried a bow and a quiver of arrows across their backs. Nicho carried the long bow and Micah carried the short one.

The previous evening, Nicho had gone to let Jeane know they would all be going hunting the following day. When he entered her mending room, she glanced up from the jacket she was working on and reminded him to watch over the younger ones while they were sharing the forest with nature. She also cautioned him to be home before the sun fell behind the nearby mountains, which of course he assured her he would. She always worried about them when they went out on their escapades, especially during this stormy time of year, but her worry was like an overflowing pia bowl lately. This was completely understandable considering the awful tragedy from just a year before, which everyone knew was still quite fresh in her mind.

Since most of the seasonal storms came from beyond the Hampa Mountains, no one ever really knew when one was coming until just before it hit. The mountains rose so high up into the cloud cover, the villagers frequently could not make out the sun setting until the moment darkness fell. Some used to say these mountains were all that stood between Uncava and a place where terrible hurricanes, typhoons that rose up to the sky, and winds that could topple the tallest and strongest pia tree, were an everyday ordeal. Aside from stories of weather, however, little was ever spoken of the 'other side'.

The two pairs of children started out on their adventure with the girls leading the way. Morning dew covered the gray, motionless valley as the sun struggled to warm the once slumbering trees. The leaves, crunchy and dry on their return trip the previous day, were now silent with dampness under their moccasins. This would soon change, however, as the glowing orb in the sky gained in intensity and its rays penetrated the mist to heat and dry the nearby lands.

Once they were deep within the Orneo Forest, but not yet at the cave, the girls led the way to the chickleberry bushes they had finally found late the previous afternoon. They worked together gathering the berries and putting them into two bags. Wanting to be sure they would have ample snacks for the day, they collected more than enough of the tasty fruit. It was decided the girls would carry these bags, one each, slung gently over their other sundries to protect them. When this was accomplished, they made their way towards the hidden cave, each of them nearly erupting with excitement. When they were about fifty feet from the entrance, Tonia stopped suddenly.

"Do you see it?"

Her inquisitive eyes twinkled as a teasing smile worked its way from one side of her mouth to the other. Her pride in her discovery the previous day was obvious.

"See what?" Micah asked in an absurd tone as Nicho shook his head. "All I see is a rocky hillside, a fallen tree, and a bush with some silly flowers plastered all over it."

"You have to know what you're looking for, Micah," Tonia replied in an admonishing tone. "Don't you remember last night when I explained that the cave was hidden and near a flowering bush?" Although she focused on the younger of her two brothers, she threw Diam a sideways wink.

Micah walked over to the fallen oak, remembering only bits and pieces of the conversation from the previous night and wishing he had paid closer attention. He began searching high and low on the rocky hillside for some crack or crevice that could serve as an entrance to the cave of which they spoke.

Meanwhile, Tonia glanced up above the cave entrance in an attempt to see the place where the birds had flown through the previous day. She was disappointed to see nothing but rocks. Not willing to divulge her secret too soon, Tonia led the way over to the flowering bush and began gathering the fallen petals which they would again use to find their way back to the entrance of the cave after they got inside. Without a word, Nicho went over and began helping them.

"Cool!"

Micah's shout of success echoed through the trees as he pushed aside the moss covering the entrance. He beamed happily, as if he was the first one to discover the cave.

"How in the world did you find this, Tonia?" he asked in a surprised tone. His pride was humbled by the sheer amazement he felt in the presence of such a fantastic discovery. "I just can't believe we've never found this before!"

"I think it has something to do with all of the snakes and bugs I've played with my whole life," she replied. "Things like that have taught me to look at everything in a different light. You would have been able to see it right away if you'd been a little more in tune with your surroundings and a little less consumed by your own affairs." She paused for a few seconds before continuing in a teasing tone, "You know, Micah, sometimes hanging out with a sister has its advantages."

Her brother remained quiet as he considered this. In his mind, he agreed with his sister, but he would never willingly admit to it.

Tonia and Diam worked together to prop the mossy brush back away from the cave entrance like they had done the previous day. Then, without any further hesitation and one at a time, they carefully climbed through the entrance to the cave.

EIGHT

"It's a lot darker in here than I thought it would be," Micah stated nervously as they stood just inside the mouth of the cave.

"I think our host forgot to light the tunnel torches for us," Diam replied in a sarcastic, teasing tone as she turned her gaze upward as if staring at something very important on the upper area of the cave. When she returned her focus back to Micah, she smirked at him. "We'll have to scold him for that when we see him," she added as she smiled at him innocently.

He scowled at her silently and stuck out his tongue in response.

Nicho ignored their banter as he peered into the darkness ahead.

"Let's take our torches out and get them lit now, before we go any further."

Diam shrugged her bag, which carried all of the torches and the rock sparkers, off her back then briefly dug through it. After finding what she was looking for, she left her bag on the ground while Tonia held each of the torches away from her body. After nodding at her friend, Diam struck the sparkers sharply against each other and in the blink of a firebug, brilliant flecks of light jumped from rock to wood, setting the short sticks aflame. Curling tendrils of gray smoke wound their way from the ends of the covered sticks toward the upper area of the cave as if trying to flee the area. Once she was satisfied with the flames, Tonia handed a torch to each of her brothers. Once Diam pulled her bag back onto her back, both of the girls grabbed one of the sticks that were propped in the corner of the cave from the previous day.

"What are those for?" Nicho asked intrigued, nodding toward the sticks.

"We were using them yesterday," Diam said. "You know how much Tonia loves spiders! She wanted to be prepared to de-web our path if needed."

"Good idea, Sis," he said. "Two sticks should be enough to beat down any hungry, hairy, giant spiders that we may encounter along the way," he joked. Tonia tried to slap him but he anticipated her reaction and moved out of her reach in plenty of time.

"If you guys get me spooked, this will NOT be a fun excursion," Tonia threatened. Micah stood near his brother, smiling, as always, with a completely innocent expression.

"Okay, Sis, I'm sorry," Nicho apologized. "If we find any big, hairy spiders, I'll try to save you by killing them with my sword first."

This time, Tonia was quicker than Nicho, and they all heard the slap as her opened hand found his arm.

"Owwww," he said, more for the drama than from the pain.

"There's more where that came from," Tonia promised.

Nicho glanced at Micah and smiled. Sometimes their sister could be so predictable.

"Come on, guys," Micah said. Without waiting for them, he turned and pushed his crackling torch into the depths of the cave ahead. "We're wasting time here."

"Diam, why don't you lead us this time," Tonia suggested.

"Micah can follow you, then Nicho, and I'll be last. Once we get to the place where we stopped yesterday I'll start tossing out flowers as we go."

She glanced down at the cave floor and could make out some of the flowers from the previous day lying in the dirt, untouched but turning brown with age. Some, however, had been trampled almost beyond recognition from their movements near the entrance to the cave. Others were dirt covered and broken.

With a nod at Tonia, Diam moved past Micah with a smirk of satisfaction and led the way deeper into the cave, heading back to the place where they found the stream. Soon, the soft trickling sounds coming from the flowing water began to penetrate the darkness ahead. They quietly approached the bend in the tunnel and Diam raised her left hand to signal she was stopping. As the muffled footsteps behind her fell silent, she slowly peered around the bend. She hesitated, nervous about what she might see while her friends waited quietly behind her. The only discernible sounds were the trickling stream and the soft crackling of the burning torches. Just as they thought she would begin to move forward again, Diam pulled back with a muffled squeak, her eyes large and surprised.

"What is it?" Nicho whispered. He knew she was on a roll today with her antics, and he found himself wondering if she had really seen something or was just trying to fool them – again. "We're just a bunch of jesters today, aren't we?" he thought with a snort.

"There's something on the side of the cavern, next to the stream!" she whispered excitedly. "It looks like a cave rat!"

She repositioned herself closer to the other three and took a step back. Slowly, the others took turns peeking around the corner at the cave dwelling rodent. Their eyes had finally adjusted to the darkness of the cave, and they were able to see the cavern in front of them in the surrounding gloom.

The unsuspecting rodent sat at the edge of the stream farthest from them, on the right side of the cavern. It appeared to be washing something or playing in the water, totally engrossed in its work.

The stream entered the cavern from the rock wall near the cave rat and exited on the far-left side of the cavern. Close to this, another dirt and rock laden tunnel continued on, leading deeper into the darkness.

The four friends looked at each other.

"What should we do?" Diam whispered.

"Let's walk out there slowly and see what happens," Micah suggested, very curious now about both the cave and the creature.

Nicho nodded and they began walking slowly into the larger area of the cave. Although they carried two flickering torches, the light provided by the flame sticks only partially lit up the large cavern. When it realized there was movement nearby, the cave rat immediately stopped what it was doing, squatted down on all four legs, and prepared to run. Its long, white whiskers twitched nervously in the torchlight.

The group of friends cautiously made their way towards the stream then turned to the left, away from the cave rat, but kept their eyes on it the whole time. None of them knew how it would react to having strangers in its environment.

Although it was not nearly as bright as being outside in the sunshine, the light emitting from their torches allowed the explorers to see the rodent fairly well. It stood motionless, waiting, watching warily, and wondering whether they were going to try to make a meal out of it or continue farther into the cave. It was small for a cave rat, with short brown and gray fur covering its elongated torso. Dark eyes watched them from a furry face, darting with nervous vigilance from one person to the next. Its tail was short and round and twitched uneasily as it watched them make their way toward the other end of the cavern. The group of youngsters couldn't tell if the tail was naturally short or if it looked this way because of an injury.

From the far-left side of the cavern, the explorers took the time to examine the area. Nicho couldn't help but think about how this would make a great place to come to in an emergency. There was plenty of room for people and what appeared to be an abundance of fresh water. Perhaps they could make a campfire in a corner, but of course they would need to check out the ventilation in the cave before doing attempting such a thing. It would be horrible for them to build a warm, welcoming fire and then have everyone die from the smoke because of inadequate ventilation, or...

"Come on, let's get moving so we can see what else we find."

His sister's impatient voice interrupted Nicho's thoughts.

They began walking, two by two, deeper into the cave, following the babbling water downstream. Soon the path narrowed, as did the stream, and they had to continue on in single file. Minutes passed and shortly the stream veered off to the right, where it flowed directly into a moss-covered line of jagged rocks before disappearing somewhere beneath. The dirt and rock littered path, however, turned here and trailed away from the stream, leaving the explorers to continue on without the chorus of liquid sounds provided them by the moving water. After a few moments, they stopped to rest.

"Well, so much for following the stream." Micah broke the silence with a sigh, obviously disappointed. "I was hoping to follow it to the end, wherever that may be."

"Don't be disappointed so fast," Nicho said as he turned to his younger brother. "We've been walking at a slightly downhill angle for quite a while, and I've got a feeling that we'll either cross or at least meet the stream again soon." They sat on rocks that lined the narrow tunnel, drinking water from their pia bottles and silently sharing a bag of chickleberries. Their torches burned nearby, quietly whispering for them to continue on their voyage.

Without warning, Nicho suddenly jumped to his feet. He thought he heard the sound of something coming from behind them in the area of the stream they had just come from. The noise sounded like a soft squeak with a fluttering of air. The hairs bristled on the back of his neck and he turned quickly, facing the direction where the sound had come from. In his left hand he held out one of the two torches, while his right hand quickly moved to the handle of his sword, ready to draw. The air around them was suddenly thick with anxiety as the others nervously followed his lead. Standing their ground, they carefully peered into the tunnel.

Nicho, the unspoken leader since he was the oldest, took a hesitant step forward as he spoke into the darkness.

"Who's there?"

Silence.

"What is it?" Tonia whispered as she leaned toward her older brother.

"I thought I heard something," Nicho whispered back without looking at her, never losing sight of the tunnel ahead.

They stood silently for several seconds, straining their ears for anything out of the ordinary. Unfortunately, the sound Nicho thought he heard did not repeat itself.

"I think we should be very careful as we continue on," he suggested. He furrowed his brow, his expression curling into a frown, as he turned back to glance at his friends.

"I don't know exactly what the noise was, but I know I

definitely heard something."

Unwilling to let fear overpower their curiosity, the decision was made to continue on. A resolute silence surrounded the group of young adults as they put away their pia bottles and chickleberries before making their way deeper into the cave.

Just when they were about to head out, Nicho stopped them.

"Hold on. I want to change the order we are walking in. Micah, you should go first. Diam, you follow, then Tonia, and I'll take up the rear. That noise..." he hesitated with a concerned shake of his head. "I want to keep an eye out behind us, just in case," he finished.

Diam and Tonia shared a look of relief, both glad to be placed in between the boys. Not surprisingly, Micah was more than happy to take the lead. He felt as though Nicho was overreacting a bit, but he didn't mind. He would play along, especially now that he got to lead!

Although the two brothers came from the same parents, they were quite different in certain respects. While Nicho was always the one to be more serious about things, Micah tended to enjoy being silly, lightening the mood whenever he could. The villagers fondly considered him a jester at his best, and of course the children of Uncava loved him.

Happy to be in the lead, Micah made some silly faces with an accompanying array of sounds, then they continued on. He quickly settled down after Nicho scolded him, and as a new seriousness washed over the younger of the two boys, they trudged through the tunnel one after the other, each of them paying much more attention to the shadowy crevices along the rocky path. After a few minutes, they spilled into another cavern. This one was smaller than the previous one, but it had a lower ceiling and lacked any signs of running water. The smells here were quite different than before. Without the stream running through it, the smaller cavern was very dry and almost musty. As dust swirled around them, it was hard not to notice the lack of moisture in the air.

There were many rocks of various sizes scattered throughout the room. In one area stood a reasonably large pile of them, all clustered together like some of the mud drop pictures they used to build as small children. Two other tunnels exited off this cavern, which led to uncertainty at which tunnel to take.

"Okay, so do we flip a stone to see which direction we should follow?" Diam asked.

"Maybe we should just keep going downhill," Tonia suggested hesitantly.

"I'm not sure which way we should go," Nicho said. "It would make it a whole lot easier if we still had the stream to follow though."

While they were discussing their options, Micah listened quietly as he moved to examine a cluster of rocks on the cavern floor. The piled stones were close to one of the cavern walls, but there was enough room for him to move freely through the space between them. As he neared the rock pile, moving his torch slowly from side to side, something overhead caught his eye.

Various shapes of rocks emerged from the area over their heads, protruding from their rocky home like dozens of jagged, beckoning teeth. Although some were flat and round many others were quite pointy, resembling small, upside-down mountains, of sorts.

Micah focused his attention on the object that caught his eye as he walked. The oddity on the ceiling appeared to be a small, round, black shape, but in the flickering torchlight he couldn't quite make out what it was.

Tonia casually glanced over at Micah while listening to Diam and Nicho discuss which direction they should go next. She saw him looking up at something dark and motionless on the ceiling, then realized he was not watching where he was going. Directly in his path was the edge of the pile of rocks.

"Micah, watch out!" she quickly shouted, but her warning came too late.

Micah had been focusing all of his attention intently on the object overhead, trying to make out what this odd, dark object was that was hiding up in the shadows. At first he thought it might be a thick cluster of dark mold, but he changed his mind when he realized the dry air wouldn't support mold. Next he thought it might be an oddly shaped mushroom, but again the lack of moisture ruined that idea. Just when he was getting close enough to the round shape to think it moved, Tonia called out to him. In that instant, he realized the dark object was more than a mere shadow.

Before he could react to her warning, he suffered the effects of one rock that had escaped his line of sight. The jagged stone protruded from the floor between the pile of rocks and the wall, and as soon as his foot made contact with it, he tripped and lost his balance. As he stumbled forward and fell, he landed on his knees on the cavern floor, where small stones and pebbles were scattered everywhere.

"Uuumphh," he cried, immediately feeling the pain of the stones as they pierced his skin. Tonia and Diam immediately ran to his side and helped him up.

"Are you okay?" Tonia asked with genuine concern.

"Man, that smarts," he said as he stood up and brushed off his leggings. "I guess I should watch where I'm going." Even in the torchlight they could tell he was blushing.

"Are you okay, Micah?" Nicho asked as he made his way towards his brother.

Rubbing his knees, Micah nodded. "We don't need anyone getting hurt while we're in here. That would be a bad thing this far away from the village. Try to be more careful, okay?" Although Nicho's tone was filled with concern, it was also admonishing.

Micah nodded in silence as he gingerly brushed more dust from his leggings.

"What were you looking at, anyway?" Diam asked as she peered upward.

"I thought I saw something up there," he replied. He pointed over their heads as he made his way back over to the place where he had tripped. This time, however, he was wary of the troublesome rock jutting out of the floor. Once he was sure he had cleared the offensive item, he stopped and turned his attention upwards. Overhead, rocks protruding downward from the ceiling around the shape resulted in its being partially hidden by dark shadows which danced and wiggled in the torchlight.

"There, see?" he asked as he gestured up at the dark, unidentified object above them. The others moved closer. Once both torches were directly below it, the circular shape was definitely easier to see.

"That's what I was looking at. Any idea what it is?" he questioned to no one in particular.

"It's just a dark rock," Tonia suggested.

"No, it's not," Micah argued. "I saw it move!"

The explorers stared intently at the dark, round object that had won Micah's attention. Although they couldn't tell what the object was, there was no longer any doubt that something was definitely there.

Nicho raised his torch, bringing it close to the mysterious black shape. Light flooded the area of the ceiling where a short time before there had been mostly shadows. They watched the dark shape as the light penetrated its surroundings. Although most of the shadows disappeared like a ghost in the light, the main shadow remained – the torchlight did nothing to dim its darkness.

"What is it?" Diam asked quietly as she took a cautious step back.

"It looks like it might be a strange clump of moss," Micah replied, looking intently at the dark shape. "For a second earlier I thought I saw two small glowing circles coming from it. That's what caught my attention."

Suddenly, the mysterious object shifted slightly to the right and the explorers took an instinctive step backward. Micah, still pretty close to the rock that tripped him earlier, narrowly missed tripping over it again, which would have sent him tumbling in the opposite direction.

"It moved!" Tonia whispered. Her voice quivered with uncertainty as she took a few extra steps back than the others.

"I told you," Micah announced in a defensive tone.

"What is it, Nicho? What is it?" Tonia asked, all but ignoring Micah's statement.

Nicho stood his ground and raised his torch a little closer to the ceiling.

The black shape shifted again, this time more noticeably. As they watched in silent curiosity, two glowing orbs slowly appeared above it, much like two small torches being uncovered by a blanket of darkness. When this happened, Nicho realized what it was almost immediately. In the light of his torch he could clearly make out the black, fuzzy body, eight short legs, and the two small, glowing, yellow eyes.

"I think it's a glow spider," Nicho stated, withdrawing his torch from the ceiling as he took a step back. "It looks like we woke it up. It was probably sleeping up there with its head tucked under its body. The two glowing circles are its eyes."

He paused for a few seconds.

"It's probably wondering what we're doing in its home. Lucky for us it's one of the harmless spiders." He paused again as he peered up at the shadowy shape overhead. "At least that's what I *think* I remember hearing back at the village."

"Well, we can turn right on our heels and get out of its home, harmless or not," Tonia said matter-of-factly. She quickly walked over to the end of the cavern farthest from the spider, all the while maintaining a tight grip on her stick. If the spider even thought about making its way towards them, she would turn it into spider mush.

The creature clinging to the rocks overhead shifted again, almost as if stretching, then began ambling slowly toward a darker, deeper crevice in the ceiling. With their curiosity satisfied, the others followed Tonia.

"So, Nicho, what did you decide for us while I was tripping over rocks?" Micah asked his brother.

"I think we should follow the left tunnel," the older boy replied in his most confident voice. "Maybe it will lead us back to the stream – or to another one."

Diam's dark eyes squinted with confusion.

"How is it we will get to the river going left, if when we last saw it, the river flowed off to the right of the path?"

Nicho, having had time to think this through, replied, "We have been traveling down deeper and deeper the further we went. That path to the right goes up. Water only flows downhill, so if we start going up, we won't come back in contact with it. We would just end up higher than the river was when we started."

"That makes perfect sense," Diam agreed, more than a bit impressed with Nicho's logic.

"Let's get moving then," Micah encouraged as he turned and

led the way towards the tunnel.

Silently, the others followed in the order Nicho had suggested just a short time before, all of them more careful now of what the cavern ceiling held as well as the floor. After a while, the tunnel slowly began to narrow until they could barely walk without brushing the wall on either side of them. They continued on in single file for a few minutes. It was Micah who finally broke their silence.

"Uh, oh."

"What's wrong?" Nicho called from behind them just as Micah stopped abruptly. Beginning with Diam stopping just millimeters away from Micah as the first human reverse domino, the children nearly walked into each other one after the other.

"End of the line," the younger brother stated as the others stopped. As they tried to peer around him, Tonia sighed loudly. They had found a dead end.

"Well, I guess we go back to the last cavern and take the other tunnel," Diam offered.

"Since this tunnel is so narrow and I can't really lead now, why don't you take the lead for a bit, Nicho?" Micah suggested. Although this made perfect sense since Nicho was at the end of the line, Micah was obviously trying to be funny.

"That's a good idea," Nicho agreed. "There's not enough room here to shift everyone without stepping on toes." They turned around and began walking in the direction from which they had come and soon they were back to the cavern with the spider. They continued on towards the other tunnel entrance without bothering to check for the now hidden creature.

As they reached the place where the path divided, Nicho stopped.

"Give me your stick, Tonia," he said to his sister, who had remained close to his heels since they had found the glow spider. Without question, she handed him the stick. They all watched as Nicho took the branch and swung it around in front of him at the tunnel entrance, brushing away remnants of what once must have been a very large spider web.

"Oh, man," Tonia mumbled. Her voice shook with renewed uncertainty. "I'm not liking this very much anymore."

"Don't worry," said Nicho. "It's just a few spider webs." Although he was worried that he was speaking a lie, he decided it was more important to not upset her by telling her what she would want to hear instead of the truth. "Besides, they're just small ones and they look like they've been here quite a while."

With a reassuring smile, Nicho handed the stick back to her then headed into the new tunnel with his torch held out in front of him. The rest of the gang followed along in cautious silence.

NINE

They continued upward through this new tunnel without saying anything for a few moments, when suddenly they heard a strange tittering sound coming from somewhere in the darkness ahead.

Nicho raised a hand, gesturing for them to stop, then held his torch out as he tried to illuminate the source of the strange noise. They couldn't see much in the gloom of the tunnel, but as they listened, the tittering softly continued.

"Who's there?" Nicho asked, unsure of what to do. The sound stopped and was followed by an eerie silence.

"Have you ever heard anything like that?" Diam asked. When no one answered her, she added, "Because I know I sure haven't."

"No," Nicho finally said in a cautious tone, "but then again I've never been exploring in a cave quite like this one, either. Who knows what could be making such an unusual noise. It sounds like an odd chirping, almost like a bird, but I really don't think any birds would be this far into the cave. Be prepared with your weapons."

Tonia stared ahead, her eyebrows clenched together in deep contemplation.

"I think I've heard it before, but I can't remember where from," she said as she tried to jog her memory.

As they stood together in the tunnel, wondering what to do, the soft tittering began again. They listened to the sounds for a few seconds when suddenly Tonia said, "I've got it! It's the sound Raguon turtles make!"

Micah looked at her questioningly.

"What are you talking about?" he asked as he rolled his eyes at her.

"Just because you love animals doesn't mean this has to BE an animal!"

"It is, though," she argued. "You know that small cave by the village, just inside the Orneo Forest?" She didn't wait for him to answer before she continued. "I was in there exploring a while back and I heard the exact same sound. I didn't know what it was but I went and checked it out anyway." She looked at them with twinkling eyes as they listened to her story.

"I found a small Raguon turtle crawling along just inside the entrance of the cave. It seemed to be looking for something. It was just a young turtle and the tittering sound may have been how it was calling for its mother." Her eyes brightened with the memory as she went on.

"I left it alone, though, because I had no idea where its mother was and didn't want to make matters worse for it." She paused briefly before adding confidently, "Keep walking. I'm sure we'll find out that the funny noise is coming from one of those turtles."

Nicho stood silently for a few seconds, unsure of what to do. If this was indeed a harmless Raguon turtle, then they would be fine. But what if it was something else? He wasn't sure he wanted to just dive right into this without carefully considering things first.

Micah glanced at his brother and shrugged.

"You know how she is, Nicho, with all of her exploring and playing with bugs that she does. If she says that's what this is, then that's probably what it is. I say let's go for it."

Nicho sighed with defeat.

"Alright," he agreed. "But let's take it slow, because I don't want Mom getting all over me if I have to tell her that one of you numbskulls got eaten by a giant Raguon turtle!" he said, feigning irritation.

They slowly continued into the tunnel, keeping a careful eye on the path ahead. After about fifteen paces, they entered another fairly large cavern, stepping cautiously around rocks and small boulders scattered throughout the dirty floor. They huddled together once they entered the cavern, and carefully examined their surroundings.

With the tunnel they came from behind them, they peered ahead and noticed two other tunnels branching off the room they were standing in. One opened up to their left, and one was directly in front of them.

While they considered their options, Tonia suddenly noticed a funny sensation in her head. It was almost as though she heard a slight buzzing noise, but it wasn't really a noise – it was more like a feeling. She'd never felt anything like this before, and her shoulders tensed with fear. As the strange sensation continued, her eyes grew wide and her lower jaw dangled open. The feeling was very much like a warm trickle down the back of her head. It reminded her of those times when, as a child, her mother would pour the water she'd warmed in the fire through her long, dark hair to wash away the dirt and leaves of the day's adventure.

Diam was standing slightly to Tonia's right, struggling to focus on the darkness. As she scanned the room, she noticed Tonia making a funny face.

"What's wrong, Tonia?" she asked quietly, not quite sure why she was whispering.

Tonia shook her head and looked at her friend.

"I don't know," she said with a look of confusion. "I thought I heard something, well not really heard it, but felt it," she frowned as she tried to explain. "In my head."

Micah looked at her, saw the expression on her face, and started giggling. "You're a nut," he teased. "You don't even know what you mean!"

Again, Tonia experienced the buzzing sensation and quickly sat down on a rock that was near her. Her fingers wrapped around the edges of the stone as if grasping for some sense of what was real.

Nicho knelt down near the rock with a look of concern.

"Tonia, do you want to go back?" he asked softly. "Maybe you ate some bad chickleberries."

His suggestion was half to comfort her, and half to comfort his own uneasiness about the situation. Knowing he promised Mom to keep the children safe, this feeling Tonia was experiencing created an unwelcome, slight tingle in the center of his belly.

"No, that's not it," she said, not sure if it was true. "I felt fine until we came into this part of the cave."

They decided to take a break, both to think and let Tonia rest. Nicho's eyes never left his sister, and he moved closer to her in case she suddenly toppled off the rock. Thankfully, she didn't.

"If you think you're going to puke, please make sure you do it over in that corner of the cavern, away from us," Micah said as he pointed at the far corner of the room. His expression turned into a grimace as he pulled his bag off his back and removed his pia bottle. He took a drink of water, all the while watching Tonia, secretly concerned about her.

"Good idea," Diam said with a nod. "A water break is just what we needed."

They all watched Tonia where she sat on the boulder with her eyes closed for a few moments, resting quietly.

Without warning, the buzzing feeling became more intense and her eyes shot open with surprise. The warm trickle was now a rush, but not down her back… the warmth seemed to flow into the center of her head.

"Where are you, Mommy?"

Out of nowhere, an unfamiliar voice materialized. It was a quiet, almost shy yet high-pitched voice that she heard.

"Mommy, I can't find you anywhere!"

"What?" Tonia asked as her eyes darted around the room.

"What?" the others questioned her simultaneously.

"Huh?" Tonia asked as her focus turned to her brothers, then Diam. Her shocked gaze looked at them one at a time, as if somehow they were the source of this new sound. Was Micah playing yet another trick on her?

"You asked 'what'," Diam replied. She glanced at her friend before tossing a questioning look at Nicho.

"Don't you hear that soft voice, asking for its mother?" Tonia asked them.

For a few seconds, all they could do was stare at her, wondering if they heard her right, infinitely unsure of what she was talking about.

"You heard a voice?" Micah eventually asked, unable to hide

his smile. "You need to give me some of those berries you were eating! Cool! I want to hear voices in my head, too!"

"Be quiet, Micah."

Nicho scolded his brother with both words and a glare. He touched Tonia's arm as he leaned toward her. "What else do you think you heard?"

"I... I don't know," she stammered, rubbing her forehead. "I've never felt anything like this in my whole life. It was a strange buzzing inside my skull, light at first, almost like a bee flying around in my head. Then suddenly it got stronger, and before I knew it, I heard a voice." She hesitated as she glanced uncertainly at Micah, aware that what she was sharing with them now could possibly lead to ample harassment from him in the future.

She stared down at the ground as she continued rubbing her head.

"This is just great," she mumbled. "I'm hearing a voice that you guys can't hear. Just wait until this gets around the village." She shook her head in an attempt to work the buzzing sensation out of her head. "I can just hear it now – Tonia, the village quack."

She covered her face with her hands in exasperation and sighed.

"Mommyyyyy," the voice cried again, louder this time.

"There!" Tonia said, dropping her hands and standing up suddenly. She was almost in tears at this point, not sure what was real and what was imagined.

"Don't you hear it?" she asked with exasperation as Nicho looked at each of them one more time, almost begging for some sort of accord. They all stared back at her, feeling her confusion yet unable to give her the answer she was looking for. One by one, they each shook their head no.

Tonia stood up and threw her arms in the air in a frustrated gesture. She covered her face again for a few seconds then peered over her fingers at Nicho. On the verge of tears now, she sat back down on the rock, unsure of what to do.

"Mommy, where are you?" the voice cried again, louder yet.

"Where are you?" Tonia asked.

As a last resort, she decided to try to communicate with the

65

voice. She ignored the others as they sat watching her quietly.

Silence filled the cavern around them.

"Where are you?"

Her voice, filled with desperation, echoed around them. Either she was losing her mind or she wasn't. Although she didn't understand it, she decided to trust her instincts. In her heart she knew what she had heard, even if her mind was screaming at her that it could never be true.

"I wish I understood what was going on," she said to the others. "I just don't get it."

As they returned her gaze, she suddenly had a thought. Her fantasy! Maybe what she was hearing was a dragon! Could it be? She closed her eyes again, concentrating on the voice she heard in the depths of her mind. As she did this, a few remnants of the morning's dream began materializing, making their way back into her conscious memory. A small dragon with sad, helpless eyes, looking up at her from…

"Maybe we should head back," Diam suggested, unintentionally interrupting Tonia's concentration.

"We've come pretty far in here…" she said, before Tonia interrupted her in return.

"Shhhh!"

Tonia's voice was suddenly commanding and she held up her right hand as if she was issuing an order to stop. She continued concentrating, forgetting the dragon memory for the moment as she cleared her mind of all thoughts. She focused only on blackness, cool and peaceful, with no thoughts and no voices, and tried her best to relax. After a few seconds, she began thinking of the voice from her dream. She reached with her mind, trying to reach out to it.

"Who are you?" she thought, completely engrossed in what she was doing. The others sat on boulders and watched quietly, each at a loss regarding Tonia's actions. Was she crazy? Was she possessed by some cave fairy? Or was it some fuzzy chickleberry or even the cave air, affecting her thoughts?

"Mommy?" the voice called out again, this time sounding excited. "Mommy, is that you?"

"No, my name is Tonia," she replied with her mind. "What's

your name?"

"Celio," the mysterious voice answered with a hint of hesitation. "I can't find my mommy. She's been gone a long time." As the voice faded to a frightened whisper, Tonia heard it begin crying softly.

The creature's cries became the familiar tittering sounds they all heard before, but this time, Tonia heard it in her head as well as her ears. The other three gathered around her, facing the direction of the strange noise. Nicho's hand was now clenched firmly around the hilt of his sword.

"Where are you?" Tonia mentally asked again. "Come out so we can see you. We can help you find your mommy." Although she spoke from within her head, she did her best to keep her voice friendly and gentle.

"Can you hear me talk to you like this?" she asked, speaking out loud this time. Her question drew stares of disbelief and confusion from her companions but she didn't notice – her eyes were closed.

"Yes," she heard the quiet, hopeful response in her mind.

"I'm here with my friend and my brothers. We won't hurt you," Tonia answered softly. "It's okay to come out. Trust me."

Nicho, Micah and Diam all sat around Tonia, watching her intently. Either she was talking to some voice that only she could hear, or she *was* having a reaction to the berries she had eaten.

After a few long seconds, they all heard a slight rustling noise coming from behind the rocks on the side of the cavern. Tonia opened her eyes just as Nicho jumped up and immediately began unsheathing his weapon. Micah took to his feet as well, grabbing his bow from his back and an arrow from its quiver in a split second. Diam stood quickly and moved closer to Tonia, one hand blindly following her hip until it found her short sword.

Suddenly, they saw the slow shifting of dirt and stones coming from around the side of one of the rocks. At first they couldn't tell what was, but eventually a small, dark head emerged from behind the cover of safety and looked at them warily, obviously uncertain about whether or no it was wise to leave its hiding place and approach the adventurers.

"What is it?" Diam asked quietly.

"I'm scared," the voice said to Tonia. It cracked as it spoke and was somewhere between a whimper and a whisper.

"It's okay," Tonia said quietly, reassuring her new friend. "We won't hurt you. Can you talk out loud?"

"I... I don't know," it said in her head. "I've never tried."

Tonia slowly slid off the rock she had been sitting on. Looking around the room, she suddenly realized they all had their weapons drawn. She held up her hand to stay them, then returned her gaze back to the new arrival.

The creature was small and its shell was brown and mottled with gray streaks. She stepped slowly towards it and the small animal quickly began retreating back to its hiding place.

"No," Tonia said in a soft, reassuring tone. "It's okay. I won't hurt you."

The creature stopped, watching her warily.

She thought for a moment then dropped to her knees. As she knelt close to the creature, she considered that if she were closer to the ground, she would likely be less intimidating.

"Can you talk to me this way?" she asked. The others watched their friend and sister with awe and amazement. Although their weapons were still drawn, they had become somewhat more relaxed.

"Nnnnn I..." the creature said as it struggled to talk to her.

"It's okay," Tonia comforted as she held up a hand again.

The young turtle was hesitant and unsure of what these strangers were that had invaded its home. The shelled creature made eye contact with the still slightly delirious girl, but held close to the rocks for protection.

"I'll talk to you and you can communicate with me through thoughts, if that's easier for you, okay?" Tonia asked quietly.

The turtle nodded in response as it cautiously watched the rest of the group, nervous about leaving the security of its hiding place. All the while, Nicho, Micah, and Diam, stared at the unfolding scene before them as they began to accept that perhaps, just perhaps, Tonia was really talking to this turtle.

"It's okay," Tonia repeated, reassuring the turtle again. She then turned and looked at the others.

"It's okay, guys," she said again. "Put your weapons away.

Raguon turtles are harmless, I promise."

Her voice, although still soft and gentle, was now filled with confidence. She hoped they would trust her judgment. At the same time, she also secretly hoped that she wasn't making a mistake.

TEN

With some hesitation, the others slowly put their weapons away. Micah kept his hand on the pommel of his short sword, keeping a wary eye on the hard-shelled reptile.

"Can you tell us what happened?" Tonia asked. The creature appeared to be very young so she kept her voice quiet and soothing. "What happened to your Mother?"

"I… I don't know."

The anxiously spoken words appeared in her mind as if they were her own thoughts, yet in a different voice. "I was sleeping, taking a nap. When I woke up, she was gone. I'm not supposed to leave this area, but I looked everywhere in here for her and I can't find her."

The turtle pulled its dark, scaly head back into the protection of its shell and began sobbing again.

"It's okay now, Celio. Don't be afraid."

Tonia did her best to comfort the frightened creature. As she listened to his cries of anguish and fear, she made a decision, which should have been expected by the others when considering her love of nature, without consulting them first.

"We'll see if we can help you find her, okay?"

Micah sighed when he realized it sounded like she was volunteering them to find someone.

"What are we doing now?" he asked without trying to hide his irritation, the skepticism in his eyes nearly overwhelming.

He would not be so quick to jump into one her fantasies without some kind of proof or reward, and although he had

70

heard his sister just fine, he couldn't help but wonder what she was getting them into.

The more she thought about it, the more listening to a one-way conversation was kind of comical, Diam mused without a word. Watching her friend talking to the turtle, then nodding her head in agreement when no one else in the group was able to hear what she heard – or thought she heard – on any regular day, would make her think her friend might just be losing her mind. Of all the crazy quests and harebrained adventures the two had been on, this one seemed to top them more than all the rest.

"He woke up from a nap and couldn't find his mom. I think the least we can do is look around the cavern, maybe explore the tunnels a bit, and see if we can find her," Tonia explained as she stood up and brushed off her leggings.

Turning to Celio, she asked, "What's your mom's name?"

"Merlia," the young turtle answered with a sniffle.

"How do you feel, Tonia," Nicho asked, suddenly remembering how overtaken she was by the sensation she had in her head a short time ago. "Maybe we should rest here for a while longer."

"It's funny," she said as she looked down at their new friend. "Since I've been talking to Celio, the strange sensation in my head has completely gone away," she answered with a shrug.

"Hmm, I wonder what caused it," Diam said as her eyes met Tonia's.

Her comment was partly in concern for her friend's wellbeing and partly a desire to feel it herself. She knew that if either of the two of them would be able to communicate with animals, it would be Tonia, but of course this didn't mean Diam wouldn't want the chance to do it, too.

"I don't know, but I'm glad it's gone. It sure was a strange feeling," Tonia answered as she turned back to the turtle.

"Okay, Tiger, do you have any idea about where your mom might be?"

"Maybe she's over by the waterfall. Sometimes she goes there to get water for us," Celio answered quietly. Although he was still sniffling, Tonia could hear a hint of hope creeping into his youthful voice.

"Waterfall?" Tonia questioned. "What waterfall?"

"The one through the darkness," Celio answered. "Over that way, where I'm not supposed to go."

As Tonia watched, the shelled reptile extended his head in the direction of the tunnel that was exactly opposite where they had entered the cavern.

"There's a waterfall?" Diam asked as a glow of excitement appeared in her voice.

Celio hesitated as he listened to Diam.

"I'm not really sure where it is because she's never taken me there. She just tells me when she's going," he answered the older girl without realizing that Diam couldn't hear his response.

"I think we should go look for his mom," Tonia said with a hopeful look toward the others. "He thinks she went over to the waterfall to get some water."

She thought of another question and turned back to the turtle.

"Celio, do you have any idea how far away this waterfall is?"

"I don't think it's very far," he answered her. "Mommy would sometimes go get water and be back just a little while later."

"I think you should wait here while we go look for her, okay?" Tonia suggested with a smile.

"Okay," Celio agreed as he began crawling back to his hiding place. Suddenly he stopped and looked back at Tonia with frightened eyes that looked like two little lumps of coal on either side of his narrow face.

"What if you don't find her?" Before she could answer, he began to whimper.

"Shh. We'll do the best we can," Tonia reassured him. "You stay here, and we'll see what we can find."

The others watched as she turned and headed into the tunnel where Celio said the waterfall could be found.

"His mom's name is Merlia," Tonia explained as her brothers and Diam moved to follow her.

"Go slowly," Nicho warned. "We don't know what's in there or what may have happened to her."

Nicho had no intention of trying to dissuade his sister from helping the young turtle, but an eerie feeling, right in the pit of his stomach, was beginning to build. Their innocent exploration of the cave was starting to look a bit dangerous to him. If a turtle had disappeared, perhaps it was eaten or trapped? The possibilities were endless. As he considered different scenarios, an unwelcomed thought struck him – what if this was all a ruse?

The two brothers shared an uncertain glance at one another, determined to go on, and yet equally determined to be on guard.

They followed Tonia into the next tunnel, which seemed somehow slightly brighter than the other ones they had been in, and it turned upward at a pretty steep grade. Within a few minutes, they heard the distinct sound of rushing water and before long they could also smell it in the air. The liquid songs were louder here, stronger somehow, than the ones they heard earlier in the cave.

A moment later they entered another cavern, also different from the earlier ones. The flowing stream looked like it might be the one they had seen earlier, but now they appeared to be much further upstream. The location of the crooked line of flowing water here was different from the last one, too. When they entered the earlier cavern the stream was on their right, flowing towards them and exiting down through the tunnel on their left. Now, however, the stream was coming into the cavern from their left and exiting through another wall on their right.

"I think this is the stream we ran into over by the cave rat," Diam announced to the group.

"I think you're right," Nicho said with a nod. "We must have gotten high enough to get closer to the source of the stream." He stared at the flowing water, still wondering where the water might end up when it flowed out of the mountain.

Once they were standing almost side by side, they stopped and looked around the new room. There were many spider webs here, and most were hanging from the ceiling or attached to nearby rocks. Tonia's eyes scanned the earthen floor nervously as she nodded in response to Diam's comment about the stream.

"Merlia," Tonia called softly as she began searching for Celio's mother. "Merlia, we're friends of Celio. Where are you?"

There was no answer.

"Merlia," Diam called as she peered around the room, but still there was no answer.

73

They began spreading out, examining the different areas of the cavern. The stream was wider in this part of the cave, but only by a few feet. The floor was strewn with boulders and smaller stones, scattered throughout the flowing water, some above and some below the water line. They could also see several different types of leaves washed up on the stream bank in addition to dozens of small, broken twigs.

The main thing in this room that caught all of their eyes was the waterfall to their left. The cool liquid was coming from somewhere beyond the upper end of the stream, whispering goodbye as it cascaded down over a wide line of rocks before it landed in a shallow pool at the base of the fall. A slight mist rose up from the pool and soft spirals emanated from larger rocks that disturbed the free flowing water. On the near side of the pool, a smaller waterfall calmly drained the trapped water, letting it slide through the channel carved by hundreds of years of erosion.

Diam walked closer to the waterfall to examine it more closely. Just seconds after she stopped and peered into the water, her voice, filled with alarm, rang out and echoed off the walls of the cavern.

"Look!"

Tonia heard the urgency in her friend's voice and quickly rushed to Diam's side.

"What? What it is?"

Diam pointed at the base of the waterfall on the opposite side of the stream.

Tonia's eyes followed the direction where Diam was pointing.

"What do you see?" she asked Diam frantically. "I don't see anything."

"There, at the base of the waterfall," Diam explained, still pointing, "In the water – do you see it?"

Tonia took a closer look, struggling to focus on the area where Diam was pointing. After a few seconds, she thought she could barely make out an odd-looking object under the water through the ripples blurring the top of the water. The unidentified object was brownish in color, slightly darker than the rocks that were near it.

Wait, was it moving?

"Oh, no!" Tonia exclaimed as her eyes filled with recognition.

Without waiting to see where everyone else was or what they were doing, she darted quickly across rocks in the stream and jumped like a gazelle to the bank on the opposite side. Instantly after she landed, she rushed over to the base of the waterfall and knelt down. With immediate yet extreme gentleness, she reached into the water with both hands in search of the object. After a few seconds, she felt her hands brush across the brown disk that had caught Diam's attention and tried with all her strength to pull it out of the water. She pulled and pulled but it was stuck tight where it was.

The cascading water landing with a splash in the area of the stream near her caused too many ripples for Tonia to see the object, or what was holding it in place, clearly. If she could only see it through the ripples!

After a few more futile tugs, she realized she would first have to move a rock that was right next to the dark object. She did this, and a few seconds later, lifted a weakened, sputtering turtle out of the water.

"Merlia?" she asked the exhausted, shelled creature quietly as she held it up to look into its eyes.

"Ack, ack," Merlia coughed. She hung her head limply as she coughed up some clear liquid then faintly muttered, "Yes?"

She paused, trying to regain the breath she held so tightly in her chest moments earlier.

"How do you know my name?" she asked as she retreated most of the way into her shell, unsure of who or what held her so high up off the ground. The others stood nearby, amazed, because they could actually hear the sound of her voice as she spoke.

"My name is Tonia. We found Celio in the cavern back there, crying because he couldn't find you," the young girl explained. "Are you okay? He was very worried about you."

"Yes, I'm okay now," Merlia answered as she turned her head and coughed again. Hearing the spoken name of her youngster, she came back out of her shell, although only halfway.

"What happened to you?" Diam asked gently. "How did you get stuck at the bottom of the waterfall?"

"I waded in the stream for a while looking for food and eventually ended up on this side. Curious about how things looked from the top of the waterfall, I decided to climb the rocky path that led to it. Once there, I went over to the edge to look down into the pool. As I got close to the edge, I stepped on a slippery rock and tumbled over the waterfall. When I first hit the water, I narrowly missed one of the large rocks which would have turned me into fish food for sure then the strong current dragged me to the bottom. Unlucky for me, however, the wave I created when I landed must have caused one of the rocks in the pool to shift. Before I knew it, I was wedged in between them and was unable to free myself."

Merlia paused as she caught her breath.

"I consider myself very lucky that you came along."

Her head slowly shifted from side to side as she passed an exhausted, grateful glance from Tonia to the others. Although Tonia held the female turtle securely in both of her hands, she felt Merlia shudder as she considered what would have happened to her if they had not found her when they did.

"Is Celio alright?" Merlia asked, suddenly remembering that she'd left him alone while he was napping.

"He's fine," Micah answered. "He was understandably quite upset when he couldn't find you."

He paused for a few seconds before he added, "Is there anything else here that you need to do here? If not, we would be happy to take you back to him."

Micah's generosity surprised Tonia and she gave him a thankful, genuine smile.

"I've had enough of the waterfall," Merlia coughed, still clearing remnants of unwanted liquid from her lungs.

"Would you mind taking me back to my Celio?" she asked sheepishly. "We are the only two Raguon turtles that I know of around here. I shudder when I think of what would happen to my Celio if anything were to happen to me. It was careless of me to climb to the top of the waterfall, but it was even more careless of me to get that close to the edge. I can promise you I will never be that thoughtless again."

As she finished speaking, tear began welling up in her eyes.

Tonia took careful steps back across the stream while carrying Merlia. As she stepped on the bank near Diam, she stopped and looked around. The path they had followed to get here continued into the darkness beyond the waterfall, leading directly under the stream at the top of it. This seemed to be the only other entrance into the small, misty cavern.

"What's through there?" she asked the female turtle as she pointed towards the tunnel under the waterfall.

"I don't know," Merlia answered. "I've never been that way. Sometimes I do hear noises coming from that direction when I'm here looking for food, but they are very faint and seem quite far away."

"What kind of noises?" Diam asked, very curious now about what they might find deeper in the cave.

"I'm not really sure," Merlia answered. "As I've said, we've never been through there, so I can't say what the noises are. They are nothing familiar – nothing I recognize. Sometimes it sounds as though there are muffled conversations, while at others it sounds almost like there are screeches, as though something is in pain." She paused as she stared into the darkness beyond the fall. "Then, at other times, it's almost as if I can hear the soft sounds of singing, but it's not a language that I understand."

She paused again as she shook her head, perhaps to shake away the mystical sounds she heard reverberating around from somewhere between her ears.

"Celio and I are alone in our little part of this world, and I do not want to do anything to endanger either his life or my own. Of course I'm curious about the noises, especially the sounds of song, but I know realistically that we must stay here and mind our own business, if we want to survive." Her voice faded into silence as she glanced pleadingly at each of them in turn, almost as though she was silently begging for them to not judge her for protecting her child. Given her recent predicament as well as their own, it was surprising how intertwined their fates were.

"We understand," Nicho said. His voice was low and gentle as he consoled the turtle. "And we can't blame you for wanting to protect yourself and your little one." The older of the two boys paused to take a breath and consider the situation. "Let's get you back where you belong. I'm sure Celio is still very upset and worried about you."

They headed back to the cavern that Merlia and Celio called home. Entering the cavern, they looked for Celio, carefully making their way to the stone where they had left him.

"Celio, come look what we found!"

Tonia's voice was loud and excited, echoing off the walls of the small, dimly lit room.

The children stood in a tight circle in the center of the room, looking for the younger of the two turtles. They did not see Celio right away and Tonia began wondering if perhaps he had wandered off. Had he followed them to the waterfall?

A few seconds later they heard a soft scratching sound, weight being shifted on a dirt-laden, rocky floor. They turned in the direction of the sound and detected a hint of movement. First a dark, dusty nose began to emerge from behind the large rock. As if in slow motion, they began to make out the curve of the mouth and eventually, the dark, nervous eyes. Celio was behind the same rocks where he had been hiding earlier, patiently waiting for their return.

"Did you find my... MOMMY!!!" he finished ecstatically as he caught sight of his mother held securely in Tonia's arms. He scooted from behind the rocks as fast as his four legs would carry him, heading straight for Tonia as she began making her way towards him.

As soon as Merlia heard his voice, she couldn't help but move her legs in mid-air, each clawed foot scooping empty space as if she were running in slow motion toward her only son. When Tonia finally got about five steps away from juvenile turtle, she bent down and gently placed Merlia on the cavern floor.

"Thank you, brave explorers, for saving my life, and for caring enough to come look for me," Merlia said with a sniffle as she nodded once, turned and began making her way quickly towards Celio.

"My Celio," she cooed to him in a soft, loving voice. "My brave Celio!"

The humans watched as the turtles finally met up with each other a few feet away from the rock where Celio had been hiding.

Mother and son extended their necks from their shells as far as they could and as Celio moved his head under Merlia's chin, they began swaying from left to right, gently caressing each other. While Celio closed his eyes and began trilling softly, Merlia smiled with happiness as tears of joy and relief ran down her dark, age-worn cheeks.

The boys were both grinning with dry eyes at the scene on the cavern floor, Micah having forgotten his earlier dismay at the upcoming search for the missing turtle. Diam and Tonia both had tears pooling in their eyes, yet still they smiled.

"Micah," Tonia said as she turned to look at the younger of her two brothers with a salty, tear-filled smile. "Do you now understand, maybe a little, why I am the way I am? There is such a satisfaction in helping someone or something in need! THIS is why I do some of the things that I do."

"Yeah, yeah," Micah said, rolling his eyes. No way would he let her see how happy this really made him feel, absolutely not. If she picked up even a hint that he understood, really understood, she'd never let him live it down. Once she turned away, however, he allowed himself to crack a slight smile. He dramatically scratched at the corner of his eye in an attempt to clear the forming tear before it trickled down his cheek.

Tonia sighed and glanced back at the turtles. Still caressing each other, neither of the reptiles seemed to notice the humans standing around them in the dusty room they called home.

Diam hugged Tonia.

"I'm glad that we helped them, too," she said with a nod.

Tonia looked at her and smiled.

"Welcome to my world," she replied as she turned to look again at the turtles. She was proud they had taken the time to find Merlia. Even better than that, they got to share in something very special – the love between a mother and her child.

ELEVEN

The young explorers watched Celio and Merlia for another moment or two then decided to sit down and have another snack before continuing their journey. In order to give the turtles some privacy, they found some rocks a few paces away. They removed their bags from their backs and began rustling through them, looking for something good to eat. Micah sat down on one of the rocks, smiling.

"What are you smiling about?" Nicho asked him as he wondered what Micah was up to now.

"I was thinking that it's close to lunchtime, and I brought a special treat for us," Micah answered, trying to be secretive as he removed his gift from his bag. The only thing the others could see was a small packet wrapped in alia leaves.

"Leave it to you to think about food," Tonia said as she punched him lightly in the arm. Her tone was sarcastic but the physical gesture was playful. "I will admit, though, that I am getting hungry."

"Well, if you're going to be *that* way about it, I don't have to share any with you," Micah said, feigning an attitude.

"It depends on what you brought," Tonia said with a sneer. She leaned towards him, trying to peek at what he was unwrapping.

"It's dried chickenbird, if you really must know. I brought enough for everyone, but if you would rather just have your sour little chickleberries, I'm sure the others won't mind if I divide your portion between the rest of us."

Micah glanced at Nicho and Diam with a nod of satisfaction.

"I'll be happy to help out by eating your portion, Sis," Nicho said to Tonia. He knew they were getting to her and struggled to hide his smile. Most times she hated when they teased her. They could be relentless.

She glared at Nicho.

"Would you like me to slap you again, big brother?"

She raised an eyebrow at him as she opened her hand and pulled it back over her head, getting ready to swing.

"Absolutely not!" he answered, pretending to be afraid. "You might make me drop my own piece!"

While they bantered back and forth, Micah unwrapped the dried meat and passed it out to them, one at a time. Tonia looked at him and smiled gratefully.

"You know what, Micah? Sometimes you really get on my nerves," she said between bites, "but right now, I just think I love you."

Diam giggled, biting off a chewy, yet tender, chunk of dried fowl. "This was a great idea, Micah. My tummy thanks you for thinking of it!"

She closed her eyes and chewed slowly, savoring the flavor.

They sat for a few moments, enjoying their lunch. Nicho ate silently, lost in thought about their next step.

"What's on your mind, big brother?" Tonia asked, licking her fingers as she finished her last bite of the meat.

"I'm thinking, like before, about which way we should go," he answered as he also finished his portion of chicken. "I'm very curious about what lies beyond the waterfall, but there is also the other tunnel that branches off of this cavern. Once again, we have two choices. What do you guys think?" He fell silent as he awaited their responses.

"I think we should go beyond the waterfall," Micah said immediately. "We know from what Merlia said that something is there – we just don't know what it is."

Tonia stood up and walked over to where Merlia and Celio were sitting, not wanting to interrupt the mumblings of their conversation. As she reached them, they looked up at her. Suddenly realizing how she must have towered over them, she squatted down to be closer to them.

"Do you know, if we were to travel down this tunnel here, what we might find?" she asked them as she pointed toward the tunnel which led beyond the waterfall. She sat down on the dirty floor as she waited for Merlia to answer.

"I'm not sure you should venture into either one."

Merlia looked up at Tonia with a tense stare and her voice was low and serious. "I've never gone farther than the waterfall, so I don't know what may lie there, but something tells me it's nothing good. As for the other tunnel, it has been many moons since I've been down that one. The last time was right after Celio was hatched," she explained, looking fondly at her son.

"There used to be other Raguon turtles like us, but they are long since gone."

As she paused for a moment, Nicho, Micah and Diam, having finished their meal, came over one at a time and sat down next to Tonia.

"Long ago, we used to live out in the forest, among the trees and the leaves. We lived there with many other turtles – our family and friends. One day, the air suddenly changed, and a terrible storm came crashing down on us without warning. It rained for many days and nights, and many of our kind got washed away in the floodwaters that rushed down off the mountains." She paused, looking at Celio again for a moment before she continued.

"Only a few of us made it here, where it was dry and safe. We took shelter in the mouth of the cave, worrying about the others as we huddled together. During the worst part of the storm, the rain fell and the sky grumbled. All of a sudden, there was a bright light and horrible vibrations as the ground beneath us trembled. We were all so very frightened! None of us understood what was happening.

"Before we knew it, the side of the mountain came falling down, dropping rocks and boulders across the mouth of the cave! There was one place where the rocks did not block, but of course it was too high off the ground for any of us to reach."

Merlia stopped for a moment as the memories of her friends forced her to look at the floor of the cavern. Sadness filled her eyes and her voice cracked as she continued.

"The handful of us that remained knew we would have to

make our way further into the cave and find another home. I think we were all secretly hoping to find another exit so we could look for our friends and family.

"Luckily, none of us had been hurt by the falling rocks and we were all able to walk. As for the others on the outside, we never heard from them again. We have no way of knowing if any of them survived."

Merlia fell silent as her dark eyes turned up from the floor in search of the faces of the strangers surrounding her. She looked at them one by one, no longer seeing them as intruders to her home. They had listened intently to her story and as she sensed their understanding, she suddenly realized these unfamiliar humans had become their friends.

"We began walking through the tunnel and eventually found a stream," she continued quietly as her eyes looked into some place deep in her memory, "but there seemed to be little food there. We had no choice but to continue on deeper into the cave.

"Soon, we came to this cavern where we are now and stopped to rest. Paleo, the leader of our small group, said he thought he could hear moving water inside the other tunnel, so we all went to investigate. By this time we had all been without food for most of the day."

She stopped and turned to look at Celio. His eyes were bright as he listened to her story.

"What happened then, Momma? Where did the others go?" he asked excitedly, thinking he might soon have some playmates.

Merlia had never shared the whole story with Celio, certain he was better off not being exposed to more than the cave around him. In the time they had been trapped here, she had come to accept that this was all he and she would ever have.

"Shh," Merlia told him. "Be quiet and listen."

She looked back at the others and continued.

"We followed Paleo through the tunnel and discovered the cavern with the waterfall. Believe it or not, it was as beautiful then as it is now."

She paused again for a moment, her eyes bright with remembering.

"Food here is still scarce, but if you sit by the waterfall long enough, eventually a small water creature will come tumbling over the edge, more often than not falling to its death on the rocks below. When this happens, we retrieve it from the stream and take it back to our home for a wonderful meal."

The female turtle shuddered as she suddenly remembered her own adventure over the waterfall, knowing she had narrowly escaped her own death.

"As I've said, Paleo was our new leader," she continued, "but there were a few other members in our group.

"Melua was a young female, my sister's friend. Gartua was one of our ancient ones, the oldest from our home in the woods. He has since gone to the woods in the sky, or so I believe.

"Then there was Antron." She paused for a few seconds before continuing with a bittersweet, melancholy sigh. "He was young, feisty, and always looking for an adventure.

"After finding the waterfall, Paleo decided we should camp there, and although I didn't anything, I did not feel comfortable in that cavern. It was cool and damp with constantly moving water. I don't know how Gartua did it with his old, brittle bones. I'm sure the moisture in the air gave him many aches and pains in his old body. I give him much respect, both then and now, for he had spent many years under the eternal skies, had seen many hardships, and never complained.

"I was also wary of the other tunnel that branched off the cavern. I followed Paleo's direction, however, and we stayed there by the stream for a while.

"Without the rising and falling of the sun, it was hard to tell for sure how long we had been there. One day we were all sleeping when Antron woke up and suddenly moved to where Paleo was resting. He nudged one of Paleo's arms with his head, waking him up, and asked him if he heard the same noise that Antron thought he had heard. Paleo listened as he slowly raised his head high up off the ground."

She glanced at those around here and saw a quizzical expression on Tonia's face.

"Sometimes we can hear better when we do this," Merlia explained as Tonia nodded her understanding.

"After a few seconds, a sound whispered around them in the

darkness," Merlia continued.

"What was it, Momma? What was it?" The younger turtle's eyes were filled with curiosity and he was totally focused on the story his mother was telling.

"Antron said he thought he heard someone talking," she said as she looked straight at her son.

"Of course, their conversation woke the rest of us from our sleep. We sat in a loose circle for a while, listening to the sounds. Although the sounds were faint, none of us had any doubt that it was someone talking.

"Paleo suggested we go see who or what it was, thinking that whatever it was would know some way for us to get out of this wretched hole."

She stopped and looked at her son again. She didn't want to scare him but felt strongly that she needed to explain this part of her story to her new friends.

"Paleo made it very clear that he did not want to spend the rest of his life in here, away from fresh air, other creatures, and the warmth of the sun."

She knew Celio could have used a few more years behind him before he heard all of this, but the time felt right to tell the truth about how they had gotten there. Whether it was right to tell him now was beside the point. The cat was out of the bag.

"Antron and Melua agreed with Paleo, while Gartua and I did not. Majority ruled, however, and within minutes the three of them were ready to be on their way, following the sounds of the voices," she continued.

"As I've said, Gartua was old and did not move very fast. He had his own reasons for not wanting to join them. I, also, had my own reasons. I did not feel well, having been very tired prior to this. I did not think I would have the energy to keep up with them myself.

"In the end, Gartua and I decided to say behind and take our chances with life at the waterfall." She looked at her friends again as a smile played at the corners of her mouth.

"I had a feeling that the two of us who remained behind would soon be three. I had to follow my motherly instincts and protect my unborn egg."

She smiled at Celio. "I do believe, my young son, that without you, I may not be here today."

The others looked at her questioningly. She bowed her head, sadness overcoming her yet again. When she finally spoke, her voice was barely a whisper.

"The three of them left that day, off to find their mystery voices, and I have never heard from them since. Maybe they made it out of this cave, out where the sun shines and the wind blows, and they have new lives of their own. Then again, maybe they didn't. The voices we heard that day may not have been good voices at all."

The others quietly waited for her to continue.

"I've heard rumors of evil creatures that live in deep, dark caves. A favorite meal of many creatures is Raguon turtle meat," she finished. As she said this, Celio gasped and his eyes were no longer filled with excitement – they were now filled with fear.

"Evil creatures?" he asked with a trembling voice as he pulled his head slightly back into his shell. "Have you ever seen any, Momma?"

"No, Celio, I haven't, nor do I care to," she answered him. Her quiet voice, although filled with sadness, was gentle and calming.

"Soon after the others left, Gartua and I found an injured fish that had fallen over the waterfall. We carried it back here, to this cavern – to our new home," she said to no one in particular. "We lived here for a few months, talking to each other and taking turns with necessities, such as gathering food or water.

"Sometimes Gartua would go to the waterfall in search of food, but I tried to do it as often as I could. He was old and frail – I didn't want to cause him undue pain from all of that walking. As time passed, his aches became greater in his old bones. I think the dampness in the air affected him more than he would admit, but it was obvious to me.

"It wasn't long before I knew the time was near for my hatchling to join us. You see, with Raguon turtles, we carry one egg within us for a few months and then it is laid in a special place that is cool and hopefully dry. Within days of being expelled from the mother, the hatchling usually finds its way out of its confining shell.

"For nourishment, the hatchling eats the egg within the first few days of life. If it survives, it can begin eating the same food as an adult turtle, but in smaller portions, of course."

She paused, looking fondly at Celio.

"When we lived in the forest, we would lay our egg on a bed of leaves. Afterward we would cover it with more leaves, in order to provide it shelter and warmth," she explained.

"In here, as you know, there are no growing trees. As my birthing time grew closer I knew I would soon have to find some place safe to lay my single, precious egg.

"It was my turn to go to the waterfall and look for food, and while I was sitting on the shore of the stream past the base of the fall, I noticed how a few leaves had washed up on the edge of the stream. They were trapped, frozen in time, caught up on a variety of rocks. There were no water creatures in the stream yet, so I scooped up the leaves in my mouth and carried them back to our cavern. I spread them out near the area I called my own, hoping they would dry quickly. Then I made my second trip to the waterfall and sat down, hopeful for an easy meal.

"Surprisingly I didn't have to wait long to see just what I was hoping to see – a large, dark shape came barreling over the top of the waterfall without warning. The unidentified object tumbled through the air as if in slow motion, its legs flailing to and fro, as the round shadow struggled to stabilize itself on ground that wasn't there. I stared at it for a second or two, and just when I realized it was a large frog, the poor hopper landed on the rocks below with a bone-cracking crunch. I watched, nothing more than a tired, very pregnant, helpless bystander as the frog bounced off a dark, jagged rock which beckoned for victims like a hauntingly, crooked finger from the pool of clear water below. Thankfully the frog did not suffer for long – a second or two after it landed, its lifeless carcass floated down the stream toward me. Not one to bypass an opportunity as good as this, I waded into the water and snatched it up as it passed in front of me.

"A large frog can feed Raguon turtles for a few days, which was perfect for me, as I would not be in any shape to go hunting for food again for a few days."

She glanced at Celio again but didn't seem to really notice

him. In her mind, she was seeing the frog, the waterfall, and many other memories from long ago. Celio, however, was still watching her, completely engrossed in her story.

"I carried the frog back to the cavern where Gartua and I lived and we had a feast! It had been a very long time since either of us had eaten any frog meat, and it was longer still since we had fresh frog meat! We both gorged ourselves on it that first day, snacked on it all through the second day, and by the third day it was gone.

"By the end of the second day, the leaves I'd brought back from the waterfall were dry, so I prepared for the arrival of my hatchling. Shortly after that, my hatchling arrived and I stayed with him until he began to emerge from his shell, which is what any good Raguon turtle mother would do. While I was busy with my hatchling, Gartua made a trip to the waterfall to bring back some fresh water. I waited all day, and he did not return. After a few more days, he had still not returned. Once Celio had eaten the remains of his shell, I covered him with more dry leaves and told him to stay there and be a good boy. Confident Celio would follow my instructions, I set off to find Gartua."

She stopped, glad to be sharing her story yet hesitant to go on. The sadness in her eyes was quite evident to everyone in the small cavern.

"I walked to the waterfall cavern and softly called for Gartua, remembering how the others had talked of hearing voices. I knew that if we could hear them, they could also hear me as I searched for my missing friend.

"I searched all along the stream, even looking in the pool at the base of the falls. I could not find him anywhere. He had disappeared without a sign or hint of where he had gone. I was frightened and knew it was impossible for me to continue my search for him. I had a hatchling to care for!

"Reluctantly, I returned to Celio without finding my friend. We lived alone, just the two of us, for many months without word or evidence from Gartua.

"One day, shortly after Gartua disappeared, Celio and I were both sleeping soundly. We had no idea what time of day it was because, if you remember, we have no knowledge of whether it's day or night without the sun or the moon to guide us. Well suddenly we were awakened when the ground started trembling. You can imagine how this frightened Celio – he began crying and quickly huddled right next to me. Not long after the ground shook, we began to hear a loud noise that sounded like large rocks falling. Within seconds, I saw a plume of dusty powder as it billowed like a dusty breath out of the tunnel that branched off of our cavern. I wasn't sure what had happened, and I'm sure you can understand how I was hesitant to go in there on my own to find out.

"A few days later, however, my curiosity got the better of me. While Celio was taking a nap, I couldn't help myself. I decided to investigate."

She paused again, gathered her thoughts, and then softly continued.

"I walked a short distance inside the adjacent tunnel. It was a dry, very musty place but also had a strange odor in it that became stronger the farther I traveled into the tunnel. Other than the odor, I didn't notice anything strange in the underground passage. I hesitated, and although I had not gone very far, I understood that I could not continue on; I could not go any farther until Celio was older."

She looked at the others with a grave expression on her dark, yellow and black-lined face.

"That's the only time I've been in that tunnel."

She looked at Celio and smiled, her eyes filled with love.

"How long has it been since Gartua disappeared?" Diam asked.

"Without seeing the sun and the moon every day, it is hard to tell, but I think it has been at least a couple of moon cycles," she replied.

"That brings us back to my earlier question," Nicho said. He scratched his head as his eyes turned to the others. It was obvious that they were as anxious to get started as he was.

"Which way should we go now?"

TWELVE

After another brief discussion, they agreed to check out the tunnel under the waterfall, if for no other reason than they knew a few things about this tunnel and essentially knew nothing about the other one.

First, Merlia believed she had heard some kind of noises coming from somewhere beyond the waterfall – this was considered as a good sign. As the children discussed this, it was decided that if someone was in the tunnel, but they hadn't come from the same direction that the children had come from, then perhaps there was another way into the cave.

Second, Gartua had gone toward the waterfall when he had disappeared, so where had he gone? Merlia spoke fondly of the old turtle and the children sincerely hoped they could find him on their way to discovering another cave entrance.

Third, Merlia's story indicated there had likely been some sort of cave-in somewhere in the other tunnel. If they decided to explore this adjacent tunnel, the young explorers suspected they would not get far before having to turn back.

Tonia looked at the others, her face filled with concern.

"Guys, can we discuss something privately before we head out?"

Although they looked from Tonia to each other with questioning glances, they eventually nodded their agreement.

Tonia led the way back towards the waterfall. When they got close to the place where they found Merlia, she stopped and turned to look at them, each in turn.

"I know you'll probably think I'm crazy," she started out when Micah interrupted her.

"We always do," he mumbled with a smirk.

Tonia stopped and gave her brother a dirty look before continuing without replying to his comment.

"I feel bad for these turtles and want to help them find a better life if it's at all possible. I want to take them with us, and if we can't find any other turtles in here, we can always let them go once we're outside the cave."

She looked plainly at the others, waiting for someone, probably Micah, to argue with her, but no argument came.

"We can't just leave them in here to wither away! You heard what Merlia said about how they used to live out in the forest. It sounds like their whole village, all their friends and family, may have died in that storm. We've got to help them."

Her eyes blazed with emotion while her voice was soft and pleading. Diam, caring for wildlife with almost the same intensity as her friend, immediately agreed.

The boys looked at each other, silently thinking it over. The turtles really weren't that large and they should be able to carry them in their bags very easily. They both also knew Tonia well enough to know that once she had her mind set on something, there wasn't much chance that anyone could persuade her away from it. The boys agreed, although with not as much enthusiasm as Diam.

When Tonia realized she would receive no argument from any of them, her face broke into an enormous smile. She went up to them, one at a time, and gave them each a tight hug. When she was done, she stepped back and looked at them, her face beaming with happiness.

"Thank you all for understanding."

Feigning a serious tone, Micah shook his head dismally as he said, "I don't know about you Nicho, but I know better than to argue with a woman that carries a big stick!"

The others laughed before they turned and made their way back to the cavern where the turtles were still fawning over each other, totally engrossed in their reunion.

After explaining the results of their discussion, the children packed their things then helped the turtles gather the small amount of belongings they wanted to bring. Before they knew it, they were ready to go.

They agreed that carrying the turtles inside a bag was the most sensible thing to do. They would need their hands to carry their torches and weapons, if and when they were necessary. Tonia picked up Celio and gave him a reassuringly gentle pat on the head. She would carry him in her bag once they moved beyond the waterfall, and it was decided that Diam would carry Merlia in the same fashion.

The group of children started walking again, one at a time. This time Nicho led, the girls were in the middle, and Micah brought up the rear. When they reached the waterfall, they stopped and refilled their pia bottles and the girls set the turtles down on the stream bank so they could also get some water. None of them knew if their travels would take them along the stream or away from it, so they made sure they had their fill of water from the underground stream.

When they finished, each turtle was gently placed inside a bag and the boys then used the utmost care when helping the girls get each of their bags situated on their backs.

"Celio, Merlia, is everything okay?" Tonia asked just before the headed out. A muffled yes came from Diam's bag, and after listening mentally to Celio's response, Tonia explained that he was doing fine.

Once they were completely prepared, Nicho led the rest of the group by heading towards the tunnel under the stream. Since the passage was quite damp, they walked with slow, careful steps, wanting to be sure that no one slipped on anything, like mud or mossy rocks. They could hear the sounds of running water over their heads and in some places, it trickled down the tunnel walls, pooling on the dirt and rocks that covered the floor.

They walked on like this for a short time, watching and listening for anything out of the ordinary as they trudged through puddles and along dirt and rocky passageways. Sometimes the passage ventured a short distance away from the stream, but mostly it followed in the same direction. The water dripping from above had grown so intense at one point that a second stream had formed along one edge of their path, and occasionally they had to cross the flowing water in order to keep moving forward.

After a while, the tunnel widened considerably before it opened up into an enormous cavern, this one much larger than those they had seen previously. They entered this room with caution, investigating with their eyes like seasoned explorers. They surveyed the ground, walls, and ceiling as they searched for any signs of life.

Due to the size of the cavern and the inability of the light emitting from their torches to penetrate the large body of darkness which engulfed the space around them, the children struggled to see through the entire length of the cool, musty room. As they stood in a small cluster, each trying to quiet the sound of their breathing, Micah held his torch high over his head, hoping to get a better look at just what kind of room they had walked into. They expected to see a lot of rocks and boulders, much like those they had seen in the past caverns, and they were not disappointed.

The first things they noticed were the large boulders everywhere in the room, or in as much of the room as they could see. There were many rocks that stood taller than Nicho, with smaller boulders scattered like a giant's forgotten gems in between. The stream had since disappeared down some hidden escape route beneath their feet, yet the soft trickling sounds of moving water still serenaded them somewhere in the distance. In the dimly lit cavern, however, they were unable to see just where the sounds were coming from. As cool, almost stagnant air caressed their skin, they continued making their way deeper into the room, stepping over rocks and in between the boulders, wondering what, if anything, they might find here.

Wouldn't it be a shame to spend an entire day, trudging through previously unexplored territory, only to come up with nothing worth talking about? Micah had been thinking of all his friends in the village that he could brag to once they returned home about their escapades, but at this rate, he wouldn't want anyone to know what they'd spent the day doing in a cool, rocky cave full of dust and less-than-fresh air! So far it had amounted to nothing more than seeing a cave rat and bruising his knee!

"We need to be very careful," Nicho warned, interrupting

Micah's thoughts with a nervous whisper. They lowered their torches and looked around the room. "I've got a funny feeling about this place."

"Why don't Micah and I check out the left side of the room while you girls check out the right? Be very careful," he repeated, "and don't venture too far. I don't want anyone to get lost."

"I think before we go any farther, I'm going to take off my long sleeved shirt and leggings. It's starting to get pretty warm in here," Micah said with an agreeable nod.

Without waiting for a response from the others, the younger boy lowered his bag to the dusty floor and handed Nicho his torch so he could remove his now somewhat sweat-dampened shirt.

As he watched his brother, a single question lingered in Nicho's mind – why would it be getting hotter in a dark, secluded cave? The others, oblivious to this thought, agreed that it was a good idea to modify their attire and, after working together for a few minutes, they were all much more comfortable and ready to continue.

They spread out cautiously, each group holding their single, flickering torch before them. With a nod and a hushed whisper to "be careful," Tonia and Diam made their way to the right, while Nicho and Micah veered to the left.

Micah paused briefly before calling after the girls. "Make sure you stay together!"

They nodded and answered in unison, "We will."

"Should we follow the wall or try to stay near the center of the cavern?" Tonia asked her friend as they peered into the darkness ahead.

"Let's follow the wall. It sounds like the water is coming from this direction," Diam answered.

The girls stayed close to each other, weaving their way over the rocks and between boulders. When they approached larger rocks that they couldn't see around, they did so slowly and always with one hand on a torch and the other on the pommel of their sword. They certainly didn't want anything jumping out at them! As they continued walking, they began to notice more spider webs, strung mostly between rocks. After a few seconds

94

of silence, Diam squatted down to look at one near the ground.

"You know what, Tonia?" she asked, bending forward to get a closer look at the web. "This one looks like it hasn't been lived in for little while. There are no cocoons or skeletons of any kind in it. It's just here," she said, using her stick to remove it from their path, "kind of like the one that Nicho cleared from the entrance to the tunnel back there."

Tonia watched her friend remove the web with a frown. The gossamer home that captured Diam's attention may have been abandoned for a week or a thousand years – the time frame didn't matter. Tonia had an uneasy feeling about spider webs of any kind – today, yesterday, last year, next year – and it didn't matter whether they found them in the forest or in the cave.

She absolutely hated spiders!

"Good," she replied. Although her friend knew she hated eight-legged creatures more than most, Tonia decided to hide how uncomfortable she was after seeing so many spider webs since they'd been in the cave. "The emptier, the better."

She gave Diam a reassuring smile and was relieved when her friend stood up and continued on.

Meanwhile, Nicho and Micah made their way along the left wall and soon encountered yet another tunnel. This one was narrow and had a very musty odor.

"Let's check this out, Nicho."

"Okay, but take it slow," Nicho replied. Although his curiosity was piqued, he didn't want to move too far away from the girls.

The boys followed the tunnel cautiously, unsure of what they might find. The pathway was clear of large boulders but was littered with small rocks and pebbles. The noticed that dust had built up at the edges of the cave, and it was obvious that no one had passed this way in quite some time.

It didn't take long before they came to a dead end where the jagged cluster of rocks overhead arched upwards, high above the rest of the tunnel ceiling. It appeared that a large part of the ceiling had collapsed here and, as a result, the path was completely blocked. They examined the blockage as they tried to see if there was a place to squeeze through and continue on. After a brief inspection, they found a few gaps and crevices here and there, but nothing they could fit through. They looked at each other for a few seconds before they finally accepted defeat.

"I wonder what happened," Micah said as his eyes roved across the scattered shards of rocks.

"It looks to me like the ceiling might have had a weak spot and it just collapsed," Nicho explained as he poked around the base of the jumbled pile of broken and jagged rocks. "I wonder if this is the other side of the tunnel Merlia talked about – the one the dust came billowing out of."

For the next few minutes the boys examined the devastated area at the end of the tunnel – Nicho checked out the right side while Micah was over on the left. It didn't take long for one of them to find something.

"Uh, oh."

Nicho's eyes were grave as he glanced up at his brother.

"I hate hearing 'uh-oh' when we're at a dead end in a dark, musty tunnel," Micah responded as he waited for his brother to continue.

"It looks like we might have solved the mystery of what happened to one of the turtles," Nicho replied, kneeling near the base of the rocks. Micah walked over to Nicho and squatted down beside him.

"What is it?" Micah asked as he turned to look at his brother. He could barely see the dark, unknown shape on the ground that had gotten Nicho's attention, so he moved his torch closer to it. It didn't take long for him to see that, whatever it was, the falling rocks had shattered a large part of it. Before Nicho could answer him, Micah could see the distinct design of a turtle shell, similar to that of Merlia and Celio.

"Oh, no," he whispered, his quiet voice filled with both sadness and dread.

A large area of the shell was buried under the rock wall that blocked the tunnel and only a small portion of it was visible. This part was broken into several pieces and was covered with a layer of dust and small bits of rock. It appeared to have been here for quite a while.

"How do we know this is him?" Micah asked quietly as he looked up at Nicho.

"We don't," the older boy responded grimly.

He picked up a small piece of broken shell. It was dry and dusty, without any remnants of the life that it had once encased.

"I'll take this to Merlia and see if she recognizes it," he said as Micah resumed his examination of the area.

"Hey, what's this?" Micah asked, kneeling to pick up a dull, gray stone that had caught his attention. It was the size of a small chickenbird egg – round, smooth, and small enough to rest easily in the palm of his hand. In the torchlight, it appeared to contain tiny, glittering flecks of light, much like the ones they would sometimes see high in the sky on a cloudless summer night. As soon as his fingers touched it, the stone immediately burst into an amazing ball of light engulfed by a mesmerizing aura of bright blue.

"What…?" Micah whispered as he quickly stood up and stumbled backwards, trying to get away from the small glowing orb. As soon as his fingers lost contact with the stone, the light disappeared like a small flame being extinguished by a pia bowl of water. He stared at the stone, wondering if he'd imagined its reaction to his touch. It was nothing more than a dull, gray rock, lying innocently on the edge of the pile of other rocks.

"Are you okay?" Nicho asked him, unsure of what had happened. He'd seen Micah stumble but wasn't sure what had caused it. He had only seen the flash of blue light that was there and then gone. He eyed his brother with a completely puzzled look upon his face.

"I'm okay," Micah said in a somewhat reassuring tone as he looked at his brother with wide, surprised eyes. It was obvious he was talking to himself as much as he was to Nicho. "Did you see it?"

Even as he asked Nicho this final question, his head moved from side to side as if to shake off a dream.

"All I saw was a flash of light," Nicho answered, not understanding what had just happened. "At least I think that's what it was. Micah, what did you do?"

Micah pulled himself off the floor and knelt down next to the stone.

"I touched this stone and it immediately began to glow,"

he said as his finger pointed at the dull, dark stone. "I'm not sure why it glowed, but I think it was because I touched it." He paused as he tried to regain his composure. "It scared me and I fell backwards."

As he finished his sentence, Micah began reaching down to touch it again.

"Wait, Micah!" Nicho shouted. "I'm not sure if that's a good idea!"

"It didn't hurt last time so I think I'll be alright," Micah said with a brave tone of renewed confidence. He hesitated briefly as his finger got closer to the stone, and although he didn't quite know what to expect when he touched it again, he could feel an unmistakable excitement rising somewhere deep within him.

"What if this belonged to a wizard," he thought. "A troll? A dragon! A king!"

On the ground the stone was dark and lifeless, but as soon as his fingers touched it, it immediately sparked to life again. A cloud of radiant, blue light surrounded the stone like a thin, colorful blanket, reminding Micah of the ocean bay where they often went fishing. It was bright and luminous, and he could feel himself being drawn toward it, almost like the valley robin was drawn to a fat, juicy worm on a warm, summer morning.

"Awesome!" Micah whispered. He stared at the glowing stone in awe for several seconds before gently reaching down to pick up the stone. With an almost overwhelming tenderness, he picked up the stone and held it in his hand.

The blue glow from the stone spilled across his hand, and as he brought it closer to his face, the color of the sky was reflected in his eyes. He smiled and looked over at his brother as Nicho took a step toward him, also mesmerized by the beautiful blue light.

"Do you feel anything?" Nicho asked. He cocked his head to the side and turned his ear toward Micah's palm. A light humming noise had begun projecting softly from his brother's hand.

Micah nodded. "It feels warm, like it's been lying on the beach in the sunshine. That's it, though. I wonder where it came from." Micah's shining blue eyes settled on Nicho's brown ones as he looked to his brother for his opinion. Being the older of the two, it was obvious that Micah hoped Nicho would have a better idea about things such as these.

Nicho, beginning to feel very relaxed, shook his head to break the spell that the stone was putting him under.

"I'm not sure, but it's definitely having an effect on me."

After a slight pause, Nicho added, "Can I hold it?"

Micah's startled gaze moved from his palm back to his brother. He hesitated, obviously unsure about relinquishing the stone to his brother's care. He loved Nicho, very much, but he had felt a strong bond with this magical stone from the moment he first touched it. When the long moment of greedy doubt finally passed, Micah gently, hesitantly, placed the stone into Nicho's open hand.

As soon as the single piece of hardened earth dropped out of Micah's hand, the glow instantly disappeared. Once again, it was just an unremarkable, dark, glittering stone.

Nicho frowned.

"I guess it likes you more than me," he said, rolling the stone around in his hand, examining it. After a brief inspection and seeing nothing extraordinary about it, he handed the rock back to his brother.

As immediate as before, the stone blazed to life as soon as it touched Micah's hand.

"I wonder why it's doing this. Could it have special powers? Maybe it belonged to a wizard!" Micah smiled as he repeated his earlier thought.

Nicho shook his head and turned around, facing the direction they had come from.

"Come on. Let's go find the girls."

With his torch in his right hand, Micah held the quietly humming stone in his left hand for a few more seconds before finally dropping it gingerly into one of his pockets. He turned and followed Nicho back out to the cavern.

Meanwhile, the girls walked past the spider webs and came to a line of decent-sized boulders that appeared to be blocking a large part of the cavern. Upon closer examination, however, they found one area where there was a partially hidden crevice. They stood listening for a few seconds and realized they could hear the sound of running water right on the other side. It was much closer now.

They inspected the gap between the rocks and decided they could both just barely squeeze through, so Diam nodded in silence and led the way. When they emerged on the other side, the girls stared at the stream, presumably the same stream as before, bubbling with life before them. They stopped to take in their new environment.

"I think this is the same stream that we passed before," Diam whispered.

"Why are you whispering?" Tonia asked as she gave her friend a funny look.

"I don't know," Diam answered, smiling sheepishly, "Because I can?"

The girls walked over towards the stream and looked around. When they were just a foot or two away, Diam saw something out of the corner of her eye. She turned toward it to see what it was.

The stream entered through an opening near the base of the wall, much like the flowing water they found near the entrance to the cave. The opening they now saw was on the far right of where they had entered and was encircled by an assortment of loosely scattered rocks. On the bank near the left end of the stream, the torchlight reflected off of a small, glittering object. Intrigued, Diam moved closer to it and as she bent over to pick it up, her shadow crossed paths with the torchlight and the object seemed to disappear amongst the gray gravel on the floor. Squinting her eyes in the light, she shifted just out of the way so the orange glow of the torch reacted with the golden flecks on the surface. Before it disappeared in the shadows again, she quickly snatched up her prize!

"Look at this, Tonia. It's a sparkly stone, and it's sooooo beautiful!" Diam said with a sigh of approval.

Tonia turned towards her with a frown.

"Now's not the time to be playing with rocks, Diam," she said, playfully admonishing her friend. "We're supposed to be looking for a missing turtle!"

100

Unimpressed with one rock in a cave filled with them, Tonia turned and continued investigating the area. Ignoring her friend, Diam picked the stone up to examine it a little closer. Small flecks buried beneath the surface of the solid object sparkled and glittered in her torchlight. She was mesmerized by the color and shape of the stone and without any hesitation, realized she just couldn't part with it. For the time being, she decided to put it in her pocket. Maybe she could make a necklace out of it, or keep it as a luck stone. Some of the village children were collecting luck stones, but as far as she knew, none of them had one like this! She pulled it out of her pocket and took another quick look at it.

Yes, this stone sure was different!

Danuth, an old man in the village, was a collector of rocks and stones, and what a collection he had! Sometimes he used an armadillo cloth that had been dried and cured as a buffer to make his rocks and stones sparkle like the stars. She would have to ask him about her new prize as soon as they returned to the village. Maybe she could sell it to him!

Diam's imagination was flying with ideas of what she could do with the stone when she suddenly froze where she stood. Tonia was squealing!

THIRTEEN

"Diam! Come look at this!"

Tonia's excited bounced off the walls and across the running water. For a split second, it sounded like it was everywhere! Diam's head spun around to find Tonia looking at something behind a large boulder near the center of the room.

"What is it?" Diam asked as she moved briskly towards her friend.

"What's going on?" a muffled voice emanated from somewhere within the bag on Diam's back. "Is everything okay?"

It was Merlia.

"I think so," Diam answered. "Tonia, our fearless explorer, has apparently found something that's caught her attention."

Tonia, originally frightened by the sight hidden behind the rocks, had quickly recomposed herself and within seconds, Diam was at her side. She grabbed Diam's torch and held it out over the edge of a wide circle of rocks.

As she made her way over to Tonia, one particular boulder blocked her view of whatever it was that Tonia was looking at. As Diam reached her friend's side, the torch illuminated the area quickly. For a few seconds, all Diam could do was stare in disbelief.

"Oh, my!" she said and backed away a couple of steps. "What is THAT?"

The wide boulder before them was about half as tall as the girls, but that didn't stop Tonia. She was already leaning over it to get a better look at her discovery.

"It's a skeleton, silly," Tonia said as she looked over her shoulder at Diam. Her eyes were empty of fear and full of adventure.

"Here, hold this for me," she said. Diam took a few, cautious steps forward and grabbed the torch Tonia was holding out to her.

"I know it's a skeleton, I am not silly, and WHAT are you doing?" Diam asked her friend. Without answering, Tonia began climbing over the boulder to get a closer look at the skeleton.

"Wait," Diam said in hopes of stopping her friend. "Let's take the bags off of our backs and let the turtles out for a little while. Who knows how long you'll be over there poking around?"

"Good idea," Tonia agreed, smiling mischievously as she slid back down from the top of the rock. They helped each other take their bags off their backs then carefully removed the turtles. Without a word the pair of girls carried the hard-shelled creatures over to the stream and set them gently on the ground next to the stream.

"We'll put you here for now until we find out more about what's behind those boulders," Diam said softly.

Merlia nodded and the girls walked back to the skeleton. Without giving themselves any time to think twice, they peered over the top of the rock like a pair of curious mud puppies.

The skeleton was relatively small, about the same size as the girls, with a wide skull, unusually shaped jaw and small eye sockets. The jaw, they noticed, protruded out farther than anything they had ever seen before.

Was it human?

Just beyond the skeleton, the rock formations grew larger, most of them much taller than the girls. There were leaves built up both at the base of the rocks as well as around the skeleton. The lifeless corpse was lying on its back, partially covered with decay. Someone had made a very poor attempt at hiding the poor thing.

"I want to get closer to it and check it out," Tonia told Diam. Although Diam thought her friend has lost her mind, she partially understood. Tonia was one of the most curious people she had ever met!

"What?" Tonia asked. Her eyes twinkled mischievously but her tone was perplexed, indicating she was unsure of why Diam would be looking at her that way.

"Oh, nothing," Diam said, shaking her head. "It's just that a few things seem a little odd to me." She hesitated, looking at her friend.

"Like?" Tonia asked, not sure where Diam was going with this.

"We're in a cave that we've never been in before. The boys are off who knows where. We're moseying along and find a strange skeleton, and you just jump right in there to check it out!" Her voice changed from a loud whisper to a shout before she reached the end of her tirade. Diam shook her head and a sighed in defeat. "What am I going to do with you?"

As Tonia shrugged, Diam added, "And Tonia, what would your mother say?"

"She's not here, the boys are not far away, and you know how I love to explore anything and everything that I can! Maybe there are some cool looking bugs under the skeleton, or treasure, or…"

Diam stopped her with a stomp of her foot and a raise of her hand.

"Ew, Tonia! That's just gross!"

In her mind's eye, Diam could see Tonia poking around the skeleton as bugs scattered here and there, interrupted from whatever things they may have been snacking on while under there. Then she saw her friend, her best friend in the whole valley, actively pursuing the bugs, trying to catch them to see what kind they were.

"Yuk," Diam added as she rolled her eyes and shook her head again.

Even though her friend sometimes did things that made scratch her head with a total lack of understanding, Diam was not in the least bit surprised. She knew Tonia well enough to expect this kind of behavior now, no matter how gross or strange it might be.

Before Diam finished commenting on Tonia's choice of activities, her friend had easily climbed over the boulder and was stepping into the makeshift grave with slow, methodical steps.

After a few more seconds, Diam handed Tonia the torch as she leaned on the rock, watching her friend as she knelt down to get a closer look at the corpse.

"I wonder who and what it was," the younger girl said, nervous about touching it but unable to quell her curiosity. "It's definitely a skeleton, but I don't think it's human."

Although it looked as though life had been gone from the skeleton for quite some time, Tonia gently brushed the leaves away that partially covered the skeleton, much like a mother brushing tears away from a child's cheek. They stared at the skeleton for a few seconds when she was finished – it was all bones and a lot of dust. A few scraps of colorful material – remnants of clothing – that partially covered the corpse crumbled away into nothing as soon as she brushed at the leaves, causing dust particles to billow gently into the air around them.

"It must have been here for quite a while," she said quietly.

Just as Diam suspected she would, Tonia poked around the leaves and the bones, looking for anything of interest. Next to the corpse, in a crack between the boulders and initially hidden by a clump of dry, brown leaves, she caught sight of a piece of tarza vine. It appeared to be wedged in between the boulders.

Ever the curious one, she reached over and tried to pull it out, but whatever the vine was attached to was wedged tightly in between the rocks and would not budge. She shifted, moving her torch closer to see if she could see the trapped item, eventually realizing it looked like a small piece of cloth.

She looked back at Diam with questioning eyes.

"Is there a crack in between these boulders on the other side? There's something stuck in there and I want to get it out." Diam moved around the rocks until she was on the opposite side of the place Tonia was talking about.

"No, I don't see a crack on this side," she answered.

She turned her attention back towards the stream bank as her eyes scanned the area for any possible tools that they could use to free the cloth from between the boulders. After a moment, she called back over her shoulder to her friend.

"Hang on, Tonia. I think I see something you can use!"

In the dim light, she walked quickly back to the stream,

hoping she'd found something useful. As she got closer, she was able to focus on the dark, straight object and smiled.

Yes! A small, sturdy looking stick had washed up among the rocks near where they entered the area. She picked it up and hurried back to her friend with it.

"Try this," she said.

Tonia took the stick from Diam with a nod of thanks and worked to free the trapped item. Not knowing what she had found, she was as gentle as she could be. She understood that if the trapped item had been here as long as the skeleton, it might fall apart as easily as the remnants of clothing had disintegrated with the gentle touch of her finger.

She placed the tool under the item and gently rocked it up and down. Although it was a bit thinner than what she would have liked to be using for this purpose, the stick definitely seemed sturdy enough.

Wanting to help her friend, Diam climbed on top of the boulder and took hold of the tarza vine with her free hand, gently pulling upward at the same time. Working together this way, they were soon able to free the object from its hiding spot. It appeared to be some sort of pouch, similar to those used to carry coins by tradesmen that occasionally visited their village. The pouch was held closed by a short, dark length of tarza vine that was woven around the opening.

Diam held the pouch out to Tonia.

"Go ahead," Tonia said, shaking her head. "Open it."

After wedging her torch in between two of the nearby rocks, Diam gently loosened the tarza vine from the neck of the bag and used her fingers to pry it open. She couldn't tell what was inside, but she could definitely feel at least two items – one was bulky and one was small. Tonia placed her torch in a rock crevice near Diam's, then cupped her hands together and looked at her friend with a twinkle of curiosity.

"Pour it into my hands," Tonia said.

Diam threw her friend a glance filled with doubt, worried about what might be in the bag. Poisoned darts? Poisonous spiders? She hesitated, thinking,"Boy, wouldn't that scare Tonia out of her moccasins!"

Diam shook the pouch gently and heard clinking sounds. Money? Gems? After another slight hesitation, she finally relented and poured the contents of the bag into Tonia's cupped hands.

Out fell a few gold coins, a set of rock sparkers, and what looked like a small, silver ring. Tonia put the rock sparkers and coins back into the bag after looking at them briefly, then took a closer look at the ring.

It was fairly small, small enough for a child's finger, and Tonia held it closer to the torches that Diam was now holding. It appeared to be made out of fine silver and held a small, green gem in the center of another, smaller ring of silver. The opaque stone was perfectly smooth and contained a slight marbling of deeper greens mixed with a few very thin streaks of white. For a few seconds, the girls could only stare at the gem when it suddenly clouded over as they watched in silent fascination. The cloudiness slowly changed to what appeared to be a swirled green and white fog, beckoning clouds filling the deep cavity of the stone. Just when the girls felt as though they might get lost in the tendrils of swirling clouds, the stone changed back to a simple, green gem in the blink of a firebug.

They looked at each other in shocked surprise.

"Wow!" Tonia said. "What was that about?"

"I don't know, but I think you should put it back in the bag for now until we can talk to the boys about it. It might be really dangerous," Diam said nervously.

Tonia nodded and placed the ring gently back inside the bag, then she pulled the tarza vine snuggly and twisted the end. She tucked it back into her pocket for later.

"Let's go see if we can find the boys. Maybe they know what kind of skeleton this is. I wonder if the bag belonged to it. Or maybe it belongs to whomever put the skeleton here?" she mused out loud.

Diam held Tonia's torch so she could climb back over the boulder. After retrieving the turtles and helping each other with their bags, the girls began walking back towards the crevice that would take them back to the boys. As they headed towards the gap in the rocks, Diam stopped and looked cautiously behind them towards the far end of the stream. She had a strange thought, actually more of a feeling, that someone or something was watching them.

Looking around, she didn't see anything out of the ordinary but couldn't seem to brush the feeling away. She shook her head in an attempt to clear it without much luck. With a sigh she turned and followed Tonia, who was waiting at the entrance to the crevice. They glanced around the area one final time before they made their way through the gap between the rocks.

As they did so, neither of the girls happened to notice the small pair of yellow eyes watching them from behind a moss-covered boulder near the far end of the stream.

FOURTEEN

Ransa had been slithering through the cave for quite a while now, mostly unsuccessful in her search for food. It was her turn today to find fresh meat for her family, which consisted of her siblings and her mother, Lusea. They were a family of cave snakes and were accustomed to living in the darkness of the cave. They lived together upstream in a small, hidden cavern, along a tunnel that ran parallel to the water – a perfect location for a perfectly happy family.

Along a small stretch of the underground passage near her home was an area where the cracks in the ceiling allowed small patches of sunlight to occasionally penetrate the darkness, cutting through the blackness like brilliant swords. On one side, smooth rocks sloped gently upward while the gentle stream meandered lazily along the other. In between was a dusty tunnel that led to nowhere, blocked in both directions by fallen rocks and stones, some twenty paces down in one direction and about fifty in the other.

Where the rocks sloped upward, it looked almost as though there had been a lot of walking done over the years, for the slope was smooth and gradual. Behind some of the rocks at the top of this slope was a small crevice well-hidden behind a large black stone. This led to the place they called home.

It was always quiet in their little corner of the cave and they were never bothered, which was likely because of how secluded the area was. They were fortunate to have found this hidden cavern and they all knew it. The places throughout the cave

109

where the sun reached in for even a minute or two each day were few and far between, indeed.

They were also fortunate for another reason – not only would the sun shine occasionally in the tunnel just outside of their home, but sometimes it would shine through two small cracks in the cavern ceiling within their home. Often, on a sunny day at just the right time they could lay in the sun in comfort and safety, if only for a short time. Ransa doubted if any of the other cave creatures were this lucky.

An additional convenience was how the cave stream flowed close to their secluded hideaway. Constant moisture in the air from the moving water led to the growth of a thick, brown moss on some of the rocks near the stream. The entranceway to their home was hidden behind a number of rocks that were partially covered by some of this shaggy vegetation as well. The moss gave off a slightly musty odor to all things in the cavern, but having lived here her whole life, the serpent did not notice anymore. It smelled like home.

That morning, Ransa had been chosen as the one to go hunting and she was quite happy to do so. All members of the family had been hunting long enough to know where to go and what to look for, and they accepted their responsibilities without argument. She was proud to go out hunting and bring enough food back to feed her entire family.

It was said that there were other Wiltoa scattered throughout the cave, but Ransa had never seen any, and it had been assumed that the rumored creatures may even have found their way into the nearby woods that Ransa and her siblings had all heard stories about. Although most of her family members had never seen this fabled place, they often dreamed of slithering through tall grass, between branches and up tall trees. Her mother had warned her that the cave was large, and their fear of the mysterious Wiltoa was stronger than their curiosity. As a result, neither she nor her siblings dared venture too far from the safety of their familiar surroundings.

Her mother's name was Lusea and she had been a constant companion for as far back as Ransa could remember, always having their best interests in mind. They had been living in their current home for quite a while, but there was a time long ago when they lived in another part of the cave. Their former home was much closer to the great abyss.

The abyss was a large, seemingly bottomless hole in the cave floor. Many of the cave creatures avoided it, because when you peered down into it, your line of vision would be lost in complete, infinite darkness. From what she'd been told, there was no bottom to the abyss, and no one who had the mishap of falling in ever returned to tell otherwise. Neither Ransa nor her siblings had ever gone exploring there – it was strictly forbidden.

There was another reason, the main one really, why that area of the cave was forbidden. It was said that the great Wiltoa snake Muscala lived there, deep in the dark shadows of the great abyss, and what an angry snake he was! They had all heard stories about him – how he would sometimes come out to hunt and was not at all picky about what he hunted. He ate anything he could find, with other Wiltoa snakes being no exception. The snakelets all knew to keep their distance from the abyss and this angry giant at all times.

Shortly after Ransa and her snakelet brother and sister were hatched, their father, Vortod, had gone hunting with his brother, Telno. Although Vortod frequently went hunting with his brother, Ransa remembered this particular time like it was just yesterday. She was exceptionally fond of her uncle, Telno, who would always save his rat tails for her. They were a favorite treat of the young snakelet.

The brothers had gone in search of a particular cave entrance where a large cluster of Shintala bird nests were rumored to be hidden. Although they'd never had any, the snakelets were told this type of bird meat was considered a delicacy, and remembering his own childhood, there was a time when Telno had the opportunity to try some. It was so good he would have been willing to risk anything for a chance to taste the truly fantastic meat again. And he would have to risk a great deal, as they could only be found near the cave entrances and it was not easy to find the mysterious birds.

The variety of food they ate was adequate and consisted of mostly bugs, small cave rats, and occasionally fish or frogs when they were able to catch them in the stream. Sometimes, however, Ransa would dream of the feast they would have if they ever found the Shintala nest clusters. Oh, how her mouth would water!!

On the day in the front of Ransa's memory, Vortod and Telno left in search of these nests. She and her fellow snakelets waited anxiously for their return, and after a few endlessly long days, Telno finally came back – alone. He slithered back into their cavern, eyes down, avoiding the eyes of both the snakelets and Lusea.

In the circle of his tail he dragged the few remaining chicklets he'd managed to hold onto in his rush to get back to the cavern.

Ransa remembered the scene well. It was like a very bad dream that wouldn't go away.

Lusea quickly slithered towards Telno, stopping just inches away from his nose. Her voice, usually gentle and serene, was low and frantic.

"Telno, where is Vortod?"

Telno shook his head as a tear slipped slowly down his cheek. It landed with a quiet *poof* on the dusty cavern floor, shattering the silence like a distant clap of thunder.

"I'm sorry, Lusea, but Vortod will not be returning."

Lusea looked at him with shocked, sad eyes, unsure of what he was saying.

"What happened?" she whispered, her voice deep with concern as pools of liquid began welling up in her eyes. Her heart was slowly breaking as she struggled to maintain her composure.

"It took us some time, but Vortod and I... we found the Shintala nests. We were able to catch quite a few of the chicklets by spraying them with sleeping venom. Once they were asleep we managed to wrap our tails around them in two groups before making our way back. The going was slow, but we were making good time, considering what we were bringing back."

He paused as he pulled his eyes up from the nearby pile of dirt on the cave floor. Although he was hesitant to continue, he knew he must.

"We were dragging the sleeping birds behind us on our way back here and before we knew it, we found ourselves at the edge of the abyss. Vortod and I had hoped we would have an uneventful trip back, but unfortunately, the venom must have only partially gotten one of the larger chicklets when we sprayed it. As we reached the edge of the abyss, this particular chicklet suddenly sprung up and began fumbling its way in the opposite direction.

"Vortod reacted quickly and turned to spray the chicklet again. He must not have realized where he was, however, and neither did I…"

Telno's words faded off to a whisper and he dropped his eyes again as he added, "Until it was too late." He fell silent as another tear traced the track of the first before plummeting into the dusty cavern floor like the one before it.

He raised face, filled with a mixture of anguish and regret, and turned to look at Lusea.

"I'm sorry," he said. Their moist eyes met for several seconds before Telno glanced at the snakelets.

"Vortod was very close to the edge of the abyss when the chicklet tried to escape. When he turned to pursue it, he moved too quickly and a large part of his body slipped over the edge, dragging quite a few of the sleeping chicklets with it.

"I no sooner realized what was happening and he was gone. I quickly looked over the edge of the abyss, hoping he might have caught hold of a rock or something on the way down, but all I saw was the deep pool of darkness below. There is no way I could have saved him." He stopped and looked at the snakelets, thoroughly disheartened. The smaller serpents hid partially behind their mother, listening to what had happened in disbelief.

Father – gone. It was unimaginable. Ransa wondered who would now protect them from the many evils contained in the darkness surrounding their cave home. After staring for a long time at the faces of each of the fatherless chicklets, Telno turned his guilt-ridden gaze back to Lusea.

"I'm sorry," he said again, his voice barely audible as it tottered on the edge of silence. By this point, several tears had worked their way down through the crevices that separated his scaly armor. What light there was in the passageway caught these moistened channels and raced across the serpent's face like jagged lines of misguided hope.

"Here, take these chicklets, the few that I managed to hold on to, and feed your snakelets. We must not let this tragedy be for nothing."

He paused as he pushed the remaining young birds toward Lusea.

"Vortod loved his family, and he was a good hunter, proud and strong. I will go back to the abyss to see if I can do anything, but it is doubtful."

Dropping his head with sadness and regret, Telno turned and slithered slowly back towards the tunnel leading back to the abyss.

Lusea stood, tall, firm, and unwavering. Though completely broken on the inside, she was not about to let the snakelets sense it. She must remain strong for them.

That night, Telno returned to the cavern after his unsuccessful search for Vortod and they ate the feast of Shintala meat with little enjoyment. Ransa had never had meat quite like it before, nor had she had any since. And for as good as it tasted, it would only serve as a reminder of the day she lost her father.

This life-altering event had happened many moons ago, but the ache in her heart was still strong and fresh. It hurt as much as if it had just happened a few days ago. It did not matter how sad she felt or how much she wanted to cry, being one of the older snakes from her clutch, she knew she had to continue on in order to survive. With or without her father, life went on. There were other members of the family to worry about – other mouths to feed. Although she missed her father terribly, her mother had raised her well. For him, she continued on.

With the excitement of the hunt shadowed somewhat by the sadness in her heart, she slithered out of her cavern and headed toward the stream. She had decided at the last minute that, instead of searching for a cave rat or a pigeon, today she would hunt for an aquatic meal. The air in the cave was quite warm, and the thought of a swim through one of the streams in the cave was more than inviting. Today she would definitely enjoy swimming in the cool, fresh water.

During this time of year, the cave temperature could get very warm. The hot season was soon to come to an end, but while it was here, she was thankful they had the stream so close to their home. She could not imagine living in this place without it. It offered them food, water, and, at times, a much-needed reprieve from the heat.

She swam along for a while, finding a small frog and a few little fish, but what she found was sparse. She found nothing really that she could bring home to her family. After a while she came to a place in the stream where it ran beneath the tunnel wall, and after a moment she realized this was a place where she'd never been before. Ransa was a little nervous about the unfamiliar area, but knew her family was depending on her to bring back something to eat. With a flick of her tail, she decided to see where it might lead.

Taking a deep breath, she dipped down beneath the surface of the vertical stones. The long, narrow shape of the creature allowed her to slither swiftly through the water and before she knew it, she was swimming underneath the wall. For a few seconds she sensed the top of the stream running immediately below the tunnel, preventing her from surfacing, so she continued onward. Suddenly the feeling of the tunnel ceiling over her disappeared, and she slowly, cautiously, tried raising her head above the water.

She felt the top of her head break the surface and the gentle current carried her softly downstream like a long, winding stick. She swam toward the stream bank, taking time to carefully survey her surroundings. Although the cavern she was in was completely dark, her eyes were used to it and she could actually see very well. Thankfully, all cave snakes could.

She peered into the darkness, making out the edges of large boulders stacked almost as high as the ceiling. She slithered through the lightless room, searching along this wall and among piles of rocks. It didn't take long for her to find a young cave rat carcass washed up along the rocks. After inspecting it for signs of too much decay, she decided it was still edible and swallowed it down with one bite. She would have to find something larger to feed the family.

Suddenly, she heard noises unlike any she had ever heard coming from the side of the cavern near the large boulders. Ransa quickly moved into the water and swam back upstream. She hid behind a boulder that was covered with dark, musty-scented moss, unsure of what to do. She had no idea what this could be.

The strange noises got closer and echoed in the darkness on the opposite side of the rock, the source hidden just on the other side. As an aura of light crept into the cavern, and she hunkered back into a corner, trying to avoid it, unsure of the source. After a moment she slowly, carefully peeked through the moss, squinting her eyes as she tried to understand what was happening. Although she had seen rays of sunshine cutting through the darkness near her home, she was not used to this kind of light.

She saw two... not one but two... things – standing creatures – holding sticks with flickering tongues of sunshine. This was the source of the light that now filled the small cavern with a soft, warm glow. She held her breath with fear, astonishment, and uncertainty. She had never seen anything like these creatures in her entire life. They were much larger than she, and Ransa had no idea if they, whatever they were, enjoyed the taste of Wiltoa meat. She remained hidden and quiet, cautiously watching the beasts with the rapidly changing light sticks.

She listened to the sounds they made. Although they appeared to be communicating with each other, their voices were muffled. She frowned from her hiding place behind the moss, unable to make out the words. She shifted her position slightly when suddenly, one of the creatures looked towards her. After a brief pause, the creature began walking towards her! Realizing her hiding spot was no longer safe, Ransa backed into the corner as quickly and quietly as she could. She tried with all her might to make her snake body meld into the cavern wall behind the boulder.

Her heart was racing. She could still partially see the creature walking in her direction and she prepared to spray it with sleeping venom. She was still young, and was not very good at spraying venom just yet, but she had to do what she could to survive. She thought she might be able to spray enough venom to stun the creature, allowing her to escape and swim back the way she had come. If she could make it back to the stream and head back upstream, she should be safe. She hoped.

The creature stopped close to where Ransa was hiding and the little snake reared back in the darkness, prepared to spray. Ransa held her breath, adrenaline racing through her veins, watching intently as the creature paused, looking down at something. What was it doing? Touching the water? Ransa couldn't tell for sure. After a few more seconds, the creature disappeared from her line of sight as it knelt down.

Ransa released the breath she'd been holding and took in another one with extreme slowness as she listened. The unusual beasts appeared to be communicating with each other, but she only heard a few words. Stone… rocks… missing turtle…

Her mouth began watering at the sound of the word 'turtle'. Maybe she could help them find this missing turtle? Hmm, now that was an excellent idea! From her corner, she smiled.

The creature closest to her stood up as it examined some unidentified object in its hand. It was looking at the object as if in a trance for a few seconds, then began to smile.

Ransa remained motionless, as still as a stone. She was thoroughly prepared to spit and run if needed. The tip of her tail began to quiver, the most obvious sign that she was quite frightened. She was thankful that she didn't have any rattles on the end of her tail like those poisonous valley snakes she'd heard her father talk about when she was younger. That would have given her away for sure.

After a moment, the creature closest to her looked back towards the other one then turned and began walking towards it. It appeared that the other creature had found something as well.

Ransa relaxed a bit and her tail stopped its incessant shaking.

It was funny how her tail, the extreme opposite of her head, could begin shaking so badly, all by itself. It was almost as if it had become a living object on its own, with no connection to her head whatsoever. It drove her crazy sometimes!

She quietly watched the tall, unfamiliar creatures as they each removed the things they were carrying on their backs and set them on the ground. After pulling something out of these objects, they took an item out of each and placed it near the stream. The moss blocked her vision so Ransa couldn't make out exactly what it was they were doing.

She watched as the creatures walked over to a large boulder in the middle of the cave and began doing something. She could see that one of them had climbed over the boulder, but the moss still blocked most of her view so she didn't understand why. She sat quietly, wondering what they would do next. When she heard the excitement in their voices, she wondered what they had found. After a few moments, the creature that had climbed over the boulder climbed back over. The creatures talked for a few seconds then walked back over to the stream.

Again Ransa tried to see what they were doing but it was no use. She didn't want to move too much and give away her hiding place so she decided to just be still and listen. She definitely did not want to be found because she was both outnumbered and outsized.

The creatures put the objects back where they had taken them from, and after helping each other, turned to leave. Ransa watched them as they carried their light sticks and headed back the way they had come.

Ransa was about to exit her hiding place when the creature that had come nearest to her earlier stopped and glanced back in her direction. It was almost as if the creature knew Ransa was there, watching them. She watched as it shook its head and followed the first creature back the way they had come.

Ransa remained in her hiding place for several moments, waiting for her racing heart to slow and allowing her eyes to adjust to the darkness of the cavern once more.

FIFTEEN

Diam and Tonia walked back to the main cavern and found their way to the entrance where they had separated from the boys. When they got there, the boys were already waiting for them.

"I thought we were going to have to send a search party out for you," Micah growled. "We were just about to start heading further into the cavern to look for you guys. You came along just in the nick of time."

Nicho was sitting on a boulder as the girls approached, munching on chickleberries and drinking water.

"Wait till you see what we found!"

Tonia shook her head in exasperation when she realized how Micah's tone had change from irritation to excitement completely out of the blue. Without explaining his attitude change, she watched as her brother reached into his pocket to retrieve the blue stone from where he had put it for safekeeping. As he withdrew his hand from his pocket, it was glowing furiously. The girls both gasped in awe.

"Wow!" Tonia and Diam whispered in unison.

Micah smiled as he unfurled his fingers from around the glowing blue object.

"Where did you find it?" asked Diam as the girls helped each other take their bags off their backs again.

"In that tunnel over there," Micah said, pointing to the passageway the boys had explored a short time before. "There's a place in there where the ceiling collapsed, and this stone was near the rocks that blocked the far end of the tunnel."

Micah's eyes filled with sadness as Nicho reached for something on the boulder next to where he was sitting.

"What? What's wrong?" Tonia asked with alarm, sensing bad news. "Finding that beautiful stone should not make you look so sad."

The girls were taking the turtles out of their bags as Micah finished talking. Without answering Tonia's question, Nicho said, "We need to see Merlia and Celio."

Without another word, the girls gently set the turtles down side by side on the dusty cavern floor.

Nicho picked up an unidentified object from the boulder next to him and placed it upside-down on the floor in front of Merlia. It was the fragment of turtle shell the boys had found in the passageway.

"I'm sorry, Merlia and Celio, but I'm afraid I may have found one of your friends," Nicho said in a solemn tone.

Merlia slowly approached the piece of turtle shell. Everyone held their breath as she slowly crawled over to the shell and smelled it. She gently touched her nose to it, and in one swift uplifting movement she slid her nose under it and nudged it, flipping the shell over.

The markings on the shell were unmistakable and her eyes slowly filled with tears. She nodded at Nicho.

"It is Gartua."

Celio scooted over to his mother and slowly rubbed the top of his head on the underside of her neck, comforting her. His eyes also filled with tears, but he tried very hard to maintain his composure. As far as the turtles were concerned, he was now the "man" of their family.

Merlia looked up at Nicho and asked if he knew what had happened. Nicho explained what they had found in the tunnel, from the collapsed ceiling to the pile of rubble, and eventually, to the blue stone. As far as he could tell, it was pretty obvious what had happened to Gartua, Nicho explained. The elderly reptile had been trying to make his way back to the cavern they had previously called home and was caught at the wrong place at the wrong time.

Merlia nodded with understanding.

"That explains the noise heard and the rumbling we felt coming from the tunnel that day. It also explains the incredible amount of dust that came billowing out of it. It is the same tunnel that I was going to try to explore but was fearful about leaving my Celio." She paused a moment before continuing. "To think I was so close to where our friend perished…"

They all sat quietly, pondering what Merlia had just said.

Suddenly, she turned her wide, dark eyes up at the group and her gaze darted nervously from one human to the next.

"Will you still take us with you?" she asked, frightened that, since their hunt for the missing turtle was over, they would now decide to leave her and her hatchling behind.

Tonia spoke up quickly, without conferring first with the others.

"Of course we'll still take you with us! I know we all agree," she paused as she looked at the others, one at a time, "that you should not have to live in this dusty cave anymore."

Diam nodded, as did Nicho, while Micah simply rolled his eyes. The younger boy knew without a doubt that he would be outnumbered if he tried to disagree. He was tempted to give Tonia a hard time, but decided this was neither the time nor the place. Having just found out that they lost their friend and companion, the turtles had enough to worry about without thinking that they might also be left behind.

"Sure you can come with us still," Micah agreed with sincerity.

Tonia, sensing her brother quelled his temptation to argue, turned away from the group to hide her smile. Sometimes Micah could be a pretty decent brother.

For the next few minutes, the explorers shared their chickleberries with the turtles while they rested and discussed their next move.

The girls were sitting on a boulder together, indulging in the juicy, red berries, when Diam suddenly jumped up, nearly knocking Tonia onto the dusty floor.

"Diam!" Tonia shouted as she stopped her fall just in time. "What's up with you? Do you have a stinger bee in your britches?"

Diam smiled at Tonia before turning her attention to Micah.

121

"No, silly! We forgot to tell the boys about what *we* found while exploring!" As she was reaching into her pocket, Tonia took over.

"Oh, man, I can't believe we forgot! Boys, you will never believe what we found!" Tonia winked at Diam as she fell silent, trying to increase their curiosity.

"Let me guess," Micah piped up, raising an eyebrow in a teasing gesture. "You found a skeleton with treasure!" He laughed out loud and slapped his knee with humor, calling her bluff.

Tonia stared at him in disbelief.

"How did you know?" Her disappointment was obvious. She couldn't believe he had guessed it so easily!

"Yea, right," Micah scoffed as he rolled his eyes at Nicho, unwilling to fall for another one of her jokes. "Okay, so tell us what you really found."

As Micah was talking, Diam pulled the stone out of her pocket.

"She's not lying, Micah, we did find a skeleton. Maybe not treasure, but we also found a bag with some stuff in it. And," she paused, "we also found this."

As she said this, she held the stone out towards them in an opened palm.

Nicho stood up to get a closer look at the object in her hand as the smile on Micah's face quickly vanished.

"You really found a skeleton?" He wasn't kidding now; he was stunned.

"We did," Tonia said. She smiled as she pulled another item out of her pocket.

"The skeleton is small, not human, at least I don't think it was, and it looks like it's been there for a while. We also found this bag in a crevice between some rocks."

She gently tugged on the tarza vine, opening the bag, and then carefully dumped its contents into Diam's outstretched palms. The ring, coins and rock sparkers tumbled gently into her hands, joining the unremarkable purple stone.

Micah looked at them in disbelief, while Nicho immediately picked up the ring to examine it.

"Remember last year when I spent a lot of time over at

122

Zatona's house?" the older boy asked as his gaze moved from Micah to Diam before turning toward Merlia and Celio to explain. "Zatona is the person in our village who makes jewelry and different collectible items." He paused for a few seconds before he added, "Zatona once showed me some of the rings she had collected, and, if I remember right, there was one like this one in that collection."

The others listened to him intently.

"And?" said Micah, waiting for more.

"And, I don't remember what she said about it," he said with a sigh, "but I think she said it was a special ring – it had some kind of special powers. I do remember that the ring was just like this one, silver with a gemstone in the center of it, but I'm pretty sure the stone in the one she had was yellow, not green."

He continued examining the ring, rotating it slowly from side to side in the torchlight. "It's definitely not for an adult human's finger. This almost looks small enough to be a child's toy."

Tonia agreed, more curious than ever about who or what this ring belonged to.

"I think this is further proof that we must be very careful and remain alert while we're in this cave. It tells me that the possibility of other creatures being in here is definitely very high," Nicho added as he handed the ring back to Tonia. She put it back in the bag and tucked it back into the depths of her pocket.

"I also found this," Diam said as she held out the stone she found by the stream. "I know it's nothing compared to the ring Tonia found, but I think it's a beautiful stone. I want to take it to Danuth and see if he can make a necklace for me with it."

Micah looked at the stone and his eyes widened.

"Can I see it for a minute?"

She shrugged and dropped it into one of his opened hands.

Immediately the stone began glowing with a bright, purple hue, just like the blue stone had done previously. The girls both gasped in surprise as Nicho looked at Micah and began to chuckle.

"What is it with you and these colored stones?" he asked his brother. "First the blue one, now the purple one. Maybe there's a hidden stone in this cave for every color of the rainbow?"

Micah stared at the stone, amazed to find it responding to

his touch just like the blue one had. As silence stretched across the room, they all began to hear a low humming noise. Micah's head bobbed in a slow, brief up and down motion as he heard the somewhat familiar sound coming from the stone.

Diam watched him and sighed.

"This is just great."

"What's wrong?" Tonia asked, confused by her friend's reaction.

"What's wrong?" Diam repeated as she looked at Tonia. "What's wrong?" she repeated again then sighed as she threw up her hands, turning to stare at Micah.

"What's wrong is that I finally found something worthwhile! A beautiful stone that I could have made into a stunning necklace, and now…" she hesitated. "Now I don't know what." She shook her head in frustration. "I don't even know what to think!"

Tonia stared at her friend for a few seconds, then burst out laughing.

"Diam, you are my best friend in the whole valley. If you want a rock necklace, there are soooo many rocks in here to choose from! The only challenge is that we just have to find you a colored rock that doesn't appear to be… umm… magical."

While listening to the girls, Micah pulled the blue stone back out of his pocket and placed it next to the purple one. The combined light created from both stones was breathtaking. The humming noise became slightly louder and the air became a little thicker. Something was definitely different about these stones.

Was it magic? Was it a dream? Was it good or evil? Was it…

"Micah, put them away for now. I'm not sure what's going on, but there's something about those stones and we don't know enough about them yet. I think we should wait until we get out of the cave before – I don't know – before something happens. There's some kind of, almost power, being created when you hold them." Nicho's words were filled with wonder and fear.

"When held in your hand individually, the stones are special. When placed together in your hand, that feeling unmistakably intensifies."

Micah shook his head, not understanding what was going on.

"Put them away for now, okay? Let me think about how we

should approach this," Nicho said. "When we get back to the village, we can definitely talk to both Zatona and Danuth. Maybe they will have some insight into what's going on."

Micah moved to put the stones back in his pocket but paused as he looked at Nicho, an obvious question in his eyes.

"Do you think it's okay to keep them together or should I put them in separate pockets?"

Nicho shrugged. "I think that their power, or whatever it is, is weaker without you as the conductor. Putting them together is probably okay."

Micah gently set the stones down on a boulder, to test Nicho's theory. As soon as they lost contact with his skin, the glowing aura from both stones instantly disappeared. Once again they looked like plain, ordinary stones.

"I guess that answers that question," Micah said. With a nod, he picked up the stones and, as the group of children suspected, the blazed back to life until he had them tucked back into the safety of his pocket.

Nicho patted Micah on the back and turned to look at the girls. "Let's go take a look at this skeleton that you found. I'm curious about it."

Once everything was packed up and the turtles were back in their respective bags, the girls led the way through the crevice once more. The girls helped each other take their bags off their backs to let the turtles out for a few more minutes, then Tonia pointed at the boulder that hid the skeleton. "It's behind that boulder."

While the boys examined the skeleton, the girls filled up their pia bottles with fresh water and the turtles waded in the cool liquid near the stream bank.

"This is neat!" Micah's voice was a bit muffled as it echoed from behind the boulder. "I wonder what kind of creature this used to be." His tone was questioning as he examined the skeleton.

Nicho shrugged and looked at Tonia. "Where did you say you found the bag with the coins and ring in it?" Tonia walked over to them and leaned over the boulder, pointing at the crevice.

"Right there."

Nicho peered into the rift between the stones, making sure there were no other hidden surprises there. He didn't see any.

"There's nothing else here so let's get moving," he said, looking at Micah. "Daylight's burning and I want to explore as much of the cave as we can."

They gathered up the turtles and their bags and headed back through the boulders to explore the rest of the cavern.

"I guess we should continue on and see where it leads us," Diam said, almost to herself.

"Yep, let's go," Micah agreed.

With that, they made their way deeper into the cave.

Sixteen

The young explorers headed out in a new direction, more excited now than ever. They were finding things they would have never dreamed they would. A real skeleton that was not human and magical stones! What other interesting objects or creatures would they come across as they continued on and explored the remaining darkness?

They wove their way through the numerous boulders, carefully examining their surroundings as they walked. When they arrived in what they thought of as the center of the large cavern, they could see how the boulders stretched from left to right in front of them, blocking their path. It looked as though they may have to turn back and none of them could conceal the disappointment on their young faces. They stopped at the wall of boulders and looked at each other in defeat.

"There's no way that our path can be blocked." Micah shook his head in denial as he looked to the left, then to the right.

In either direction he could not see the end of the earthen stone wall that had halted their progress. Unfortunately the light from their torches was not strong enough to penetrate the thick, black shroud which covered the rest of the cave, and they could not tell if there were any hidden openings in the obstruction.

As Micah faced the wall, he made a suggestion.

"Girls, you go to the right again, and Nicho and I will go to the left. Look high and low for a way around this darn thing. If you find a way through, give us a shout, and we'll do the same."

The girls nodded and Micah started out with Nicho close

behind. Nicho stopped suddenly and turned back, watching as the girls began to make their way in the opposite direction.

"Let's make sure we stay within earshot of each other. I'm still a little uneasy about this cave," he told them.

The girls verbally agreed and continued on their way, with Tonia following closely behind Diam. Diam held her torch out in front of her, watching where they were walking, and Tonia held hers near the rock wall, looking for any sign of an entrance. They had nearly reached the end of the wall when the girls heard Micah call out to them.

"Tonia! Diam! Come back this way. We've found an opening!"

The girls had nearly reached their end of the cave. They had not found anything interesting along the way; no skeletons, magical stones, or turtle carcasses. Tonia realized that they had also not found the stream again.

When Micah called out to them, they immediately turned and began heading back towards him. In a few moments they had reached the opposite end of the cavern where the boys were anxiously waiting for them. As the girls reached them, the boys began leading the way around the troublesome roadblock. The opening they had found was narrow and nearly at the end of the rock wall. There was barely enough room to squeeze through as they made their way around the rock barrier.

When they finally rounded the corner, they heard a sudden high-pitched squeal from directly in front of them. The sounds echoed through the cavern, making it sound as if it was coming from somewhere over their heads. Micah, having taken the lead, immediately drew his short sword in his right hand as he held up the torch in his left. Nicho responded immediately in the same manner. The girls, startled for only a second, also drew their swords and huddled closer to the boys.

In the gloom of the cave before them they could see nothing. They remained still and quiet, prepared to defend themselves against a possible, unseen attacker.

SEVENTEEN

"What are you doing in my home?" a rumbling voice hissed angrily from somewhere in front of them. The children stood in a close huddle as a string of garbled words erupted through the middle of the squeals.

"My eyes! My eyes! Take it awayyyyyyy! **Take it awayyyyyy!!!**"

The instant they heard the first sound of trouble the children froze in their tracks. It didn't take long for them to realize this was a blessing in disguise.

Directly in front of them was a gigantic gossamer web. It stretched from floor to ceiling and across most of the path they were traveling, faintly glittering in their flickering torchlight. In a few places they noticed remnants of small cocoons caught up in the web – meals that had been wrapped with careful and expert precision. Although they had seen their share of both spiders and webs during their frequent adventures in the nearby forest, the empty shells hanging in the web before them looked quite different than any kind of cocoons the explorers had ever seen.

A sudden movement caught their attention near the top of the web. As if they were a cluster of puppets being maneuvered by a single hand, the children's focus moved in unison toward the direction of the movement. Surprisingly they saw a creature struggling to escape but it couldn't – it was wrapped tightly in layers of shiny webbing which held it like glue to the outer edge of the web. Short bursts of infantile squeaks could be heard coming from somewhere behind a strip of webbing that partially covered the lower part of the struggling creature's face. After staring at it for a few seconds, they realized it was probably a bat, still alive and squirming, its eyes completely filled with fear.

Except for its head, the struggling creature's entire body was totally encased with the web owner's special touch. Although its wide, terrified eyes could be seen gaping at them over the top of a thick line of white webbing, the bat's mouth had been sealed with the sticky material, preventing it from crying out. In spite of this, they could still hear its muffled struggles as it unsuccessfully tried to free itself.

Scattered throughout the web were other cocoons, these much larger than the multitude of the smaller ones they'd first spied. These larger gossamer-covered objects all appeared to be non-living. One appeared to be another bat, one was definitely a small cave rat, and yet another one was like nothing any of them had ever seen before. This last, unidentifiable carcass appeared to have been a trophy on the main web for many, many moons. It hovered a few feet above the ground in spite of being only partially wrapped with broken, disorganized strands of silk. Through the stringy disguise, they could see that the entire carcass held within the partial cocoon had been reduced to nothing but a skeleton, with a large head and short body.

Like the bat, these other cocoons were completely wrapped except for their heads. One difference, however, was the mouths on the deceased ones were no longer sealed. It was obvious that there was no need for the coverage since the meals were no longer alive.

As the explorers cautiously gazed around the area, they realized something that made them shiver. If it had not been for the squealing sound they had heard, which had stopped their forward movement, Micah, being in the lead, very likely would have walked right into the web!

After hastily examining the web and its trapped snacks, they continued looking around, each with a hand on their weapons in case they needed to defend themselves. After the initial outburst from whatever was hiding from them and the squealing sounds from the trapped bat, the room finally fell silent. There was no sign of the spindly creature that lived in the web anywhere around them. Regardless of this, they held their ground, still on guard. Tonia watched the cocooned bat as it struggled in silence now, frowning at the sight.

"Who and what are you?" Nicho called out to the creature that had spoken out from the dark shadows from somewhere in front of them. He held his sword firmly in his hand as he waited for a reply.

"Show yourself!"

Except for the occasional sound of the struggling bat and the torch flames licking the air, the cave was filled with silence and stillness.

"Show yourself!" yelled Nicho one more time.

"The liiiiiiight… it hurtssss my eyeeeeeessssss…"

The creature's response was a mixture of hisses and squeals. Nicho turned slightly to his left, the direction of the sound, his body automatically taking a defensive stance. The sound seemed to be coming from within a sunken area in the ceiling on the other side of the web.

Nicho looked at Micah and mouthed the word 'bow'.

Micah nodded and quickly sheathed his sword. Just as quickly he prepared his bow and withdrew an arrow from his quiver, immediately ready to fire.

"We WILL NOT darken our torches and DEMAND that you show yourself," Nicho said to the creature. "We are not here to hurt you. We are only here to explore the cave and are searching for some missing friends of ours."

For a long moment, an uncomfortable silence filled the darkness beyond the large web. The mysterious creature was apparently thinking over its options.

Tonia quickly looked over at Nicho then stepped forward without a sound, silently handing her torch to Diam. Using the stick she had been carrying since entering the cave, she reached carefully up to the top of the web where the bat was still struggling in its gossamer prison. As soon as her stick made contact with the webbing, she realized it felt as though it was made from rubber trees. Although the narrow, silky strands appeared to be quite flimsy, they actually felt very sturdy. As a result, she wasn't sure she would be able to do what she had in mind.

As she continued prying at the silken threads, she got some

of it entangled on the end of her stick. She twisted her branch this way and that when suddenly, her manipulation caused the webbing surrounding the bat to break away from the rest of the meshwork. The result of this was a web-wrapped, still-struggling bat now stuck at the end of her stick. Not understanding what she was doing, the bat continued to struggle as she hurriedly moved it closer to the ground. The bat stared at her, its eyes dark, wide and terrified. An ornament at the end of the stick, it squirmed and twisted as it continued struggling to free itself from the confining web.

Although she felt bad that she was scaring the suffering creature even more, she couldn't help but smile, knowing she would soon free it from its sticky prison. Suddenly remembering how she had been able to communicate with the turtles, Tonia quickly closed her eyes and concentrated, focusing all of her energy on reaching out to the bat.

"It's okay. I'm not going to hurt you. I'm trying to help you. Please trust me!"

Within seconds, the terrified bat became still. Its eyes were still wide with fear, with several red and orange reflections dancing on their surface, but Tonia sensed it was trying very hard to calm itself.

The creature hiding on the other side of the large web hissed angrily, but Tonia ignored it. Feeling as though she must hurry, Tonia moved quickly as the other explorers took a step away from the web.

She hated spiders. Absolutely hated them.

She focused on the trapped mammal at the end of her stick, but knew if she didn't move quickly, her fears would soon get the better of her. She lowered her stick after stepping away from the web. She carefully leaned the branch up against a rock behind them on the side of the cave, increasing the angle until the bat was flat on the rock's surface. She worked quickly and gently to free the cave-dweller from the sticky material which held it securely at the end of her wooden rod. The frightened bat shook with fear as it watched her, but it did its best to stay this fear as she worked diligently to release it.

After almost a minute, Tonia had separated the bound creature

132

from the stick, but its body was still partially covered by webbing, restricting its movements. Tonia set herself to work again, trying to untangle the binding threads. While she was working, she noticed the webby mess covering the bat's mouth but decided against removing it just yet. She didn't want her finger bitten off by this terrified creature. She smiled at the bat as she pulled and tugged, and continued sending it soothing thoughts.

Diam watched her friend work, keeping a close eye on the other side of the web at the same time. Occasionally, she would also glance behind them to make sure nothing was sneaking up on them, possibly getting ready to lay ambush to their group. So far, there was nothing.

Before long, the bat's body was released from the matting and the only thing left was the binding across its mouth. The bat struggled to keep its balance on the rock as it frantically began using one clawed hand at the top center of its wing to scratch at this remaining binding. In less than a second, the final piece of the sticky, white material was gone and the bat stretched out its wings as it prepared itself for flight.

Watching it curiously, Diam whispered, "Is it okay?"

"I think so," Tonia replied.

She smiled at the bat then took a step back until she was at Diam's side, giving the creature space to calm down as well as herself a good distance away from whatever might be hiding above.

Diam handed Tonia her torch and patted her on the back with approval.

Nicho had remained quiet as Tonia worked, but now that she was done, his voice boomed out in the cavern, startling the girls.

"Creature, show yourself! I am a man of my word, and I give you my word that as long as you do not give us a need to, we will not try to harm you."

The explorers heard a slight rustling sound in the darkness beyond the web as a dark shape began to emerge from its hiding place behind the large rock on the ceiling.

"The light hurrrrrrrrrrts my eyesssssssss," the creature repeated. The children stared at it, weapons ready, as the dark form slowly made its way down to the cavern floor. Although they were prepared to defend themselves if need be, as he watched the creature climb down the wall, Nicho had a feeling it wouldn't be necessary.

It was a spider, as they all suspected. The hair covering its body was dark grey and thin in the torchlight, and its legs were unusually long. It was the size of a large mud puppy, but that's where the similarity ended. The creature's eyes were hidden behind thick, closed lids, set deep into its hairy face as it squinted in the torchlight. The thin legs twitched and shuddered as the disgustingly impish spider ambled cautiously across the floor.

"What are you doing in my home?" the spider asked quietly. It stopped when it reached the center of the cavern, lifting a leg up to shield its eyes from the torchlight while attempting to look at them.

"We're looking for some lost friends of ours," Tonia answered quietly as her stomach began churning in disorganized flip-flops. She couldn't believe she was this close to a spider – and not just a simple, tiny garden spider, but a GIANT spider – and as her words faded into silence, all she could do was stare at it. Her hand was wrapped tightly around the handle of her sword, resulting in the blood draining completely out of her knuckles until they were as white as the web. She took another step back without realizing she had even done so, her earlier show of bravery completely subsided now that the bat was no longer in danger.

"What kind of friendsssssssss?" the spider prodded inquisitively. "Maybe I've seen them pass by, or maybe they're jusssst... hanging around." Although the group couldn't see the smile on the spider's hairy face, they could definitely hear the faint hint of mockery in its voice.

"They are Raguon turtles and there were three of them. They've been missing for many moons now," Nicho answered. "We do not wish you any harm, we only wish to pass by and continue our hunt for them."

The spider cracked an eye and looked at them with uncertainty, unsure about what to do. It shifted its position and looked up at its web. It stared at its home in shock for a few seconds before they heard a low grumble coming from the spider's direction. The children quietly watched the spider as it surveyed the fresh damage done to its home when Tonia rescued the bat. The spider snarled with disbelief, angry that its afternoon snack had disappeared.

They kept their weapons drawn and ready as the spider sat motionless, anger now becoming apparent on its face. Micah's fingers trembled slightly as he gripped the taut string that bound the end of the short bow. His arrow was trained on the eight-legged critter before them.

"What happened to my fine web?" the spider grumbled angrily.

Tonia peered over her shoulder at the rock where she had placed the bat as she worked on it – it had vanished. She turned back and glared at the spider, her eyes shining with satisfaction, confident in her decision to release the trapped mammal.

"I released the creature that was entangled there. I apologize, but I could not just stand by and watch it suffer." She glared defensively at the multi-legged creature.

"Do you know how often I catch fresh food in this DREADFUL place?" the spider yelled with another growl that sounded more like a gurgling whine. It dropped the arm to the floor that had been shielding its eyes as it slowly became accustomed to the brighter environment. The light projecting around the flaming torch pierced the spider's familiar darkness like an unwelcomed stranger. The children could clearly see the beady, devilish, spheres glaring at them now.

"Sometimes I wait many moons!" the spider bellowed angrily. It paused as its beady, onyx eyes scanned the faces of the intruders, spending enough time eyeing each one, sending chills down their spines.

"Are you trying to destroy me?"

Before they could answer, the spider began easing its way in their direction like a child sneaking up on a flydragon, the arachnid's eyes now fully open, angry and full of hungry vengeance.

"Wait!" Nicho yelled. He raised his sword slightly as he held out before him. At the same time, Micah pulled the arrow back as far as he could, taking aim directly at the spider's head, and waited patiently for the signal from Nicho to let the arrow fly.

135

He tried hard to steady his bow, but his elbow was beginning to tingle with exhaustion.

"Stop!" Nicho ordered. "We are NOT here to destroy you!"

The spider ignored him and continued its slow, purposeful advancement. After a few long, silent seconds filled with tension, they could just start to make out a small, salivating grin on its angry face.

Micah's grip instinctively, if not intentionally, released. The arrow flew, narrowly missing the spider's head. It ricocheted off the hardened floor, then to a rock, before making its way back toward the adventurers. Luckily, the shaft found a home in the sticky mesh of the web that filled the space between them. Surprised, the hairy foe stopped moving and glared at the one with the bow. It had moved close enough to them that it could reach out and touch the web separating it from its adversaries if it wanted to.

The adventurers had separated somewhat, turning one potential target into four. Tonia remained behind the others, trying very hard (and succeeding, for the time being) to not show her fear.

The spider reared back on its four hind legs and spread the remaining front legs out in a wide arc, a gesture which made it look larger and more ominous. Its eyes continuously shifting from one explorer to the next, eventually settling on Nicho, the closest of the opposing party. Realizing where he was in relation to the others, Nicho stood strong and confident, his sword drawn and ready for combat.

After a moment's hesitation and carefully considering that it was outnumbered, the spider brought down its legs and returned to a less threatening position. It continued to rock slightly from side to side for several seconds as it focused on the group of children.

"You only want to pass through?" it finally asked as it turned back to Nicho.

"We give you our word," the boy answered. "We only want to pass through as we try to find another entrance to the cave other than the one we entered through."

The spider's eyes widened at once and it asked with

excitement, "Where is this entrance you speak of? I will know this before you may pass by… I **must** know this!"

Realizing they had information that the spider obviously wanted, Tonia took a step forward as a rush of confidence flowed through her. As far as she could tell, it sounded as though the arachnid would let them pass once they explained how to get to the cave entrance. With a slight nod of her head, she made a decision to try something.

"Follow this tunnel back along the stream. When you get to one of the small caverns you will find an exit that will take you out of the cave," she explained, her words simple and direct.

The spider's eyes brightened with the thought that it might be possible to finally escape this prison-like home it had lived in for so long! Its face suddenly softened in appearance and it attempted to fake a smile towards the group.

"Since you have shared this information with me, then I shall return the gesture in kind. I give you permission to pass through my home and will do my best to tell you what I know about this part of the cave," the spider said, less aggressive now. "Follow this tunnel behind me and you will come to another cavern. In this cavern, you will find many tunnels."

The arachnid glanced over its shoulder into the darkness behind it for several seconds before turning to peer at them with an obvious smirk.

The spider chuckled as its voice dropped to a whisper, "From there, one of the tunnels will exit out of the cave. I'm sure that… before you get there… however… you will find many interesting things! You must be sure to watch your every step!"

As it fell silent, the hairy creature suddenly jumped up onto the cavern wall and climbed effortlessly up to the rocky ceiling on its eight spindly legs. On its way to the upper part of the wall, the spider knocked parts of the web down that were anchored to the side of the cavern without a second thought. Their host quickly moved above their heads and began scrambling away, not caring that its former home was beginning to collapse behind it. In a split second, the spider was past them as it headed off in the direction from which they had come. As the web gently cascaded to the floor, the spider disappeared from sight.

The explorers were once again alone in the cavern.

"Darn," said Micah. "By the time I realized what that sneaky creature was up to, it was gone!" He lowered his bow and arrow, but still held it ready, in case the spider was tricking them and decided to come back from behind them. They looked at each other, then at the broken web.

"I say we continue on," said Micah after a few seconds, returning his bow to his back and his arrow to its quiver. He drew his sword and brushed aside the dangling strings of remaining web. "Let's see where this new tunnel goes."

EIGHTEEN

During the entire confrontation with the spider, the turtles had remained quiet. Merlia chose this moment to break her silence.

"Is everything okay?" she asked in a quiet, concerned voice.

"Yes, everything is fine," Diam answered her. "We happened upon a road block with eight legs, but the barrier is now down and the big, bad spider has left the cavern. We're going to continue on and see what we can find."

Merlia fell silent once more and, surprisingly, Tonia heard nothing from Celio.

"He must be sleeping," Tonia thought, although how anything could sleep through the confrontation with the spider was beyond her.

They made their way around the damaged gossamer strands, each holding the frayed web aside for the person behind them. In single file they wandered into the tunnel where the spider told them they could find the next cavern. The stream they had come across twice earlier could not be heard at all. It was completely gone, as if it had never existed. The only sound they now heard was the faint crackle of the flames from their torches and their footsteps crunching through the dirt and gravel as they made their way through the dusty tunnel. They walked for a few moments, and just as the spider said, they finally came upon another large cavern. Oddly enough, this one contained very few boulders, but the cavern floor was almost familiar, littered with smaller rocks and pebbles. The air here was warm, dry, and musty, which was not a surprise.

As in the previous cavern, the area of their new location was so large that the light from their torches was not strong enough to allow them to see the entire area. As they looked around, they noticed a few other tunnels nearby, each of them branching off into random directions.

Tonia finally broke the silence.

"Well, boys, which way do we go now?" Looking around, she added, "This must be the cavern that the spider was talking about."

Nicho nodded his head in agreement before he spoke.

"From the way the spider talked to us and the tone of its voice, I really think we should stay together. Remember it said 'watch your every step?' For what it's worth, I believe we should follow its advice. I'd rather be careful and find out the spider was just trying to scare us than not be careful and end up regretting it. Based on the feeling I got from the creature, though, I don't think it was kidding."

They continued walking through the cavern, now more careful than before of where they were going. They ventured towards the left and soon noticed various tunnels branching off into darkness. Nearing the wall closest to one of the tunnels, they all stopped.

"If we're going to continue searching for another way out of the cave, we'll need to head down one of these tunnels, I think," Tonia offered. "Nicho, do you want to separate again, like we did before, or stay together this time?"

"I definitely want us to stay together. Since there are so many more tunnels branching off of this cavern, our chances of getting lost have increased quite a bit. We should definitely stay together." Nicho's voice was quiet but firm.

They decided to try the tunnel closest to them. Like the cavern, there were few large rocks down this path, but there were numerous small rocks scattered throughout. The air here was dry and musty, too, and Diam found herself wondering what had happened to the stream.

Soon they came to a place in the tunnel where it branched off in several directions, forming a large intersection. They stopped, unsure of which way to go as Micah made his way forward from the tail end of the group, and continued past them. After realizing they weren't following him, he stopped and glanced back at the rest with a questioning look.

"What's wrong?" he asked, looking at Tonia. "You're not scared, are you?" Without waiting for his sister's response, Micah tossed a quick wink at Diam.

"You should know better than that," Tonia admonished him. "I'm just not foolish enough to continue on without considering our other options."

Micah stopped, appeared to be deep in thought for a moment, then turned forward and began walking again.

"Okay, done," he said as he moved further down the path.

"Micah, hang on," Nicho said. "Let's talk about this."

Micah stopped and frowned at his brother.

"Why? If we go straight, there should be less of a chance of us getting lost, because all we have to do is go back the same way," Micah rationalized. "If we start going through tunnels, turning left and right along the way, we'll get lost for sure." Micah's voice was serious but there was an unmistakable yet slight whine to it. He stared defiantly at Nicho as he waited for a response.

"Micah, do you remember when Diam and I told you about this cave? Part of the deal we made was that you promised to be on your best behavior and to not get on our nerves! Do you remember that?" Tonia asked with obvious irritation.

Micah turned from Nicho to Tonia as his face flooded with an expression of innocence.

"What?" he asked with a shrug.

"You're in such a hurry to get going but we shouldn't be! We'll be rushing to get to a place that we don't even know where it is, or IF it is, and we'll end up getting into trouble for sure."

Tonia sighed. It made perfect sense to her and all she could do was hope Micah would understand. They didn't need to have a serious sibling argument while they were deep in the middle of nowhere.

"She's right, Micah. I think we should sit down for a minute, let the turtles out for some air, and have a snack," Nicho suggested, wanting as much time as he could get to ponder their options. Tonia nodded and without waiting for Micah to answer, she began to help Diam take her bag off her back. When Tonia finished, Diam did the same for her. Micah, frowning, came back and silently joined them.

They sat quietly together on the cavern floor for a few moments, enjoying the break and thinking about what they should do next. There were definitely more tunnels to consider here and they all agreed they didn't want to get lost. The girls shared their water with the turtles and before they knew it, they were all packed up and ready to go again.

"Okay, Micah, lead on," said Nicho as he gestured for them to move forward. "Just please go slowly and be very careful of where you step."

The tunnel took them deeper into the cave as it wound through the dark passageways like a black, waterless river. They passed a few spider webs here and there but none of them showed signs of recent life. After several minutes of hearing nothing but their feet crunching across stones and dirt, they reached a three-way fork in the tunnel. Surprisingly, Micah stopped and waited for everyone to decide which way to go without being asked.

Tonia watched him silently, wondering if perhaps he wasn't feeling well. She had learned to expect him to react exactly how she didn't want him to in most situations, and this was one of those situations, indeed. She thought it very odd that he was now working with them so willingly. Did her earlier scolding make a difference in his cooperation levels? She shook her head in answer to her own question, deciding Micah was probably more inclined to be preparing other ways to get on her nerves instead of being a willing participant in their excursion.

Without a word, Nicho pointed toward the tunnel on the left. Micah nodded, turned and led them in that direction. Diam noticed Micah's odd silence and threw a questioning look at Tonia, who only shrugged at her friend and followed Micah. They walked for quite a while before they wandered around a wide curve in the tunnel and Micah stopped. On their right was an opening in the tunnel wall. It ran from ceiling to floor and looked barely wide enough for them to fit through, even one at a time. Micah moved his torch into the gaping darkness. As light from the flickering flame pierced the darkness, they could see a small room. After looking around the perimeter of the new room, Micah decided it was safe to enter, so he cautiously stepped through the opening. One at a time, the others squeezed through the natural doorway.

The new room appeared to be a small cavern with a very low ceiling. Nicho was the last of them to enter, and as he squeezed through the opening, a noise suddenly erupted in the air above their heads! Instinctively, they all ducked down, immediately noticing how the air near the ceiling began swishing around their heads. Accompanying the movement of air was an ominously strange sound of wing beats.

Careful not to burn each other with their torches, they knelt down close to the ground. As soon as the initial surprise wore off, Tonia knew exactly what was happening.

"Bats," she explained to the others. "This must be one of their homes and we startled them."

"Wow," said Diam with a sigh of relief. She leaned against one wall of the small room as her heart left her throat and went back to where it belonged in her chest. The boys silently agreed, and they all stayed low to the ground until the last wing beat was gone.

"I guess maybe we should have knocked first," Micah said with a chuckle as he stood up. "At least next time we know what to do."

The rest of the group got to their feet and waited for their eyes to readjust to the dim light of the torches. Not surprisingly, the air was musty here, too, and it also had a hint of some strange odor like nothing any of them had ever smelled before.

"What is that smell?" asked Diam as her nose crinkled up like a knobby prune. "I think I remember smelling the same scent a little while ago."

"Yeah, me too," Tonia agreed as she shrugged her shoulders.

They began to look around the room. About ten paces into it, there was a decent drop in the cavern floor. It looked like a trench that had been dug as a stepping hazard, possibly as a means to prevent someone or something from going further into the room. This odd, recessed part of the floor stretched from left to right across the center of the room and the floor beyond it was scattered with stones, some quite large.

If not for the bats surprising them, someone might have tripped in the trench, leading to an injury. Tonia could not imagine one of them breaking their leg this far into the cave and having to be carried or dragged back to the village. What a pain in the mud puppy tail that would be!

"I wonder why anyone would feel the need to dig something like this in such a little room." Micah pondered aloud. He turned to look at the others as questions floated through his head. His eyes were bright with curiosity. "Maybe there's something hidden here that they did not want to be found!"

"You could be right, Micah," Nicho agreed. "Let's check it out."

They made their way past the trench and began looking around the rocks. It wasn't long before they found something.

"Wow – look what I found!" Nicho exclaimed as he knelt down to pick something up off the floor. The others quickly came over to see what it was.

Nicho had picked up the object and was holding it in his hand. It was another colored stone like those they had found earlier, but it was a different color. This one was dark green. Also like the others, it had small, sparkling flecks embedded deep within its surface. As the four children stared at the stone, Nicho frowned.

"What's wrong?" asked Diam.

Without answering, Nicho held the stone out to Micah. The younger boy looked at him questioningly for less than a second before he suddenly understood. As the girls watched, Micah silently extended his hand and opened it.

The second Nicho dropped the stone into his brother's hand the room began glowing with a stunning shade of emerald green. Nicho nodded his head as he smiled.

"Uh huh, just like I thought. Micah, I don't know what it is with you and these stones, but I believe we might be onto something."

Micah smiled as he placed the green stone in his pocket with the blue and purple ones, causing his pocket to briefly light up with a green hue. As soon as it the stone lost contact with his skin, the glow disappeared like an extinguished candle. They

144

stood in a crooked circle as torchlight became the only source of illumination in the room.

Micah looked at the others and shrugged with mild disinterest, but his thoughts were racing wildly with curiosity and wonderment as to what these colored stones could mean.

Why would someone, or something, bring stones such as these into this cave, only to drop them in different areas? What purpose did they serve? Were they used as gems? Had they once been placed in a crown belonging to a powerful King in some faraway land? Could they belong to a Mundunugu?

His imagination was spinning with unanswered questions.

As Micah glanced at the dozens of scattered rocks in the room he remembered the times that he, Nicho and Tonia used to sit around the village campfire, listening to the stories told by the old ones.

One such story was about a Mundunugu named Scurio, a powerful medicine man who had a special way with dragons, or so it was told. Scurio was a legend, a great caster of spells and magic, who lived during the time of dragons. Another story Micah remembered was about a miniature dragon named Gruffod, owned and loved by Scurio. One day Gruffod simply disappeared, never to be heard from or seen again. The story explained how the little dragon had been out flying one day, drifting leisurely around the valleys and mountaintops. Here and there, villagers would sometimes see him high in the sky as he flew.

Later that day, however, he disappeared without a trace.

It was said that Scurio could sometimes talk to his dragon with his thoughts, and he called and called for Gruffod to come home, but never got a response. Scurio canvassed the countryside looking for his dragon, without any luck. Gruffod was never heard from again. This saddened Scurio beyond belief.

Dragons of old were mostly wild, but there were those that shared their lives with humans. Those that were tame were frequently permitted to fly freely, as they needed to, to hunt or just practice their flying skills. Everyone knew it was difficult to keep a dragon that did not want to be kept!

Like Tonia, Micah loved listening to these kinds of stories. The mystery of whether dragons had ever existed totally fascinated him.

Micah came out of his daydream, back to the present. He watched as Nicho turned and began looking around the rocks again for anything else of interest. The girls stood silently side by side for a moment then began to do the same. They soon found a suspicious mound of rocks that had been arranged in an odd shape, wide at the base and narrower at the top. Looking at them, Tonia thought it possible that they had been shaped this way naturally, but she didn't think so. Knowing others had been in this room before led her to believe that the mound was made this way for some special, unknown reason.

As the girls worked together to move the rocks away from the mound, the boys continued looking around. Suddenly Diam backed away, catching Nicho's attention.

"What's wrong?" he asked when he saw the look of surprise on Diam's face. "What is it?"

The girls had rolled one of the larger rocks away from the base of the mound, revealing their find. Tonia stayed right where she was as Diam backed away a step.

"Another skeleton," Diam answered, somewhat amazed that her friend wasn't startled in the least. "That girl is as tough as a dragon sometimes," she thought with a small smile, proud of her friend and wishing that sometimes she could be more like her. Now, however, encouraged by her friend's lack of fear, Diam returned to Tonia's side.

"I wonder if this one is like the one we found a little while ago," Tonia mused as the boys joined them.

Although the larger rock they had moved had been laid across the top of the skeleton, entombing most of the bones, many smaller rocks surrounded the rest of the bony structure. Once they shifted some of these smaller rocks around, they were able to see that this skeleton was similar to the last. It, too, was barely covered with old and withered remnants of the clothes it once wore, but it didn't take long for Tonia to notice that there were a few things different with this corpse.

Slightly larger than the last skeleton, this one was lying on its back with its legs straight. The creature's hands were both centered on its chest, wrapped around what appeared to be some kind of stick. Tonia reached down and removed the object, realizing too late that it was some sort of short, handmade spear and not a stick. As she withdrew it from the skeleton's chest, dust surfaced from the corpse's bones where the weapon had been lodged.

"I could be wrong, but I think that whatever kind of creature this is, someone or something wasn't very fond of it," Tonia said. She stood still, staring at the spear, amazed at the violent story it told them.

"Let me see it," said Nicho, holding his hand out for the weapon as Tonia handed it over willingly.

"Hmmmm," Nicho said quietly. He pulled his torch closer to the weapon, spending numerous silent seconds examining the object's handle. "I see etchings of some kind, but they're faint and it's hard to make out what they are in some places. They look very intricate, though, like someone took a lot of time carefully carving them into the handle."

Tonia and Micah leaned over for a closer look. After a moment, Micah shook his head.

"I've never seen any kind of drawings like this before."

Tonia stared at the etchings as if in a daze, remembering a conversation she had once with Zatona in the village. Somehow they had gotten into a discussion about other tribes and the different styles they used when decorating pottery. This was when Zatona had told Tonia a story about how, long ago, certain members of royalty would be very intricate in their artwork on weapons. Unfortunately, Tonia couldn't quite remember the details.

She sighed, aggravated with herself. She should have paid more attention to stories like these! Then again, how was this young girl to know she would find herself in a situation like this? A situation where she would need to remember something she had thought of as a neat story about the past and nothing more? She shook her head and glanced up at Nicho. He had removed the bag from his back and carefully placed the spear in it for safekeeping. He wanted to hold onto the weapon because it was one of the only clues pointing to what might have happened to both of the skeletons they had found.

After looking at the handle with the boys, Tonia turned her attention back to the skeleton. Maybe this one could provide them with more information as to what it was or where it came from. She gently prodded the dusty bones with her stick, looking for clues or any evidence about what might have done such a horrible thing.

She found nothing.

As she was looking for clues, she heard Celio making a noise in the bag on her back. After a few seconds she realized it sounded like he was coughing. Within a few seconds, she felt the somewhat familiar, slight buzzing sensation in her head again. She closed her eyes and heard her name being called, barely more than a whisper floating behind the darkness of her closed lids.

"Tonia?"

"Yes, Celio?" the young girl answered, not realizing she was actually speaking. The others looked at her, wondering what was going on.

"Can you let me out?" he asked. "I'm not feeling very good." He started coughing again.

Tonia opened her eyes and found Diam staring at her with a quizzical expression.

"What's up, Tonia?"

"He's not feeling well and wants to be taken out of the bag," Tonia answered.

Without a word, Diam moved behind Tonia and helped her with her bag, gently placing it on the cavern floor. Tonia handed Diam her torch and gently set Celio down on the cave floor near the wall, out of the way so he wouldn't get stepped on.

Celio looked at Tonia gratefully then closed his dark eyes and receded into his shell partway.

"He doesn't look very good," Tonia thought.

"What's wrong, Celio?" she asked.

"I feel sick," he answered, coughing again.

"Celio? What's wrong with you, my son?" Merlia's worried voice projected from somewhere within Diam's bag. The girls worked together to take Diam's bag off her back before placing Merlia next to her son. The mother turtle nuzzled her youngster, talking to him gently the whole time.

Suddenly, Celio began coughing repetitively, at times uncontrollably. During one of these coughing fits, an object flew from his mouth without warning and rolled across the dusty cave floor.

"What was that?" Tonia asked with surprise. Diam shrugged before she knelt down and picked up the object.

"It looks like a rock," she said as she held her torch closer to the object. Within seconds, the others noticed a huge smile lighting up her face.

"Why are you smiling?" Tonia asked. She was kneeling next to Celio, gently rubbing his head and shell, but quickly stood up and walked over to her friend. "What is it?"

"You'll never believe this," Diam replied as she held the object out in front of her just as Nicho and Micah joined them.

They all looked at the single object, completely entranced. When they realized what it was, Tonia said stepped back with surprise.

"No way!"

Diam simply smiled and held the object out to Micah. The younger of the two boys had not had a chance to see what the object was but he trusted his sister's friend. Without a word, he raised a curious eyebrow as he extended his hand. The others watched in silence as Diam dropped the object into Micah's open palm. Silence surrounded them as, just like before, the object made contact with the young boy's skin and the entire room began to glow. The instantaneously colorful aura was one of soft, amber, much like the first moments of sunshine leading the way into a gorgeous summer day.

They had found another one of the magical stones.

As soon as Micah realized what was happening, his face broke out in an enormous grin. "We're getting quite a collection of these stones," he thought as he nodded.

Tonia looked at Celio in amazement as the glow continued to gently light the cavern, chasing away the shadows from just a moment before.

"Where did you find this, Celio?" she asked as she knelt down next to the young turtle. Feeling better, he had emerged from his shell while they were all staring at the stone. He tilted his head upward as his dark eyes met Tonia's.

"I found it back in the cave where you placed us next to the stream a little while ago."

"Back at the first stream? When we set you both down near the water when we found the first skeleton?" Tonia asked. "I don't remember seeing you eat anything near there." She continued to look at him with a questioning expression.

"I bet it was when we were playing with that skeleton," Diam answered with a knowing smile. "You were so engrossed in playing with bones, and I was so focused on making sure you were being careful, we both neglected to watch the turtles." Her explanation ended with a guilty sigh.

"Or it could have been when we were trying to free the bag with the coins and ring from the rock crevice," Tonia suggested.

Merlia looked first at Celio, then at the others.

"Even I neglected to watch him closely enough," she said as she lowered her head with shame. "As his mother, it was my job to make sure he was safe, but because he was so close to me and I was interested in seeing what you both had found, I failed in my job as a good mother."

She looked over at her son with obvious love.

"My Celio, I am so sorry I did not keep a better eye on you." Her voice turned to a low coo as she lovingly rubbed the underside of her neck across the top of his head in a slow, gentle sweeping motion.

"I'm sorry, Mother."

Celio's voice could only be heard by Tonia and Merlia, but spoken words were not necessary for the rest of the group to understand what was happening.

"When they were playing around the rocks, I decided to drink some water," Celio explained. "While I was looking in the stream, I spotted a beautiful yellow object and even though it wasn't floating, I thought maybe it was a piece of fruit that had somehow made it downstream."

He lowered his head in silence for a few seconds before raising it to look up at Tonia with a sheepish expression.

"I swallowed it in one bite!" He was obviously proud of this, which brought a small smile to Tonia's lips. "But I never even got a chance to taste it," he finished.

Tonia stared at him and tried to keep a straight face, but suddenly started giggling. "Little turtles weren't much different from little people," she thought before she explained to the others why Celio had swallowed the stone.

Micah only partially listened to his sister while his eyes examined the glowing stone. Once again, he wondered what all of this meant.

Why did the stones react the way they did with him – first the blue stone, then the purple stone, then the green stone, and now the yellow stone? How many of them were there? Were all stones like these found just in this cave? And was it possible for them to even find all of the colored stones, if there were a limited number of them? After a few seconds, he handed it back to Diam.

Like before, the warm amber glow immediately disappeared as soon as the solid piece of earth left his hand. As they expected, the remaining light in the room was that created by the flickering torches.

Micah continued staring at the stone as Diam held it in her opened hand. He could now see it clearly without the bright aura affecting his vision. Small flakes sparkled deep within it, just like they did with the other stones. He also noticed that this stone was definitely smaller than the others. If it had been any bigger, Celio probably would have died from choking. He was amazed that the young turtle had been able to swallow it in the first place.

"Celio, do you feel well enough to ride again? I think we should get moving." Nicho's voice was gentle but firm. He was obviously anxious to move on. "We'll have to head back to the village soon. I think it's getting close to late afternoon."

Merlia spoke to Celio for a moment then turned towards Diam with a nod.

"Yes, we're ready to go again."

They helped each other place a turtle in each of their bags. Within moments, they were back to adventuring through the cave.

Nineteen

The four explorers exited the small cave one at a time through the narrow opening in the wall and followed the tunnel to their right. It wound around, first to the right and then to the left, in an oddly curved pattern. In a few moments, they reached another four-way intersection. After a slight hesitation, Nicho gestured for them to keep going straight. As they continued on, they encountered yet another intersection. Just past this Nicho stopped and looked at the others, his face crinkled into a frown.

"This is not good."

He tapped his foot nervously on the ground as he glanced back at the intersection behind them. His eyes examined their options before he finally turned and peered into the intersection in front of them.

"There are a lot more tunnels in here than I expected. I think we should turn back soon and come back another day," he suggested, feeling as disappointed as the others now showed on their faces.

Micah had wandered a short distance into the tunnel to their right. He was listening to his brother but was still anxious to keep going.

"Hey guys," he yelled back at them, "there's another cavern over here. Come on!" The girls glanced at Nicho and he nodded with a sigh as they hesitantly turned and headed in the same direction as Micah had gone. Micah smiled when he saw they were following him, and with a muffled, "Yes!" led the way into the large cavern. A few steps into it, he stopped, holding his torch

152

high up over his head.

Within seconds, the others were behind him. They stopped and looked at the surrounding area in both awe and sadness, unable to believe the horrible scene before them.

Scattered about the room were countless skeletons. Some were big and some were small, while much of the rest was just parts, with a leg here or a skull there. It appeared that some great battle had taken place in this room.

Diam looked at Tonia, who was looking around with bright, curious eyes, and shuddered.

"This is amazing!" Tonia said with an almost overwhelming excitement. "These creatures were in here for who knows how long, and we never even knew it!"

She took a few careful steps forward, staring at one pile of bones before moving onto the next. Diam watched her, shaking her head. Sometimes her friend got excited about the strangest things! They separated slightly, looking for clues to what had happened.

Like the two skeletons they had previously found, the ones they now examined were mostly bones with small fragments of clothing scattered here and there. These corpses also appeared to be the same type of creature as those they had found earlier.

Scattered throughout the room, though much less frequently, were various weapons. Swords, spears, and arrows could be seen strewn about – some were broken and some were whole. A few were just lying on the cavern floor, but many had been thrust violently into the bodies of the skeletons, undeniably the cause of death. With some of the skeletons it was difficult to tell how they were killed, until they looked closer. Only then were they able to make out the hilt of the murderous weapon, lodged between the bones, which had been used to end one of the many lives before them.

Diam looked at her friend and saw Tonia kneel down to look at something. Curious, she walked over to see what Tonia had found. As she reached her friend, Diam touched her on the shoulder, letting her know she was behind her. Tonia looked up at Diam with tears pooling in her eyes.

"Some of these…" Tonia began to explain, but without

finishing, she turned abruptly and looked back down at what had caught her attention, unable to finish her sentence. Her view blocked by Tonia's body, Diam knelt down next to her friend to see what had saddened her so deeply.

Lying on the dusty cavern floor she saw another skeleton that was quite a bit different from the others. This one was very small, as small some of the new babies they sometimes saw in the village. The tiny corpse was alone on the dirty ground, with the nearest skeleton being a few steps away.

Tonia sniffled before she got quickly to her feet and walked farther into the cavern.

"I just don't see how anyone could do that to anything so small, regardless of what kind of creature it is," she said angrily. "And what happened here that would cause so much death? Why would someone carry so much anger?"

She shook her head, emphasizing her lack of understanding.

Diam glanced down at the childlike skeleton, then stood up and quietly followed her friend. Together they continued to examine the rest of the cavern. It appeared to be isolated from the main part of the cave by a curving line of boulders, which stretched ominously from floor to ceiling. These boulders were connected together in the shape of a crude circle, and as they followed the line around, it took them back to the tunnel by which they had entered.

Spearheads, broken arrows, and fragments of clothes were just some of the items they found while exploring. The room appeared to be one where the mysterious creatures may have been living, but it was hard to say if it had been a temporary or permanent residence. The old, dry bones looked as though they had been there for quite a while.

Not finding anything else of interest, they decided to go back through the tunnel and continue their hunt for both the missing turtles as well as a different entrance to the cave. With racing thoughts and heavy hearts, they carefully continued on their journey. In the tunnel shadows nearby, none of the children noticed the small, dark creature clinging to the ceiling just outside the room with the skeletons. It had been watching them silently, its dark colors aiding in its ability to blend in with the darkness of the tunnel.

The children quietly worked their way back to the previous intersection and took the tunnel to the right to see where it would lead. As they walked, the tunnel wound around and around, reminding them of how the old village men walked after drinking too much ale. Before they knew it, they had re-entered a large cavern and immediately noticed a line of tall, large boulders on their right.

"I think this row of boulders is the same one from the previous room with the skeletons," Nicho suggested.

"I think so, too," Micah agreed.

They had all seen their share of skeletons today to last them a lifetime, and thankfully this room didn't have any bones in it. They carefully spread out but found nothing of interest – no skeletons, no burial mounds or magical stones. The room appeared to be completely empty of anything except for the dirt covering the floor.

"This is really odd," said Diam. "One room has all kinds of things, rocks, skeletons, even weapons, but the next room has nothing. What's been going on in here?"

"I don't know, but let's keep moving," Nicho answered from the far-left side of the room. "Here's another tunnel entrance over here."

He was standing next to a tunnel near the edge of the room, close to where the boulder wall ended. As the others reached him, Nicho led the way into the narrow passageway. As soon as they entered it, they noticed yet another fork. This time Nicho led them towards the right without any sign of hesitation. In the back of his mind, a pestering voice whispered that they would need to turn back soon.

He thought about the past few hours and decided the most difficult thing to deal with was the lack of daylight. They really had no idea what time it was or whether it was day or night. He smiled to himself then thought, "It's a good thing we're young because some of the older village people would never have been able to keep going like we have today."

Shortly they came to a place where their tunnel intersected another one. One passageway went almost straight, one turned

155

to the right, and a very short tunnel went to the left but the last one abruptly came to a dead end within just a few feet.

"Shhhh, listen," Tonia whispered as she held up a hand to get their attention.

They stopped, listening carefully. After a few seconds, none of them had heard anything. They looked at her questioningly as Micah asked, "What?"

"I thought I heard voices coming from one of those tunnels," she said, referring to the intersection before them. She took a few steps forward, listening carefully, but now only heard silence. They decided to take the right fork, and after a few minutes they came to another intersection. Without a word, they continued straight through it.

Micah's advice from earlier seemed to be one thing they agreed on, Tonia thought with a small smile.

Before long they entered yet another large cavern. As they all stepped in and looked around, they could see another large line of boulders to their right. They decided to follow the boulders and see where it would take them.

They all were getting a sense of the late afternoon hour. They all knew they should soon be heading back to the village, but strangely, no one suggested it.

The boulders began winding to their right and in the gloomy distance they could partly see another tunnel entrance to the left. They stopped and considered which direction they should take. This was becoming an all too common occurrence.

"I think we should go to the left and start heading back," Nicho said, ever conscious of the late hour and unable to keep it to himself anymore. The others agreed.

The air surrounding them had suddenly become cooler, reemphasizing the lateness of the day. Before beginning again, Nicho suggested that they stop and put their jackets and leggings back on. After helping each other, they continued on, walking into the left tunnel. Soon they came to yet another intersection, and they continued straight through it without stopping.

Within minutes they approached something strange... something none of them had ever thought they would come across in a place like this.

They had found a cave pond.

The pool of dark liquid before them was an odd round shape and almost encompassed the entire width of the tunnel floor. There was just enough room for them to skirt around the edge of the pond, one at a time, if they decided to continue on and head through the tunnel on the opposite side.

Not surprisingly they noticed another tunnel to their left.

They moved closer to the pond and peered into it. The water was as smooth as glass, without even the slightest hint of a ripple. The light from their torches glistened and sparkled across the motionless surface of the still liquid. As they stood near the edge of the water, their torchlight also reflected across it, dancing across the tunnel wall on the opposite side.

None of them could see any place where incoming water fed the pool.

Tonia, with a questioning look in her eyes, was the first to speak up.

"Nicho, how can there be a pond in here without water running into it? That just doesn't make sense to me."

Nicho looked first at the pond then at Tonia with a shrug.

"I don't know. The water would have had to get here somehow, but without a stream or something feeding it, I just don't know how that can be." It was the only explanation he had to offer his sister.

"Maybe there's a stream running somewhere underneath it," Diam suggested.

Micah's voice suddenly broke the silence from the back end of the group.

"I suppose it is possible that if an underground stream fed the pool slowly enough, it wouldn't make any waves or ripples."

Micah approached the edge of the pond and knelt down to get a closer look at the water. Tonia walked up behind him and put a hand on his shoulder as he did so.

"Wait, Micah. I don't think you should get so close. We don't know what's in there."

Micah peered into the pond for a few seconds, then stood up and backed away. He wasn't sure if Tonia was right, but he sure didn't want to find out. Something definitely seemed odd to him about the entire thing.

He looked at Nicho and shrugged again.

"Now what?"

"We should continue on," Nicho said briskly as he began making his way around the pond. The others followed, Diam, Micah, and lastly Tonia.

Without a word they passed the motionless pond without stopping, carefully walking around the edge as they made their way to the tunnel opposite the one they had entered through. They walked on, making their way through the winding passageway until it again forked with another tunnel. They took the right fork and soon found themselves inside of another large cavern. They continued walking through this new room without stopping and it wasn't long before they noticed three new tunnels to choose from off to the right. As they walked a little farther, they began to make out a boulder wall ahead as it became visible in the distant gloom. They stopped, trying to decide which way to go.

Nicho was starting to feel very nervous about the time but tried not to let the others see. To make matters worse, with the new tunnels to choose from, he found himself at a loss.

"Wait!" Tonia said, her voice brimming with excitement. "I think I recognize that rock wall in front of us. Didn't we come into this cavern before?" She turned to look at the others. "From over there," she said, pointing towards the tunnels on their right.

"It's possible, but which tunnel was it that we came through?" Nicho asked, chiding himself for not paying closer attention earlier in their journey.

Tonia and Diam both shook their heads, but Micah disagreed.

"I think it was that one," he said as he pointed at the tunnel in the center.

Tonia interrupted them when she mumbled, "Uh oh."

The others looked at her questioningly.

"Oh, geez Tonia. What's 'uh oh' now?" Micah asked with irritation.

Tonia looked down at the bag hanging around her midsection, opened it, and grabbed a handful of what it contained.

Browning flowers.

In their excitement of exploring the cave, then finding the

turtles and the colorful stones, none of them had remembered the flowers. It seemed that their idea of how to avoid getting lost while in the cave had been totally forgotten by all of them.

Ignoring his sister's concern about the flowers, Micah looked at Nicho with piercing, expectant eyes.

"Okay, big brother, which way should we go?" the younger boy asked. Nicho shook his head with uncertainty.

"I can't believe we got lost. I thought I was paying close enough attention to where we were going," Nicho admitted with a sigh. "We don't have much of a choice. Let's keep moving and see if we can find anything familiar. Maybe luck will be on our side and we'll find our way back to the waterfall."

He looked at Tonia and Diam. He knew them both well enough to understand the looks they were giving him. They were nervous but were keeping it to themselves – for now.

"Tonia," Nicho said to his sister, "I need you to start dropping a flower every few steps. That way, at least if we walk in circles and find some of the flowers that you've dropped, we'll know we were here before."

"Better late than never, I guess," she said with a nod. "We *all* forgot about the flowers, Nicho, so don't feel bad about it. I'm sure we'll be fine."

Nicho smiled at her. Although he was thankful that she understood, his doubt remained heavy and unwavering.

"Would anyone like to take the lead?" Nicho asked.

The girls immediately shook their heads and both looked at Micah, waiting for his response. Micah looked at Nicho, considering the question, then he shook his head as well.

"I was happy to lead us earlier, but right now, big brother, I think it's all you."

Micah gestured for Nicho to go ahead then added comically, "After you." He gave a silent bow towards his brother.

Nicho attempted to smile but couldn't. Instead, he paused while he considered the three tunnels in front of them, and after a moment he decided they would take the last tunnel, closest to the boulder wall. He looked at Micah, then at the girls. Sometimes being a big brother had its privileges, he thought, but this was definitely not one of them.

TWENTY

The tunnel forked as soon as they entered it and Nicho led them to the left without a word. They followed him in silence and continued straight through the next intersection.

Tonia was next to last in line, in front of Micah, and every few steps she dropped a flower here and there as Nicho had asked. She tried her best to drop the browning pieces outside of where Micah was walking so he wouldn't step on them. It wouldn't be any good for them to come across the flowers again if they were squashed and unrecognizable. Hoping to avoid this, she decided to toss the petals to her right, reminding herself to remember to look towards the outside of the tunnels as they continued on in case they came across the flowers again.

After a while they arrived at a large intersection where four tunnels crossed their path. They stopped and looked at Nicho.

"If we had a four-sided coin, we'd be all set," Micah mused. Nicho smiled and proceeded forward into the second left fork. The light from their torches led them through the darkness of the cave tunnel into another small cavern. Directly in front of them they were quite surprised to see a large, gaping circle of blackness along one side of the cavern floor.

It was very large hole, extending almost completely from one side of the cavern to the other. Along the remaining edges of the path surrounding the dark pit, their torches reflected off of the different sized rocks littering the area. Nicho held up his hand to have the others stop behind him then cautiously made his way over to the hole. He stepped carefully on the rocks around the edge of the abyss, wanting to get a better look down the depths of the chasm. When he got a step away from the edge, he stopped and leaned over slightly as he peered into the darkness below.

"Nicho, I don't think…"

Tonia began to protest her brother's actions but before she could finish, a tremendous rumbling erupted around them as the floor beneath them began shake violently. Nicho realized too late that he was standing too close to the edge of the gaping hole. Before he could step away, the loose rocks beneath his feet began to crumble. His face instantly clouded with a combined look of shock and fear. He scrambled to regain his footing as his feet began to slip over the edge of the hole. Nicho reacted by releasing his torch as he tried to regain his balance. As if in slow motion, his torch fell from his grasp. It hit the outer edge of the hole and began spinning swiftly, end over end. It disappeared out of sight as it tumbled into the depths of darkness below.

"Noooo!" Nicho yelled. He glanced back at the others as helpless understanding flooded across his face while fear filled his eyes.

Micah, Tonia and Diam all jumped forward and tried to grab Nicho's left arm as it flew into the air. Their reaction, however, was too slow. They watched helplessly as Nicho slid off the edge of the hole and was swallowed immediately by the ring of darkness. Seconds later they heard an audible *thump*! The others immediately fell to their stomachs, staring into the dark chasm as they called after their friend. As a plume of dust rose from the pit of blackness, silence surrounded them. They could see and hear nothing from below.

"Nicho!" Tonia shrieked, lying on her stomach at the edge of the pit, trying to see her brother. Although her mind knew he had fallen well beyond her reach, Tonia's arms took on a mind of their own as they stretched into the darkness, reaching out for him in wave after empty wave. Her hands opened and closed; opened and closed; and after a few seconds, her arms finally withdrew, pulling back toward her body, her hands empty. She called out to him, over and over as she peered into the darkness. She could see nothing as tears streamed down her face.

The tremors which caused Nicho to lose his balance finally

ceased as suddenly as they had begun. The tunnel was now silent except for the whimpers from Tonia. After a few long seconds, she turned and looked at Diam and Micah in disbelief. The look on her face was reflected back to her from theirs.

What had just happened?

After a few moments they could vaguely make out the flickers from the torch as it struggled to stay lit in the depths of the abyss. The torch appeared to have fallen into a spot that was either under an overhang or partly in a tunnel. When the dust finally began to clear, they could vaguely make out a body in the nearby shadows, lying motionless in the dust.

"Nicho!" Tonia yelled frantically. "Nicho, answer me! Are you okay?"

They continued looking into the darkness over the edge of the abyss as the feeling of complete helplessness engulfed them.

"This can't be happening," Diam thought.

"Is everything okay?" Merlia called out from the bag on Diam's back. "What's happening?"

"Nicho?" Diam called into the darkness, but only whispers from the silent, gloomy shadows answered.

"Nicho fell into a deep hole in the tunnel floor," Diam explained as Merlia returned to her silence.

Without a word, Micah got up on his knees and crawled back a few feet. He removed his bag and began hastily rummaging through it.

Diam looked back at him and asked, "What are you doing?"

"Did we pack any tarza vines?" he asked the girls. "I can't remember." He was trying hard to maintain his control, but both girls could hear the uncertainty and fear in his voice.

"Nicho?" Tonia called out again, clearly on the verge of tears. "Nicho, please answer me! Are you okay?"

Diam scooted back next to Micah and began going through her own bag, shaking her head with doubt. She was almost sure that tarza vines, especially long ones like what they would need in this situation, were something none of them had thought to bring along. Unable to find anything of use, she left her bag on the ground and crawled back to Tonia, who was now crying unashamedly.

"Tonia, come on. We've got to keep ourselves together if we're going to be able to help Nicho. Let's look through your bag. We're looking for tarza vines, but I don't think we packed any. It's worth a try, though. Come on."

Diam encouraged her friend to scoot back towards Micah. As if suddenly remembering Micah and Diam were there with her, Tonia looked up at them with a look of total anguish, her face a smudged mess of grime and tears. With a slow, hesitant nod, Tonia reluctantly dragged herself away from the edge of the abyss after one last glance down into the darkness. She crawled over to where Micah was sitting, still riffling through his bag with no luck. Diam helped her friend with her bag, and after gently placing it on the dirty floor, Tonia used her shirtsleeve to wipe fresh tears away from her eyes.

"What are we going to do, Micah?" she asked. Her chin quivered as she stared at her younger brother who was now in charge.

Micah shook his head as if arguing with someone.

"I know we didn't pack enough tarza vines to be able to reach that far down into the hole. We don't know where we are so we can't even go back the way we came to try to make it into the forest and find some vines that we *can* use!" Micah would have tried to conceal his desperation, but right now he was beyond that point. The more he talked, the louder his voice rose with anxiety and confusion.

Tonia could feel herself beginning to panic but felt helpless to stop it. Seeing this, Diam put a steady hand on her friend's shoulder, which calmed her somewhat.

"Tonia, take a deep breath! We're not going to do Nicho any good if we fall apart! Get control of yourself and help us figure out what we are going to do!" Diam gently admonished her friend.

Tonia nodded and closed her eyes. Struggling to compose herself, she took a deep breath, opened her eyes, and after a long moment, turned to face Diam.

"Okay."

After a brief discussion, the girls decided to go back into the tunnel a few steps and put the turtles down for some fresh air.

Diam looked down at Merlia with a pleading look of urgency,

"Please stay here with Celio. We don't need to worry about him falling down into the hole with Nicho. We need to get back over there."

"Go," Merlia answered reassuringly. "We'll stay right here."

Without waiting for Diam, Tonia turned and joined Micah back at the hole, where they tried to figure out what to do about their predicament. A moment later, they came to the expected conclusion that indeed they did not have what they needed to rescue Nicho. Even if they did, Micah thought, they didn't know if Nicho would even be able to climb out on his own. If he was seriously hurt...

Tonia interrupted his thoughts when she began crawling back over to the pit of darkness. She got to the edge, looked over, and called out, "Nicho? Are you all right? Please, answer me!"

She immediately noticed that while they had been looking through their bags, the torch that had fallen into the hole had gone out. Tonia's question bounced off the rocks in the darkness below and was only answered by silence. She stayed where she was and covered her face, about to cry again.

Without warning, the rumbling in the tunnel surrounded them again out of nowhere. Afraid of falling down the hole with her brother, Tonia immediately scooted back and joined the others. In addition to the tunnel shaking around them, they now heard another sound, which was indistinguishable at first. As the rumbling subsided, the other sound increased, and soon they all recognized it for what it was... an evil, guttural growl.

"Who has the nerve, the absolute **gall**, to wake me from my sleep!" an angry voice bellowed from the depths of the pit of blackness. The explorers looked at each other in shock. Who or what was the owner of this angry voice?

"My slumber is NOT to be interrupted, under ANY circumstance!" the infuriated voice boomed. As suddenly as the rumbling began, it stopped with an unexpected silence.

They had all drawn their swords as they backed away from the hole a bit more, moving into the mouth of the tunnel they had entered by. They looked at each other, unsure of what to do. After a few seconds of uncertainty, Micah took a slow step forward, sword pointed towards the abyss.

"Nicho?" he called out worriedly, unsure of whether or not his brother was even alive.

"Nicho?" Tonia and Diam called out in unison, each taking a step forward, joining Micah.

They heard the growl once again, quieter but still ominous, followed by another endless, eerie silence.

Without warning a creature's immense head began to emerge through the center of the black hole in the tunnel floor. It was massive, and as it moved higher and higher into the air, it turned to look at them, eyes squinting in the remaining torchlight.

"Ahhhh," the creature hissed, sounding as though it had just found something it had lost. "You, my friendsss, are playing a very dangerous game by awakening me from my much-needed ssslumber!" The creature's words rolled menacingly off its tongue as it peered warily at them as it hovered in mid-air in the center of the dark hole. The only part of its body that they could see was the head and part of a thick neck, all of it light in color and apparently hairless. The head was round and large, with dark, evil, red eyes, and a thin slit for a mouth.

"Are those scales covering its skin?" Tonia thought. Just then, the creature turned and looked at her, making the hair on the back of her neck prickle her nerves. They stared at each other for a few uncomfortable seconds, but eventually the creature turned its attention to Micah. None of them knew exactly what it was until a moment later, when a blurring streak of something the color of blood shot from its mouth, wagged in the air for a several seconds, then retreated back to the safety of the creature's mouth. A few seconds later, it did it again. This time they knew for certain they were watching forked tongue, tasting the air around them. The creature was, without any doubt, an extremely large cave snake.

"Who are you?" Tonia asked, a hint of nervousness apparent in her voice.

Diam and Micah noticed her voice trembling but hoped the creature didn't.

"You come into MY home without being invited, awaken me from my sssleep, and now you expect me to happily answer your questionsss? HA!" The angry creature released a laugh, but its eyes were not laughing. They were glaring at Tonia.

"**DO YOU KNOW WHO I AM?!**" the cave beast bellowed. They looked at it silently as Tonia shook her head.

"No," she answered quietly. "We have not been in this cave before today, so no, we do not know who you are." That, she thought, is why she had asked the creature who it was in the first place.

The creature glared at Tonia with distaste for several seconds before closing its eyes and sighing audibly. It appeared to be slumping back down into the hole like a turtle retreating into its home, when it suddenly straightened, rose higher into the air than before, and bellowed in a loud, confident voice, "I AM MUSCALA!" As its statement bounced through the air around them, the creature continued lifting itself out of the hole. They watched in stunned silence as the reptile began slithering the front half of its body across the tunnel floor while the back half remained hidden in the darkness below. It didn't take long for the tail end of the creature's body caught up with the rest of it.

The creature was indeed a snake, but it was much different than any other snakes any of them had ever seen, including Tonia. This one was abnormally huge, with a body that was easily as long as all of them combined and twice as wide.

As the hissing reptile continued to approach the nervous children, they held their swords out toward it in a defensive gesture. The snake stopped a few feet from them and released a chilling, sinister laugh.

"You think your puny weaponsss scare me?" Muscala asked in a taunting, humorous tone. "They could almossst be toysss."

Micah protectively positioned himself in front of the girls. The snake watched him quietly then lowered his head, squinted his eyes, and began closing the gap between them.

"Wait!" Tonia yelled as she stepped from behind Micah and moved to his right side. After realizing what Tonia was doing, Diam repeated the motion in the opposite direction.

The snake stopped and turned a curious eye towards Tonia.

"Why should I wait?" he asked. "When a snake asss large asss I sleeps, it is not hungry. But," he smiled, "once awakened, essspecially if awakened before it isss ready, a meal is the firssst thing that it cravesssss." As Muscala said this, his tongue flicked rapidly in and out of his mouth, re-emphasizing that he was not thinking about the weather. His eyes moved from one child to the next with a hungry stare.

"My brother fell down in the hole where you came from," Tonia said as she pointed a shaking finger at the abyss. She was nervous and knew it was obvious, but held her ground. "We only want to get him out of there and we'll be on our way."

The snake looked from her to the others as his tongue continued to wildly spear the air – in and out, in and out.

"Yesssss, I know of the one you ssspeak about," Muscala replied with a mischievous smile.

"You know?" Micah question was filled with surprise. "Is he awake? Is he okay?" he asked as he took an excited step towards the snake.

Muscala rose up a bit in defense of Micah's movement towards it.

"Be careful, Micah!" Diam cautioned.

"Please tell us if he's okay?" Tonia pleaded. "We only need to get him out of the hole and we will be on our way."

"Sssssss." The snake's eyes were gleaming as it smiled at the young girl. "I'm sorry, but that isssss impossible."

When Muscala's words finally sank in, Tonia's face flushed with anger, causing her eyes to begin tearing once again. Without thinking, she took another step towards the snake, sword firmly in one hand and torch in the other. Muscala stopped her with a loud hiss and a baring of long, shiny fangs.

"If you want your brother to remain in thisss world with you, you will think whatever thoughtsss you are thinking again." He fell silent as he held his ground.

"What do you want?" Micah asked the snake.

Tonia could tell by the tone of his voice that Micah was not happy at all about their current situation. The snake eyed them cautiously, tongue still flicking, then smiled, knowing he had the upper hand.

"This brother… he isssss special to you?"

"Yes!" Tonia answered without hesitation.

Who would have known that a single word could convey so

much?

As soon as the word was out of her mouth, she realized with regret that she should have waited. She did not trust this creature and now feared it would use whatever means it could to get what it wanted.

"It obviously wants something," she thought as she admonished herself.

The snake watched her for a moment before it began to shake its head.

"No." It paused then looked at each of them, one at a time.

"No," it repeated, licking the air, tasting their fear. "The question ssshould not be, 'isss he special to you.' The question ssshould be, '*how* special isss he to you?'"

He paused again as he gave them a smile of innocence. He had them right where he wanted them.

Sensing some kind of impending manipulation, Micah suddenly lost patience with the snake.

"What do you want!" he yelled as a mixture of anger and hatred flashed in his eyes.

"Yesss," Muscala said, still smiling. "It seemsss as though he isss very special to you, isn't he?" The snake paused but did not give them time to answer.

"Good! I will tell you what I want," Muscala gloated as he shifted, backing away from them slightly. At that moment, they heard a weak moan as it drifted up through the darkness engulfing the dark hole like a blanket.

"Ohhh," they heard again, but as they continued to listen, only silence followed.

"Nicho!" Tonia squealed with relief. She ignored the snake as she dove back to the edge of the abyss, where she collapsed in the dirt and peered over the edge. Muscala remained where he was, calm and smiling, watching her.

"Nicho! We're here!" Tonia yelled into the darkness. At that moment she wanted nothing more than to see her brother, but all she could see was a sea of blackness.

"Uhhh." A weak response floated up from the depths of the abyss. Then she heard a single word that nearly made her break into a fresh bout of tears.

"Tonia?"

Nicho's voice was faint and weak, but he knew she was there.

"Nicho! Oh, Nicho! You fell into the abyss in the tunnel floor and we're here, at the top of the hole. We're going to try to get you out! Don't move too much, okay?" Again, she heard only silence.

Remembering the snake, she backed away from the edge of the dark hole, stood up, and faced Muscala with unmistakable anger and a new determination in her eyes.

"Okay, Muscala, tell us now! What do you want? I want my brother back up here and out of that hole – NOW!" The smile faded slightly from the snake's face as he slowly leaned towards the girl with the sudden burst of brevity.

"What isss your name?" he hissed, glaring at her.

"Tonia!" she answered firmly and without hesitation.

"Yesss, so I thought," he hissed, then turned towards the others. "And you?"

"Diam." Tonia's friend answered quickly, hoping she sounded as confident as Tonia looked.

Muscala nodded slowly and turned to look at Micah, waiting for his response.

"Why?" Micah asked, surprising the giant snake. "Why do you need to know our names? It's not important, unless we've won some kind of contest and you're going to give us a prize!"

The snake had appeared to be settling down a bit, but with Micah's response, they could all see the instant anger flashing again in the serpent's eyes.

"WHY?" the snake thundered, questioning the child's tenacity. "I will tell you why!" Muscala began moving the upper half of his body from left to right in a side to side rocking motion.

"Uh oh," Tonia thought.

Twenty-One

"Have you ever heard of the 'Dragon's Blood'?" Muscala asked as he continued to rock back and forth. He licked the air, tasting something that briefly held his interest then looked at them enigmatically as he stopped his movements until he was directly in front of them. They each shook their heads back and forth in denial. Muscala sighed and began slithering in a figure eight pattern along the floor of the cave around them. A grid of scales swam over itself, gentle torchlight catching the ridges like stars moving across the night sky. His iridescent scales shown with different shades of blue and purple and the children could see their reflection in his eyes.

"The 'Dragon's Blood' isss a very powerful amulet that disappeared yearsss ago, probably before any of you were even *thought* of. Before disappearing, it had been around for many moonsss, more than you or I could even dream of.

"For a long time the amulet wasss the prized possession of Lotor, a very powerful and knowledgeable wizard." He stopped talking briefly, raised his head up as if listening for something, then continued. "The amulet wasss beautiful, made out of the bessst king's gold that shone like the sssun, even on a cloudy day.

"Somehow, the amulet disappeared and Lotor wasss very angry. He rounded up a whole squadron of mercenariesss from the countryside to go out and find hisss beloved amulet, all to no avail. They looked high and low, near and far, but the men could not find the amulet anywhere.

"Before long he decided to try another strategy, ssso he offered

171

a generousss reward for the amuletsss safe return. Surprisingly, he got no responssse.

"After a while, a rumor ssssurfaced which told of a group of kalevala which had found the amulet and were sssecretly keeping it. Word quickly spread throughout the valley of thisss new information. It was sssoon discovered that these creaturesss, the kalevala, lived deep within a well-hidden cave somewhere within the Orneo Foressst. Lotor was very powerful but he wasss also very sssmart. Asss a result, little essscaped him and he soon discovered the location of thisss hidden cave.

"He sent hissss mercenariesss out again, armed with knivesss, spearsss, arrowsss, and swordsss. They wore armor made of giant turtle shellsss. He was determined, at all costsss, to get hisss amulet back."

Muscala stopped his figure eight motion in front of them. They could see that his face had softened somewhat, but the reflection in his eyes showed the children's expression had not changed.

"The mercenariesss entered this hidden cave, found the cavern where the kalevala resssided, and demanded the return of Lotor's amulet. The leader of the kalevala, Pauzel, after questioning hisss people, denied having ssseen or heard of the lost gem. If he was lying, it wasss a grave missstake!

"The kalevala were a gentle creature, alwaysss striving for peace and tranquility. The mercenariesss disregarded thisss, however. When Pauzel denied having the amulet, the leader of the mercenariesss, Ugla, ordered hisss troops to kill every kalevala they could find, large or sssmall, old or young."

He paused again, this time lifting his head high in the air, as if for effect. Then he lowered himself and resumed looking at them expectantly.

"Di... di... did that hap... happen in this cave?" Diam stammered.

"Yesss," answered Muscala.

"I think he's referring to the cavern where we found all the skeletons," Tonia said sadly. The others nodded, thinking the same thing. It still angered her when she thought of the tiny skeletons she had found.

There was a calm, silent stillness emanating from the abyss.

The explorers had unknowingly dropped their swords down to their sides. Almost as if in a trance from the snakes glowing eyes, they had grown more complacent, or perhaps were just too afraid to try to stand up to this giant, slithering monster. Although their weapons were now dangling down as an afterthought, pointed towards the ground, they still did not trust the snake enough to re-sheath them. Diam glanced towards the tunnel where they had left the turtles, and could vaguely see them in the tunnel entrance, motionless and listening quietly.

"So, what happened with the amulet?" Diam asked, regaining her composure.

Tonia nodded and wanted to ask Muscala what all of this had to do with them, but she sensed if she did so it might anger him again. If they weren't careful, none of them would make it out of this cave at all, she thought worriedly.

"That isss my predicament, don't you sssee?" Muscala answered. "Once the kalevala were ssslaughtered, Ugla had no other cluesss to the gem's whereaboutsss. He returned to Lotor empty-handed and wasss immediately taken out into the nearby forest and beheaded.

"As for Lotor, he wasss very angry indeed! When he realized that threatening and killing would not resssult in the return of his preciousss amulet, he decided to change hisss strategy once again." He paused, lost in thought as the others waited quietly for him to continue. After a moment, the snake began again.

"Lotor sssoon offered a more generous reward, larger than the firssst, but this time he included a bonusss… a place by hisss side," Muscala explained as he smiled dreamily. "To have a place at the ssside of the mosst powerful sorcerer in the valley… ahhhh, yesssss. THAT, my friendsss, isss what I want."

He fell silent and gazed down at them, his thin lips curving into a small smile.

"Okay," Micah spoke up, "so where does this leave us?"

Muscala turned and looked at a nearby wall as he pondered the boy's question for a long, quiet moment before finally continuing in a strong, confident voice.

"You, my friendsss, are going to help me find that amulet!"

"And just how are we supposed to do that?" Diam asked,

realizing all too late her tone was far too acidic for this conversation.

Muscala nodded once and slowly began encircling them in his figure eight pattern as he had done earlier. Just when they thought he hadn't heard Diam's comment, he continued, startling them.

"Sssomewhere in this cave residesss the Wiltoa, a family of cave snakesss that is much, much sssmaller than I. They, I believe, found the only sssurviving kalevala." He stopped in front of them and looked from one to the other, his tongue flickering in and out of his mouth as he attempted to taste their scents.

"Yesss, this one kalevala wasss special. She," he paused, "she wasss the one who had possession of the 'Dragon's Blood'."

"How do you know?" asked Micah in a doubtful tone, simply trying to understand. Without warning, Muscala swung his massive head around until he was just inches away from Micah's face.

"Are you quessstioning *ME?!*"

The snake's voice erupted into the air, filled with anger as it flooded the room. Micah stood firm and quickly responded, "It was just a question!"

The snake glared at the boy, his tongue flicking haphazardly in the air as his breath shot wildly in and out through his wide, round nostrils with every quick breath he took. Diam thought the sound was similar to those of one of the village children breathing through a tightly rolled alia leaf as they tried to make a whistling sound. After listening to this for several, achingly long seconds, Muscala noticeably settled down.

"I am sssorry if I seem a bit… defensssive," the snake said apologetically. "You can imagine that I am not used to visitorsss in this part of the cave."

As the snake said this, Tonia saw that Micah had an odd look on his face. She knew her brother very well, and could imagine him saying, "A BIT defensive?" Luckily, Micah held his tongue.

Muscala resumed with his curving figure eight motion around them as he continued his story. As he did so, the repeating pattern of light on scales seemed to flow much like a stream of water across a log in the sunshine. In this case, however, the ribbons of light flowed upward, disappearing over the curve of his back like

174

a reverse waterfall.

"I am a large sssnake, and I am usually here, in thisss part of the cave, alone," he explained. "During the course of many moonsss, everywhere you go, you will find creaturesss of importance; those who were created to lead othersss. I, as you can plainly sssee, am one of them."

He stopped in front of them, paused for effect, and puffed out his upper body with an almost overwhelming look of pride. Just when they thought the long silence would never end, they heard Nicho call out to them from the depths of darkness somewhere below.

"Hey!" he cried out, his voice sounding a bit stronger than it had earlier. "Guys? Where are you?"

The others moved to the edge of the abyss and got down on their stomachs, peering into the blackness. Although they could still see nothing, they heard faint scuffling noises drifting up through the darkness.

"Nicho?" Tonia shouted. Not as trusting as his sister, Micah kept a close eye on Muscala. "Nicho, are you okay?"

"I think so," he answered. "A little sore, but I think I'm okay. I don't particularly care for the total darkness down here, though. I found my torch. Can one of you toss down some rock sparkers? Hopefully I can catch them."

Diam had already scooted back before he finished his sentence. She hurriedly rustled through her bag in search of the requested items. It didn't take her long to find them before she was scooting back to the edge of the dark hole. She then held her torch over the circle of blackness as the three children strained their eyes in an attempt to pierce through it in search of their friend. Tonia cried out as she began to make out the shape of her brother in the darkness. She cried out again as she finally noticed the whites of his eyes.

"Nicho! I'm so glad to see you!" she yelled down to him, then as an afterthought, "Or, at least to see part of you!"

They heard Nicho chuckle.

"I'm going to drop these down to you, okay?" Diam offered as Muscala watched their interaction with silent curiosity.

"Sure," Nicho answered. "Hopefully, I'll be able to find them."

"Here they come," Diam said as she cast the rock sparkers into the darkness. Nicho managed to catch one, but the other fell into the dust somewhere close to his feet.

"Oh, great," they heard him mumble as shuffled around in search for it. Diam tried to help by holding her torch as far over the abyss as she could reach.

After a few seconds, they heard Nicho's triumphant voice.

"I found it!"

"Ahem!"

Diam jumped at the sound of the snake's voice. Surprisingly she had almost forgotten he was there.

"I believe we have sssome unfinished mattersss to discuss."

He was gazing at each of them with wide, expectant red eyes.

"Sit tight, big brother. We're working on getting you out of there," Tonia called down to Nicho. She scooted back with the others so they could finish talking about their 'unfinished matters' with the crazy reptile. Before she had settled into her new location, the snake continued as if he had never been interrupted.

"Other creaturesss within the cave know very well that I am a leader, and occasionally, they report to me with interesssting information." His voice was low and pompous. They stared as he took a deep breath and let it out slowly, as if waiting for the children to sigh with amazement from his words.

"As I'm sssure you know, at timesss I can be a very hungry sssnake, with no regard to the creaturesss I consume." He paused. "And when I am hungry, I can assure you that I am not picky.

"For these creaturesss that provide me with valuable information, however, I tend to make exceptionsss. In return for quality information, I overlook them or their families as potential mealsssssss."

He paused and let his words sink in, extending the hissing sound which accompanied this last word. The children could almost hear the smile in his voice as he resumed his pattern of circling them.

"They mussst be careful, however. If they come to me with information that I find as, shall we say, lesssss than important, they have a very high potential of becoming my next meal themselvesss." As he passed in front of them, they weren't surprised to see he was smirking.

"One lucky creature came to me many moonsss ago," he continued, "and told me a ssstory about a lone, surviving kalevala who had possession of a beautiful ssstone. He further explained that thisss kalevala, whom he called by the name of Kaileen, had befriended a family of snakesss, the Wiltoa of which I ssspoke earlier."

As he completed yet another figure eight in front of them, he suddenly stopped, his eyes wide and serious.

"Listen carefully, for here isss the proposal I make to you." He paused and appeared to be considering his next words.

"You need your friend, your brother, to be ressscued from my beautiful home. I need to find the Wiltoa, and Kaileen, ssso I can take possession of the amulet, if in fact the amulet and 'beautiful stone' are one and the sssame. Once I have possession of thisss amulet, I can return it to Lotor. Once that has been done, I am sssure he will gladly offer me the place by hisss side that I ssso rightly deserve!"

He paused as his smirk curved into a wide, arrogant smile.

"My proposition isss simple, really. You want your friend, yesss? Find mine and bring her to me." Muscala paused again as his narrow, haughty smirk slid back across his face.

"No Kaileen, no Nicho."

Evil was very evident now in his glaring, blood-colored eyes. Tonia saw Muscala's smile and knew he was proud of both himself and the situation. She also understood they had no choice but to help him. She stared at him as her blood ran cold in her veins.

"If we agree to do as you ask and succeed in finding these… these other snakes and your precious kalevala, do you agree to help us get Nicho out of that wretched hole?" Although she knew they didn't have a choice, Tonia's voice was confident as she questioned the snake's offer. It did not bother her in the least that she might be offending the serpent's precious home.

Without hesitation, Muscala nodded.

"Yesss," he replied with a satisfied smile. Believing he was about to get his way, the snake visually relaxed as he continued his fluid, curving motions around them.

Micah, after listening quietly to the conversation between his sister and the snake, looked at Muscala and frowned with an obvious question wavered in his blue eyes.

"You will also tell us how we're supposed to find these Wiltoa, right? Especially since we have absolutely no idea where we are?"

"Yesss, of coursssse," Muscala answered as he floated to a stop before them. He lowered himself until he was eye level with the boy. The gentle back and forth movement of his head and side to side swaying of his neck caused Micah to begin rocking his own head from side to side, as if he slowly falling under some kind of unspoken spell.

"Ssso, do we have a deal?" the snake asked in a smug, quiet voice.

"Where do we go to find these cave snakes?" Diam responded without answering his question. The sound of her voice seemed to interrupt the boy's movements. Micah blinked as if trying to focus on what she had said and his gaze fell away from the snake.

As if he hadn't heard her question, Muscala closed his eyes for a long moment, still swaying from side to side as if in time to another soundless song. After a few seconds, he finally answered.

"That isss sssomething I will tell you shortly."

"Wait a minute," Tonia said, a sudden look of confusion falling across her grime-smudged face. "If you already know where these Wiltoa live then why do you need us at all?"

Muscala's eyes darted open and rolled toward the girl within their sockets, his head following the same direction shortly after. They heard him hiss in response before he finally answered her with dry, emotionless words.

"The tunnelsss I am familiar with and can fit through in that part of the cave have been blocked off. The only other way to get to where the Wiltoa live isss to ssswim downstream a short distance, until the moving water opensss up into a part of the tunnel where smooth rockssss line the sssides of the tunnel itself."

He paused and tilted his head as if listening to some sound coming from the dark hole in the floor. After several seconds, he turned back to the group of children with a small, satisfied nod.

"You will know you are in the right part of the tunnel when

you can sssee small patchesss of sunlight breaking through overhead, allowing jussst a little bit of light in. Although this is only what I have heard, I have never ssseen this part of the cave, ssso the information I am giving you may be… lessss than accurate.

"In some placesss, the stream becomesss very small, much too sssmall for a muscular, ssstrong creature of my sssize and girth." His voice came alive and shadows in between his scales rippled in the light of the torch as he shivered with pride. "In those placesss, my body, unfortunately, will not fit. I know this simply becaussse I have tried."

"So, let me get this straight," Micah spoke up with a shake of his head. "We go through the tunnel and follow the stream, find the passageway with the sunlight, find these snakes, find some creature named Kaileen, bring her back, you give us our brother, and we can be on our way?" He fell silent as he raised a questioning eyebrow toward the snake, who was still gently rocking from side to side.

"Yessssss." Muscala's affirmative hiss was almost a whisper.

"What if this takes us days to accomplish? Will you give us your word that you will take care of Nicho and bring **NO** harm to him until we get back?" Tonia asked, her eyes anxious and filled with doubt.

The snake waved his head in a wide arc as he turned to look at the young girl. At the same time, Tonia took a step forward which took her mere inches from the snake's face.

"I want your word, your solemn word, that absolutely NO harm will come to my brother," Tonia's voice turned into a hiss as she clenched her teeth. "If you give me your word, one creature to another, that he will be safe here, we will agree to go try to find your amulet."

Muscala looked at her, unaffected by her bravery, and his narrow mouth curved into a smile. He nodded.

"You have my word."

Tonia immediately walked past the snake toward the dark hole in the tunnel floor and, after falling to her stomach again, peered into the abyss and tried to get a glimpse of her brother. The first thing she noticed was that he had succeeded in lighting his torch while they had been talking to Muscala. The second thing she noticed was the dark stain on his shirt. She wasn't sure it was blood, but the darkened areas on the fabric seemed to cling to him.

"Nicho! Are you okay?" she asked him with a shriek, frantic worry replacing the calm brevity of just a moment before. Micah and Diam quickly joined her at the edge of the opening in the floor.

"Yeah, I got some scrapes when I fell, but I'm okay. Lucky for me, we put our long shirts and leggings back on when we were in the other part of the cave." Tonia couldn't hide the distraught look on her face. Nicho saw this and smiled up at her, offering reassurance.

"Really, I'm okay."

Tonia trusted that Nicho would not lie to her and breathed a sigh of relief.

"What's going on?" he asked.

He had not heard the entire conversation between the snake and the trio above him because he had been lighting his torch, so they explained to him what they were going to do. After a moment, Muscala approached them at the edge of the entrance to his home and interrupted their discussion.

"Since you are outsidersss, you will have no way of knowing thisss, but you will just have to take my word for it. The moon has risen in the night sky. Let's get sssome rest, and then we can ssstart fresh tomorrow."

With that, Muscala began making his descent into the hole in the cavern floor. They saw Nicho draw his sword and immediately take a step back as he tried to give the serpent plenty of room to pass. The trapped boy leaned against the wall and held his breath.

Muscala chuckled at Nicho's reaction as Tonia cried out above them.

"No! Wait! We want to start now!"

The snake ignored her as it seemingly floated down to the bottom of the abyss. Once there, Muscala stopped in front of Nicho.

"You, my new friend, are a guessst in my home for the

next day, week, or however long it takesss for your friendsss to complete the quest I have given them." Muscala smiled innocently at Nicho, breathing slowly in and out as he did so. His breath smelled like rotten eggs, dead fish and stagnant air. Nicho held his breath again, hoping it wouldn't take long for the snake to leave.

Muscala didn't seem to notice the boy's reaction. "While you are a guessst in my humble home, you may help yourself to many of the amenitiesss, save one."

Nicho glanced around the room, wondering what 'amenities' the snake was talking about. The rocks? The dust? The many bones littering the dusty, dirty floor around him?

"Do you see thisss tunnel behind me?" Muscala asked with a smirk.

"Yes," Nicho nodded as he glanced toward the tunnel around the snake.

"Good," the reptile replied in a quiet, satisfactory tone. "That isss the one place where you are NOT welcome in my home." The snake's eyes glinted with some kind of question but Nicho couldn't quite read it. Was it a warning? A death wish? A challenge? A promise?

"If I senssse that you are even thinking about coming where you *are* not and *will* not be invited, I will devour you without hesssitation! And, trussst me, it will not be a pleasant experience... for you," the snake smirked. The forked, red tongue shot from Muscala's mouth and wavered in the air, the tip gyrating in a tight, small area just inches from Nicho's face before it finally disappeared back into the snake's mouth.

"I will do it while you are alive, one bite at a time."

This, Nicho knew, was a promise.

With a final smile and a nod of his large, reptilian head, Muscala turned and slithered into his tunnel without even a glance back at the boy.

"Muscala?" Tonia called out, but the snake did not answer. Tonia sighed in exasperation.

"Well," Micah said, resting his head on his hands as he continued to look down at his brother. "Now what?"

"If I could get down there..." Tonia started, but Nicho

abruptly stopped her.

"Tonia, if you could get down here, we wouldn't be in this situation. I don't think we have much of a choice except to wait until tomorrow," Nicho's voice was tired and full of despair.

As Tonia let out a sigh from up above, Nicho added, "Does anyone have any chickleberries? Mine got bruised a bit during my recent trip." He looked at his bag in the corner. It was speckled with damp spots all around the bottom edge. "Squashed might be a better word to describe those berries," he thought.

Diam sat up and scooted back, reaching into her bag. It didn't take her long to find her berries tucked away beneath some other sundries. She took a handful out then carefully dropped the bag of berries down to Nicho, which he caught with ease.

"Thanks," he said graciously.

As Nicho opened up the bag of berries and began munching on them, Micah couldn't help himself.

"That's a good idea, big brother. No matter how bad things get, food ALWAYS helps." Even in this dark situation, the children shared a laugh at his shenanigans.

Micah retreated to get his and Tonia's bags while the girls sat next to the edge of the hole. Accepting Micah's suggestion, Tonia went over to get the turtles, bringing them closer to where the group was sitting, but not too close to the abyss. Then they all sat quietly for a few moments, enjoying a snack together, including the turtles.

Tonia smiled at Celio, who was gulping down berry after berry.

"You're really enjoying those berries, aren't you, Celio?"

He nodded and continued eating like it was the last meal of his life. Celio had never eaten chickleberries before. Having lived in a cave his whole life, he barely remembered the last time he had fruit of any sort.

Diam glanced around the cavern as she munched her own handful of berries. After a few moments, she wiped her mouth with the back of her hand and glanced down the hole at Nicho.

"Did you hear what Muscala said about it being dark outside?" When the others nodded, she looked at Tonia and frowned. "Your mom's going to be worried sick!"

"Yeah, and after all we've been through this past year, I hate to think about what's going through her mind right about now," Tonia agreed. A look of sadness fell across her face like a gray blanket and she nearly broke into tears. She wanted nothing more than for Nicho to be okay and to be home, in her own bed.

Micah nodded as he said, "What a day today has been."

After finishing their snack they decided to take the snake's advice and try to get some sleep. None of them expected that this would be easy, and each of the younger children wished nothing more than to have Nicho out of the hole and out of danger. Before they called it a day, they propped one of their torches over the abyss in between some cracks in the wall but extinguished the rest. Not knowing how long they would be wandering around inside the dark tunnels, and even though they had a few extra torch wraps in their bags, they didn't want to waste torch fuel if they could help it. The lone torch provided them with enough light for all of the explorers to be somewhat comfortable as they tried to sleep.

Although none of them thought they would be able to sleep, surprisingly, they all did. Within just a few minutes of settling down, they were all fast asleep.

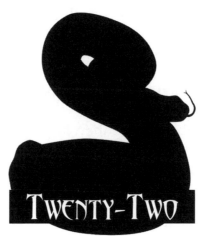

TWENTY-TWO

When Jeane awoke that morning, the house was quiet, just like any other day. She got up, washed her face, and began her daily routine of cleaning, laundry, and tending their animals and the garden.

By that afternoon, the children had not yet returned, but she did not worry. Often the girls were out exploring and the boys were either with them or off with their friends. They could be out all day and she wouldn't hear a word from them. She learned to appreciate these quiet times, because when all the children were in the house together, it could be a real hullabaloo!

While Jeane was cooking supper, she was surprised to hear a knock on the door. She wiped her hands on her apron and went to see who it was. When she opened the door, Andar was standing in the doorway, smiling at her. She greeted him with a similar gesture as well as a hug.

"Andar! How are you? Many moon wishes to you!" she said as she wrapped her arms around him.

"And many more to you, Jeane," he responded in kind.

After talking for a bit, Andar asked, "What are the children up to today, Cousin?"

Jeane gave him a questioning look.

"They're out in the forest hunting... why?"

Andar made a noise, which sounded almost like a muffled grunt.

"Well, Micah stopped by last night and asked to borrow some short swords, bows, and arrows," he explained, his wiry eyebrows curling with doubt. "I ask only because I wasn't sure if hunting was what they were really doing. You know how boys can tell stories sometimes." His gruff expression softened a bit in the candlelight. "I would expect stories after all the ones they've listened to around the village campfire."

"I definitely agree," Jeane said. "They mumbled something to me last night about hoping to bring home a valley pheasant." She smiled at the memory then returned to the fire where a large pot was bubbling above the flames. She gave a quick stir then gently extracted a spoonful of the broth. Blowing on it, she sipped loudly from the stock which she had made with fresh alia, some herbs from the garden that the girls had gathered for her, and a few of the flowers from the ipa-ira bush which grew behind their home. These petals were usually fragrant enough to entice the children to come home, wherever they might be.

She was proud of her children. They had all grown up quite a bit during the last year, mostly because they had to. It had been a long, hard year.

"You sure do have a good litter of kids there, Jeane," Andar said, proud of his cousin and how she had raised them. It had been a long road for all of them lately.

"Thank you, Andar," she whispered quietly. "I definitely do."

Andar's face clouded slightly and his expression hardened again. "How are things since Bazel disappeared?"

Like his, her face clouded with the memory.

"Hard," she admitted. Her eyes suddenly became shiny with tears.

He moved closer and set a rough, calloused hand on her arm. "You know if you need help around here, with anything at all, just say the word." Although his face was wrinkled from the sun and grooved with bird-like grooves around his eyes, his voice was gentle and reassuring. "I can come over most any time. I could just drop in here and there to help, but don't want to intrude."

"I know," she said as she tried to smile. "I appreciate that; I really do."

She nodded as a tear slipped out of the corner of her eye and she quickly brushed it away. "The whole village has been great."

"Have you heard any more about what happened to that

husband of yours?" Andar asked.

"No," she answered sadly. "All I know is last summer he went hunting in the Hampa Mountains by himself and he never returned."

"I'm sorry, Jeane," Andar said. He leaned over gave her another hug.

"I am, too," she replied with a sniffle. "He was a wonderful husband and father. A big, strong man to look at, but so very gentle of heart." She wiped another tear away as she walked to look out the kitchen window. "I miss him so, as do the children."

Andar decided to stay and help Jeane with supper, and they enjoyed each other's company immensely. Since their mothers were sisters, they grew up together and had been raised almost like brother and sister. Although they had lost touch for many years after Andar's mother moved away from the village, the past several years had been much like an ongoing reunion. They were closer now than they had ever been, even as children.

As the time to eat neared, Jeane began to worry. The children were never late for supper. After everything they had been through, they knew better than to cause her to worry.

While she finished final preparations for their evening meal, a twisted, bundled knot of trepidation began to grow in the pit of her stomach.

TWENTY-THREE

Before falling asleep, Tonia made sure she had rock sparkers and an extra piece of torch cloth nearby in case she had to re-light the torch while they were resting. They slept close to each other, with Tonia lying between Micah and Diam, and had taken special care to choose a resting place far enough away from the blackened pit to avoid someone rolling into it as they slept. The following morning, the trio of explorers began waking up to the soft flickering noises of the lone torch, which had surprisingly continued to burn throughout the night.

Tonia woke up first and, after rubbing the sleep away from her eyes, she lay still for several moments, allowing her body time to wake up.

In her half-awake state, she vaguely remembered scattered wisps of the dream she had been having as she woke up the previous morning. A voice calling out to her as she walked… to where? From where? She lay on the dirty cavern floor in the torchlight, watching the flames as they flickered high and low, creating shadows which danced like faceless ghosts on the wall just a few feet away.

The dream.

She closed her eyes as she tried to remember. An image of color sparked across her mind for less than a second and she tried to focus on it but it was gone like the wind before even had a chance. It looked like a pair of sad, glowing eyes but she couldn't be sure – were they green? No. She shook her head, trying to find the memory. Were they blue? No, they were blue-green.

Good – she remembered the color of the eyes, but now what? Who did they belong to? What did they mean? She tried to recall the memory that was suddenly nagging and chipping at the outer edges of her subconscious mind, but, as was true for most dreams, the more she tried to remember it, the further it slipped away.

She opened her eyes and glanced over at Micah. He was facing away from her but was also beginning to stir. She watched as he stretched silently then slowly rolled over in her direction. His eyes opened slowly and looked at her, startled for a second, until he remembered where they were and his sister was staring at him.

"Ugh," he groaned, stretching again. "I wish we would have prepared for a night in a dark cave when we were packing our things the night before last. I think I would have slept much better with a bedroll." He grunted again and sat up.

"Me, too. I'm sorry I didn't think to bring some hay for us," Tonia said teasingly.

Diam heard their conversation and she, too, began to emerge from her slumber, rubbing her eyes as she pulled herself into a sitting position. After staring at the flickering torch for a long minute, Diam began digging in her bag, looking for something to eat. What she wouldn't do for a meal consisting of more than chickleberries right about now, she quietly thought.

They sat in a circle and talked softly as they snacked on berries and dried chickenbird. They sipped water they had collected from the stream the day before while they patiently waited for Nicho to wake up.

"I wonder how long we'll have to sit here waiting for Muscala to finish telling us where we need to go." Diam's questioning thought passed through her lips before she knew it. She was as anxious as the others to get started. They all knew the sooner they got started, the sooner Nicho would be with them again and they could find their way out of here.

It didn't take long for their muttered conversation to wake Nicho, who began stirring at the bottom of the abyss. Tonia finished her last bite of meat and crawled over to the hole, carefully peeking over the edge.

"How are you feeling today, Big Brother?" she asked.

"Like I got run over by a dragon," he said, surprisingly managing a tired smile.

Like the rest of them had already done, she watched as Nicho stretched in hopes of working out the countless kinks which had settled into his sore muscles while they were sleeping.

"Do you want some chickenbird?" she asked.

"Absolutely," he said as he stood up. "You don't think you guys can eat a fancy breakfast while I sit down here, all alone, in this dusty bedroom of mine, do you?"

She chuckled as she got some chickenbird from Micah then tossed it down to Nicho. He caught it and sat back down, eating in silence.

After they finished their breakfast, they packed up their things then began preparations to set out on their quest. All of the children took the time to ensure that their weapons were secure, their bags were arranged properly, and they could get to what they needed in a hurry if necessary. Just as they finished, they heard a rustling noise coming from the tunnel which led back into the cave. Micah jumped up and drew his sword. In the shadows of the tunnel, they suddenly saw Muscala slithering in their direction.

"Good morning, my new friendsss," he hissed. Although he portrayed a gracious host, they all knew it was just an act. "I trussst you had a good night's sssleep?"

He stopped, tongue flicking quickly as he looked from one to the next.

"I bet he can smell the dried chickenbird," Tonia thought but chose to remain silent.

"We slept fine," Micah said without any sign of emotion. "How did you manage to get into the tunnel behind us? The last time we saw you, you were heading down into your home through there?" He pointed at the gaping hole in the floor.

"I have lived in thisss cave for many, many yearsss," Muscala explained. "I know of more than a *few* alternate tunnels through which I travel, sssome above ground, sssome below."

He paused to inspect their belongings. "I sssee you are preparing for travelsss of your own?" He smiled at them,

189

nodding his scaly head, but his ruby-colored eyes were filled with suspicion.

"Yes, we are ready for you to tell us where we need to go," Tonia said quietly. Diam nodded as she repositioned her bag.

"Very well, then," Muscala said, "I will give you the ressst of the information you will need and have ssso patiently waited for."

The others listened quietly, each wondering how long it would take for the snake to give them the necessary details. Muscala seemed to enjoy the fact that he was able to keep them waiting.

Tonia sighed. "This snake is the most arrogant, self-centered creature I have EVER met," she thought with a frown, irritated with both the snake and their situation.

"You mussst go back through that tunnel," Muscala started, nodding in the direction they had come from the previous day.

"When you reach the place where the tunnel forksss, you must continue into the left tunnel. Sssoon enough the tunnel will come to an end, and when it doesss, you will find the stream."

He paused to see if they understood his instructions. Receiving nothing but silence and intent stares, he nodded and continued.

"This isss the stream you mussst go through to find the Wiltoa, and once you find it, you will notice it quickly becomesss very narrow. I have not been able to go any farther than where you will find yoursssselves at this point in your journey."

He stopped again, sizing them up.

"You should not have any problemsss fitting through the narrow opening at thisss part of the stream. Unlessss, of course, it continuesss getting even more narrow asss you go along."

Muscala paused and closed eyes, deep in thought.

"What happens if the stream gets too narrow for even us to get through?" Diam asked.

The snake looked at her and his thin lips spread into a wide, mischievous grin.

"Well, I guessss I would have to find sssomeone else to complete my quessst, and your friend, Nicho, will sssimply..." he paused as his sly expression quickly folded into a gloating one, "perish."

The snake finished with a half-smile, turning to look into

the pit with a look of... what? Satisfaction, Tonia surmised. It didn't take her long to realize the look was not one of pride or uncertainty – it was one of hunger.

Micah glared at the snake angrily but sat still, biting his tongue.

Instead of saying anything that would make matters worse, he looked at Tonia and Diam after several seconds and muttered, "Come on, let's get moving."

Micah stood up, turned and walked over to retrieve the turtles. He then helped the girls put them back inside their respective bags, each of them ignoring the snake completely. When they were ready to leave, they crawled over to the abyss and gave one last look over the edge. Micah dropped down an extra torch, more snacks, and some water.

"We'll be back as quickly as we can, Nicho. I promise," Tonia said, and after some thought, she added, "Do you want my sword?"

She heard movement to her left but somehow knew it was the reptile. He had begun his figure eight movements again as he smirked at them in silence just a few short paces away.

"No," Nicho said confidently. "I'll be okay, Sis. Just hurry back as soon as you can."

"He's trying to be brave and not show us he's scared."

Tonia's thoughts comforted her as her love for her older brother swelled in her heart more than it ever had before.

"We will," Micah said as he got up and brushed off. "Come on, Tonia."

Tonia smiled a quick smile at her brother then got up. As she began following Micah and Diam into the tunnel, she heard Nicho's booming voice echo up at them from the pit.

"BE CAREFUL!"

"We will," they trio of adventurers said in unison, and without looking back, they began their search for the Wiltoa and Kaileen.

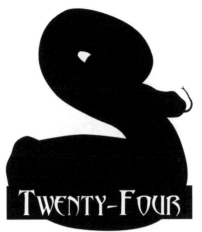

TWENTY-FOUR

Micah took the lead again while Tonia brought up the rear, both carrying a torch. Diam walked between them without any source of light, and every once in a while she would turn and glance back at Tonia. She knew her friend was desperately worried about her brother. To make matters worse, none of them knew if they could really trust that sneaky reptile not to hurt him while they were gone.

Tonia pondered things as they walked. She wondered what other plans the snake had in store for them. What would they do when and if they actually found these other cave snakes and the creature called Kaileen? She had too many questions floating around in her head and too few answers. Perhaps this was all a dream…

Shortly after they started out they met the part of the tunnel where a few other tunnels opened into it. They followed the snake's directions and continued into the left tunnel. As they neared the stream, they found themselves in a somewhat familiar place, once again listening to the soft, rippling sounds created by moving water.

"Sounds like we're heading in the right direction," Micah observed.

Almost as soon as the words were spoken, their eyes fell upon the bubbling stream immediately in front of them. They stopped and watched it briefly as it sparkled softly in the orange glow of torchlight. Although it seemed familiar, this time the water flowed into the tunnel from their left and gently followed the path a short distance downstream to their right. It might be the same stream, but it was definitely in a different area of the cave.

"At least the description of the area the snake gave us was a fairly accurate one," Tonia mumbled as she lingered near the stream while Micah and Diam moved past her. It would not surprise her if they discovered that the snake had made up the entire story of the creature and the amulet, if only for the satisfaction of sending them on a wild mud puppy chase. Then again, as Muscala described the death of the creatures by the uncaring mercenaries, the room he had described sounded eerily like the room where they had found the skeletons, she thought. She shook her head and silently followed behind Diam and Micah.

Within a few hundred feet of finding the stream, they noticed how it narrowed incredibly in width while it grew slightly taller in height. In some places the tunnel walls were dripping with moisture, and scattered here and there along these damp walls were the same clumps of dark colored moss they had seen by the waterfall. They continued quietly on their way, feeling confident that, so far, they were heading in the right direction. It wasn't long before they found there was barely enough of a path remaining at the outer edge of the stream for them to walk on. Before they knew it, walking through the running water was the only way to continue moving forward.

They stepped into the chilly water and quickly found the farther they walked, the deeper it got. First it covered their ankles, then their knees, and before they knew it, the cool liquid was up to the middle of their thighs, making them shiver with the cold. They continued walking slowly through it this way for a few minutes, and then, slowly, the depth of the stream finally began to recede.

"Whew," Micah gasped as he crossed his arms across his chest and rubbed the opposite arm, trying to warm himself up. "I was starting to worry that the water level would keep climbing and we would have to start swimming."

"Me, too," agreed Diam, "and how would we swim and still keep the torches lit?"

"We would take turns riding on Micah's back, of course!"

Tonia offered quickly as she glanced at her brother. He caught her eye and she offered him one of her most innocent smiles before adding, "The rider would just hold both the torches, which would solve THAT problem!"

Micah stopped and childishly stuck his tongue out at her.

"How about we take turns with who plays the horse?" he suggested with a smirk. Both girls immediately shook their heads in denial.

"I always get stuck with the bad jobs," he mumbled, and both the girls laughed playfully as Tonia splashed Micah with a thin spray of water.

They continued on and gradually a path began to appear on the right side of the tunnel. Although the air temperature in the cave was not uncomfortable, they were all relieved to get out of the water as they stepped onto the dry path. They definitely did not want to walk around all day in wet clothes. The sooner they got out of the water, the sooner their clothes would dry – or so they hoped.

As they moved along the winding path, they noticed the tunnel had widened again. At the same time, the ceiling seemed a bit lower, almost similar to the top of the cavern back at the abyss. After a few more minutes, the tunnel took a sudden turn to the left and then to the right. Without warning it suddenly opened up into a larger passageway, which Tonia thought looked almost like a small cavern, yet it didn't.

Most of this tunnel appeared to be dry, but along the right wall she could see a few large, smooth rocks which extended roughly towards the ceiling.

The stream continued flowing along their left, traveling behind some larger rocks for a short distance before continuing on next to the tunnel that stretched out in front of them. They decided to sit on some of the smaller rocks sandwiched between the large rocks and the stream for a few minutes to rest and give their clothes some time to dry off.

"I wonder how much farther we need to go," Diam said quietly. Visibly uncomfortable with the circumstances that led them here, she added, "I sure hope we're at least going in the right direction still."

"I think we are," Micah answered. "The narrow stream was just like Muscala described, so I think we're close to where we need to be."

Tonia nodded. "What do we do when we finally find these snakes?"

"I'm not sure," Micah replied with a frown of concern. "Hopefully we'll find them soon though. I'm worried about leaving Nicho back there with Muscala for too long."

"Me, too," Diam agreed. "The sooner we get this done, the better." As an afterthought she added, "I bet your mom is worried sick."

"Yeah, I know she is, but there's nothing we can do about it right now except hope we're on the right path and can find these Wiltoa quickly," Tonia said as she shook her head.

As she listened to her friend, Diam leaned back on the rock she was sitting by and rested the back of her head against it. She closed her eyes for several seconds then opened them. As her eyes focused on the area overhead, she noticed a small ray of sunlight making its way into the cave through a single crack in the ceiling.

TWENTY-FIVE

Ransa remained in her hiding place near the stream until she was sure the two strange creatures were gone for good. After a few more minutes, she began to relax and her heart rate slowed. When she was certain it was safe, she began making her way out from behind the boulder where she had been hiding. She knew she should head home but her curiosity got the better of her. Before she knew it, she found herself crawling toward the rocks that had captured the creatures' attention.

Her tongue flicked rapidly in and out of her mouth as she smelled the stagnant air.

Mixed scents lingered here – she definitely picked up the scent of the strange creatures that had been here, but she could also smell some kind of fruit. A berry of some type, she would have guessed. There was another, much fainter scent, animal-like, that had been stronger over by the water, but she couldn't quite make out what it was. For now, she focused on the creatures who had been here before.

She tilted her head and gazed up at the rocks where the creatures had spent a lot of their time, looking for any way to get over the tall, smooth barricades. She had always been a curious creature and really wanted to see what those other creatures had found! The rocks were too tall for her, however, so she slithered around the outside of the stone enclosure in search of a crack or hidden entrance.

She found none.

Disappointed, she continued exploring around the rocks as

she prepared to make her way back to the water and continue her search for food. Just as she was about to leave the mysterious rock enclosure, something caught her eye.

At the bottom corner of one section of the impenetrable structure she found one particular rock which looked like it had a small opening behind it. From a distance, she thought the rock looked a little odd so she slithered over to it in order to take a closer look. When she reached it, she placed her nose against the stone and pushed gently.

Nothing happened.

She paused for a few seconds then pushed again. This time she pushed with a little more force.

It moved!

She pushed even harder and after a few seconds, the rock began rolling away from the opening, revealing what appeared to be a small entrance beneath the enclosure.

She hesitated only a moment then quickly entered the opening. She remained cautious as her tongue whipped frequently through the air in front of her face, searching for any signs of danger. She didn't detect any but remained on guard, ready to begin slithering backwards if she sensed even the slightest hint of trouble.

Not far into the opening she came to another rock which also blocked her path. Again, she pushed with her nose. This one cooperated with her and moved quite easily. She crawled past it and was surprised to find she was exactly where she had been trying to go.

In front of her she could now see the object that had attracted the attention of the other creatures. A skeleton. She circled it slowly while looking at it, and then stopped suddenly as her yellow eyes filled with remembrance.

Although Kaileen was not a forgotten pile of dried up bones like the skeleton before her, the little snake knew beyond a doubt that this corpse belonged to one of Kaileen's kind. Her friend's facial structure was very similar to the skeleton, especially when it came to the protruding jaw. Ransa's eyes filled with sadness as she wondered if this was one of Kaileen's relatives.

After a final look around, Ransa headed back the way she

TWENTY-SIX

Living in complete darkness is normal when it's the only way you've lived your whole life. Many creatures that spent their lives within the cave lived just this way, and it would probably never occur to them that there might be any other way to live. Since they lived in complete darkness all the time, their eyes became naturally accustomed to life without light. As a result, most cave-dwelling creatures had excellent night vision, even under their circumstances.

Kaileen was a kalevala, and, as far as she knew, she was the last of her kind. A terrible tragedy had befallen her and others like her when she was younger. Although she knew she couldn't change the past, she tried her best not to think about it. Unfortunately, it didn't always work. Sometimes, especially when the cave was silent and sleeping, she would find herself remembering those times when things were different – when she had lived happily with her family and friends. Her life was good then, until…

She pushed the memory away.

During those times when she found herself remembering a cornucopia of events from times gone by, she would force herself to push the unwanted memories into a cave-like part of her mind. In her mind's eye, a forgotten memory would creep up on her like a snake about to pounce on an unsuspecting cave rat and she would see the past with vivid clarity, but when she pushed the memory away, she would then see only blackness.

Blackness was good.

Sometimes, when she was lucky, her heart would harden like

a large, lifeless stone by not allowing her to feel any of the pain and emptiness which now seemed such a dreaded part of her everyday life. Unfortunately for Kaileen, this didn't happen very often. The pain and emptiness were persistent, almost always there, even as she slept. Her family and friends haunted her in her dreams and she could do nothing but stand by as nothing more than an invisible, emotional observer, helplessly watching the events of that fateful day unfold right before her eyes. She could scream, cry or yell at her family and friends from deep within her dream, but in the end there was nothing she could do to prevent the heart-wrenching tragedy from happening over and over again.

The first few months of life for a new kalevala could be quiet difficult. Although the cave was filled with darkness (or so Kaileen believed), countless different predators lurked in the tunnels surrounding their home. Sometimes the young ones were taken, or killed, or both. This, however, was both an accepted and sad part of life for the kalevala, and it was also the reason why they celebrated Half-Year Day.

Her dream, the one that haunted her day after merciless day, always began with Boreas. His day, the day he had looked forward to for many moons, had finally arrived. It was Boreas' turn to celebrate his Half-Year Day because he was the youngest kalevala. During this celebration, he had been happily playing with friends in the cavern, reveling with the knowledge that the celebration on this particular day, although shared by all kalevalas, was his and his alone.

The dream. The heartbreaking memories. The nightmare.

In her sleep, Kaileen begins tossing and turning, her eyes twitching and blinking behind closed lids, her subconscious mind filling with the memories she daily tries so hard to suppress.

Unable to wake up, Kaileen lives through the events of that evening again, for the hundredth, thousandth, or millionth time. Like she expects, the dream begins with her part nothing more than a ghostly memory, a bystander watching the events unfold. This changes quickly, however, and she resumes her place in the dream, reliving it one more time.

In the center of the room, she spied Boreas jumping up and

200

down with excitement after opening his gifts when she heard the sound of a commotion beginning at the entrance to their cavern. Torchlight suddenly filled the room as all of the kalevala squinted and tried to shield their eyes from an invasive, unfamiliar brightness that was such an oddity to them. Through squinted lids Kaileen listened to the conversation quietly from the back of the cave where she had been playing with her friends. Between the unwelcome brightness and the numerous bodies between her and the commotion near the front area her home, it was difficult for her to see what was happening.

After the uninvited creatures crowded the entranceway to her home, Pauzel, the leader, approached the strangers and began talking to them in a deep, familiar voice. The leader of the strangers introduced himself as Ugla.

She jumped up and down as she tried in vain to see over the group now huddled closely in the center of the cavern. All she could really see was the intruders carrying sticks of light, the effects from this odd brightness making her eyes feel very strange. The glowing sticks were very bright, much brighter than anything any of them had ever known. It blurred their vision, which was somewhat uncomfortable, but it also seemed to remain in their eyes even after they looked away. This was a very disconcerting feeling. Thinking back, she knew the invasive light in their home must have caused all of the kalevala much discomfort in their heads. As a result, for the first time in their lives, their vision was no longer excellent.

Pauzel asked Ugla to give them a moment in order for their sight to adjust to this strange, new sensation caused by their light sticks. For a few moments, all was well. It seemed as though Ugla sympathized with them and was going to allow the requested time.

As the kalevala's eyes adjusted, they could finally focus clearly on these creatures that had invaded their home. They were slightly taller than the kalevala and had a much broader build, with wide shoulders and thick legs. Their muscular upper bodies and upper part of their legs were covered with a heavy, shiny garment.

Her heart jumped into her throat when she realized that each and every one of the strangers blocking the entrance to her home carried various weapons with obvious confidence. She could almost smell their confidence and smugness, filling her senses, making it hard to breathe.

She closed her eyes for several seconds, glad she stood at the rear of their cavern, farthest away from these menacing creatures. If she was any closer she doubted she'd be able to breathe at all.

While the kalevala's eyes adjusted to the change in the environment, Ugla described the reason for the intrusion. A very important gem, an amulet, had been taken from their leader, who happened to be a highly respected and powerful magician named Lotor. Ugla explained that Lotor had heard a rumor detailing how the amulet had somehow made its way into this cave, and now Lotor believed one of the kalevala had possession of his prized jewel.

Believing she could hear the conversation better if she was at a higher point in the room, Kaileen scrambled up onto a rock and peered across the heads of her friends and family, listening intently to the unfolding conversation.

Behind closed lids, her eyes twitched and rolled as she remembered how Ugla looked as he spoke to Pauzel on that fateful day. No matter how much time passed – days, weeks, years – it felt like it had happened just yesterday. Ugla's voice was loud and booming and his eyes squinted wickedly across the faces of her people. Even from the back of the cavern where she stood, Kaileen did not trust this creature who questioned their leader. As uncomfortable as she was, all she could do was listen to the stranger with an almost overwhelming trepidation as he persisted in questioning Pauzel.

"We firmly believe the amulet we seek is here, somewhere among your people. If any of you have possession of this amulet and hand it over now, without a struggle, no harm will come to any of you."

Although Ugla's words were reassuring, his tone was quite threatening. Pauzel turned and looked at his people. After a few seconds, he clasped his hands in front of him and his familiar voice echoed everywhere around them as he spoke.

"Does anyone here have possession of the gem Ugla speaks

of? If you do, you must hand it over to him now so he may return it to its rightful owner."

A gentle wave of rumbling voices filled the cavern as the kalevala looked at each other before slowly shaking their heads in denial. Wanting to be certain he understood their response, Pauzel addressed them once again.

"No one knows anything about this amulet?"

Murmurs of denial wafted through the group of kalevala again. Satisfied, Pauzel turned back to Ugla and repeated the words of his people. They had no knowledge of such a gem.

The kalevala were a peaceful and trusting society. The result of their docile nature was quite unfortunate, for none of them had any idea of the incredible evil that had wandered into their home.

A nervous wave of whispers rolled through the kalevalas when they sensed something was not right. Without a word from Ugla, many of the accompanying soldiers had set their hands on their weapons, although they did not draw them. Instead, they waited for a sign from their leader, and before the kalevalas knew what was happening, Ugla gave his soldiers the sign they were looking for.

Before the gentle creatures living in the cavern knew what was happening, the damage had been done. In an instant, Ugla drew his sword. With a single, rapid swipe of the expertly sharpened blade, Pauzel crumpled into a lifeless heap on the ground.

The kalevala watched silently as their leader fell to his death, in both shock and disbelief at what had just taken place. In mere seconds, reality set in. The group of kalevalas began screaming as they ran frantically around the cavern in hopes of escaping the imminent pain and death, which now filled their senses like a thick, heavy smoke.

Kaileen covered her mouth and without thinking about what she was doing, tucked herself behind one of the taller, nearby stones. Her mind, although shocked at the scene before her, screamed a single word to her.

Run!

The only tunnel leading into their home was filled with armed mercenaries. Regardless, some of the kalevala tried to run past them in hopes of escaping the same fate that had tragically fallen upon their leader. Watching as they began trying to push their way past the intruders, Ugla called out a short, simple order to his troops.

"Kill them all!"

His soldiers obeyed without hesitation.

From the back of the room, Kaileen disbelievingly watched as the scene unfolded before her. Within seconds after Pauzel fell to the dusty cavern floor, she realized this was not a game and followed her first reaction. She darted out from behind the rock and ran to the only place she could think of. It was the only place where she thought she just might have a chance to be safe.

Living in this small cavern most of her life, Kaileen knew every nook and cranny. She knew of one small place on the other side of the cavern behind the rocks that would take her through a hidden crawl space. This led to a tunnel that would take her to another part of the cave. She glanced back at the group of kalevalas and was horrified to see them dropping like flies. They were being slaughtered! She remained frozen for several seconds before she was bumped into by one of the younger members of her group.

It was Boreas.

"Run, Kaileen!" he yelled as he tripped and nearly fell headfirst into another one of the large rocks in the room. She helped him get up but he pulled out of her grasp and headed in the opposite direction.

The soldiers were only a few feet away. They were swinging their swords and maces as they wiped out her friends and family, one by one. She was going to run after Boreas but it was too late. She was out of options.

The crawl space was just a few feet away. If she waited any longer, the soldiers would see her.

She had to go now!

Without a second thought, she quickly ducked behind the rocks and entered her secret hiding place on her hands and knees. She shimmied between the rocks as fast as she could, whimpering softly as she tried without success to block out the screams and cries of her friends and family behind her. This sound would haunt her, awake and asleep, for many, many moons.

Soon she reached the tunnel on the other side of the cavern wall. She stood up and began running through it, unsure of where she was going, but feeling the need, the almost overwhelming, desire to survive. The one thing she was sure of was that she had to get away, as far and as fast as she could.

Around her waist she carried a bag. It contained all that remained of her personal belongings – a few smooth rocks that she sometimes used when playing with her friends. Among these rocks was another very smooth rock that she had found next to the stream when she was on a long hunting trip with her family. This special rock was smooth, yet had a border of some sort around it which she was not able to remove. From the day she found it, she thought of it as her lucky rock, carrying it with her at all times.

As she ran, her heart breaking with the loss of her family and friends, she hoped her luck had not run out.

TWENTY-SEVEN

Kaileen ran and ran through the winding tunnels of the cave, as fast as she could, until she came to a place where she finally could no longer hear the horrible screams and desperate cries of her family and friends anymore. She stopped for a moment, resting her hands on her knees as she bent over, struggling to catch her breath. She stood this way for several seconds when she suddenly thought she heard the sound of approaching footsteps. Like prey being chased by a predator, she bolted upright and began running again.

She had to get away from the pain in her heart, the fear, the death, the anger…

She ran for several minutes without paying attention to where she was going. When she came to an unfamiliar stream, she finally slowed and, with little thought, she followed the direction of the flowing water. It was quiet here with the exception of the sounds of gently flowing water and soon the stream led her to a place that looked safe. It was a smaller cavern but had a few large rocks here and there that she could hide behind if she realized the heartless, murdering invaders had followed her.

After taking a quick drink of water, she curled up behind one of the large rocks and wrapped her arms around her legs. She sat like this for a few moments, catching her breath, her heart still pounding in her chest. She did her best to control her emotions. If she began to cry again, she didn't know if she would be able to control her gut-wrenching sobs. As far as she could tell, she had gotten away from the strangers who had turned her life into a turmoil of anguish and confusion, but if she began crying again, her sobs would no doubt lead them right to her. Of this she was certain.

As her breathing settled down, she focused on the sounds of the soft gurgling stream and the incessant beating of her heart. She closed her eyes and tried to calm the ache bubbling up inside her, filling her very core. No matter how much she tried to avoid the unavoidable pain, fresh memories of the gruesome tragedy she had just been witness to snuck into the room with her, surrounding her like an unwanted blanket of sadness. It became too much for her and she began crying into her knees. Her tears ran down her face, her arms, and her legs until they mixed with the dirt and pebbles surrounding her on the dusty floor. She somehow managed to control her anguish, emitting only soft, quiet cries as the pain and sadness flowed through her body, her entire being consumed with an overwhelming grief. It felt as though a giant cave spider was ripping her heart out, one aching piece at a time.

She sat this way for a while, allowing the tears to flow from both her eyes and her heart. Tears fell for her mother and father, her siblings, her friends. She cried for Boreas, too. As she remembered the young kalevala that was being honored today, her tears evaporated from her face and were quickly replaced by an almost blinding anger that settled into the deepest corners of her heart. Today was supposed to be a day of celebration, not of death! Today had been his day!

She sniffled and decided to rest where she was for a while before trying to move on in her search for a new home. She knew she couldn't go back there... back to the place of so much devastation, even though she doubted the evil strangers would linger there. All she knew was right now she had neither the strength nor the will to find out if they did.

As her heart nearly overflowed with emptiness caused by those who had murdered her friends and family, an odd, unexpected thought struck her. Maybe, if she was very careful and quiet, she could go back there. Perhaps she could head home and follow the strangers back to wherever they had come from? Her mind drifted back to the light sticks the strangers carried with them and how she had never seen anything like them before. Where did they come from that they would carry sticks of light such as these?

She tried to remember the things they said – something about a Lotor; was that a person? A creature? A magician?

The long, hard cry she'd had left her drained both emotionally and physically. As she settled herself against a rock she closed her eyes again, listening to the soft sounds of the flowing water which surrounded her like a gentle cocoon.

Before she knew it, Kaileen drifted off to sleep.

It seemed like moments later when she felt something tickling her arm in the darkness. She brushed at it and tried to go back into her dream of one day long ago, floating carelessly in a time when she had been on an adventure with a hunting party… with her family.

In her dream, they had been meandering together through the tunnels as they searched for something for dinner. They decided to follow the water as it flowed and after a while, stopped to rest. She and the other young ones began playing with rocks, smooth, cool shapes in the darkness, trying to see who could find the smoothest one for their game of hop rock. She managed to find a few nice stones before fate led her like an invisible magnet to her lucky rock. She found it among countless other ones, close to the edge of the stream bed, almost as though it was waiting for her.

It was common for some of the rocks they found to feel different from each other, especially after being tousled in current of the almost constantly flowing water. Surprisingly, some of the rocks were covered with different sized patches and layers of course material, which made them rougher than others. All the little ones knew the smoother the rock, the better for hop rock.

Kneeling next to the stream bed, she placed her hands in the water as she searched for the perfect rock. Her fingertips suddenly brushed across one that felt a lot like one of the other rocks she had found earlier, yet, in a strange way, this one felt somewhat different. Although she suspected it was just an odd rock, she couldn't be sure so she took it out of the water and placed it in her pouch until later.

After resting for a while, the group of hunters moved on as

they continued their search for prey. Soon, one of the men found a piglet that had apparently been separated from its mother and got lost in the cave. After wandering around for a few days, the piglet was weak from lack of food and didn't stand a chance against the hunters. The men pummeled it with rocks in an effort to bring the small animal down and soon they heard it crying out from both fear and pain. Without hesitation, they pounced on the creature without any further hesitation. In order to save the poor creature from any further suffering, they killed it quickly. Afterwards they cleaned it, skinned it, gathered the meat, and headed back to the others with their prize.

From that day on, Kaileen considered the rock she had found her own, personal, lucky rock.

She lay in her curled up position in the part of the cave she now considered her home, trying desperately to get back into her dream. She wanted – no, needed – to float freely through dreams of happy events, instead of being weighed down by a heavy, black cloud of sadness and loss. She closed her eyes, hoping more than anything that her body would take her back to the dream, back to her family. Just when she thought she might be finally close to drifting off, she felt the strange, tickling sensation once again on her arm.

She sat bolt upright and clumsily grabbed for a nearby rock, trying to focus her way through her sleepy dream to defend herself. She didn't know what had tickled her arm, and she held her breath, waiting in silence for it to happen again.

She heard a soft sound in the dark a few feet away, almost like a whisper, and a quiet voice spoke to her in the darkness.

"Are you okay?"

Kaileen's breath caught in her throat and she wondered if she was simply in another dream. She was not prepared for anything to talk to her like this, especially when it was this close! It sounded almost as though it was right next to her. Why hadn't she heard whatever it was as it approached? Then she remembered her dream... and suddenly understood.

Again the whisper came to her from the darkness just to her right.

"Are you okay?" the faceless voice repeated.

209

Kaileen wasn't sure what to do but decided the voice was real. It was not in her dream. Now the question was, should she respond or try to throw her rock at it? Was it one of the creatures that had slaughtered her friends and family, searching for her still after all this time? She doubted this, thinking it not very likely that the enemy would tiptoe into her new hiding place, then whisper to her, asking if she was okay. If it were one of those creatures, and if it had known she was there, it probably would have killed her where she lay dreaming.

She decided to take a chance.

"Yes, I'm okay," Kaileen whispered back. "Who... who are you?"

She tried to sound confident, but her voice shook with obvious hesitation.

"My name is Ransa," the whispering creature answered back. "I heard you crying and was worried that you were hurt and needed help. Then you became quiet for a while. I was afraid to come see if you were okay, but felt like I had to."

After a slight pause, the mystery voice continued, "What do they call you?"

Kaileen was silent for a moment, afraid to trust this new creature. A partial memory struck her then, her father's face, and her mind flooded with the memories of what had happened earlier. Her resolve crumpled into a puddle of emotions at the base of her heart and she began crying softly again.

"What is it?" Ransa asked. Her voice was soft and soothing. "What's wrong?"

As she listened to the creature whimpering in the darkness, Kaileen's emotional walls crumbled with a sob once more, and she broke down and told Ransa everything, including her name.

"I don't know what I should do. Should I run away, as far as I can go? Should I go back to see if my family and friends are still alive? Should I go and see if I can find those evil, (sob) evil creatures who did this and follow them to this Lotor, then have my revenge on him?" The kalevala's anguished voice rose with each question.

"Whoa, whoa, whoa," Ransa answered, feeling Kaileen's pain and sadness, but also understanding that her mind was much more clear than Kaileen's about everything right now. "I think your last thought is definitely, absolutely NOT an option! Do you want to end up just like your family? If they showed no hesitation to kill your leader… what was his name? Pudel?"

"Pauzel," Kaileen mumbled through her tears.

Ransa nodded her acknowledgment, not realizing the gesture was covered by the lightless shadows around them. "Don't you think, if they killed Pauzel without any hesitation like they did, that if you *could* find them, they wouldn't kill you the same way?"

Ransa's voice was both stern and gentle. After giving her words a few seconds to sink in with her grieving new friend, she continued.

"Kaileen, I know it hurts you, what you've been through. Your family and friends…" Ransa paused. I cannot imagine your pain, but there's nothing you can do for them now. It sounds like they were both outnumbered and overpowered."

She stopped, waiting for Kaileen to respond, but the kalevala remained silent.

"You," Ransa continued softly, "*you* must go on!"

She said this without realizing that, ironically, she would tell her new friend these exact words again in the not-so-distant future, under much different circumstances.

Ransa listened for a response from Kaileen, but heard nothing in return except for the rustlings of a hand running itself gently through the mixed dirt and pebbles on the cave floor and the soothing sounds of the bubbling stream along the far wall. Although she knew the grieving creature was still next to her, Ransa couldn't see what she was doing to make the sound on the floor, but she hoped it meant she was listening to Ransa's words. She decided to continue, adding more force and energy to her words.

"Kaileen, you must live like they no longer can! If these horrid creatures did indeed kill everyone in that cavern, and if you are the only remaining creature of your kind, then it is **vitally** important for you to survive!"

Her words echoed through the darkness around them. Both creatures sat together, side by side but not touching, as the last whispers of Ransa's words fell silent and the only sound left was the gentle trickling of the stream.

"Why don't you come with me? Come live with me and my family for a while, until you are ready to move on," Ransa suggested. She couldn't help but want to do something for this creature, especially after knowing what a horrible tragedy she had been through.

They fell silent again and a few moments later, the sun began making its way through the cracks in the tunnel ceiling. The unexpected sight brought back an instant memory of the fateful light sticks, those hateful objects that had been the beginning of the end to life as she knew it. Kaileen jumped up, frightened that the murderous, evil beings who had invaded her former home had found her and she darted behind a large rock and buried her face in her hands, whimpering with fear.

Kaileen's actions startled Ransa, who had no idea what had frightened her new friend.

"What's wrong, Kaileen?" Ransa asked quietly as she moved to the nearby rock.

"Shhhh," Kaileen whispered. "I think they're coming! The room… the same thing that happened before… the light!"

"The light?" Ransa whispered back in confusion.

She turned and looked behind her, trying to see what had frightened her friend but there was nothing there. Her eyes scanned from side to side and she was about to say it was nothing when she suddenly realized what the terrified creature was referring to.

"No, no, Kaileen, it's okay! That's the sun coming though the cracks in the top of the tunnel. Trust me, it's okay."

"Sun?" Kaileen asked quietly as she lowered her hands, turned slightly and looked around the room. "What is sun?"

Ransa was surprised. She had known about the sun most of her life. It was almost hard to believe that there might be other creatures here who did not know what it was.

"The only part of the sun I've ever seen is through these cracks here and through others like it within my home," Ransa explained. "I've heard that the sun is much brighter and hotter outside the cave, but I've never been there."

"What is 'outside the cave'?" Kaileen asked as she wiped a

line of moisture from her cheek, more confused than before.

"Boy, do I have a lot to teach her," Ransa thought with a small smile.

As Ransa answered Kaileen's question, the sunlight continued creeping into the cave. It wasn't long before Ransa was able to finally see what her new friend looked like.

Kaileen was larger than Ransa, and the snake could clearly see that the kalevala's eyes were soft brown and filled with an almost overwhelming sadness. Her lower jaw protruded out in front of her and she had a short, stubby tail.

Although she had never seen anything like her, Ransa sensed she had nothing to fear from this creature.

"What?" Kaileen asked when she noticed the snake was smiling at her.

"What kind of creature are you?" Ransa asked. "I've never seen you or any creatures like you in here before."

Kaileen lowered her head for a moment before she slowly met the snake's warm, friendly gaze. "I am a kalevala," she said proudly, as tears again began pooling in her eyes.

"And you?" she asked after struggling to maintain some semblance of control over her emotions.

"I am a Wiltoa... only one of many different kinds of cave snakes," Ransa answered. "I live with my family just over there." She nodded in the direction of the smooth, rocky slope that was just becoming visible in the surrounding gloom.

Kaileen nodded. Now that her eyes had adjusted to the light penetrating the shadows around them and she finally understood she did not need to fear this light, she was also able to get a good look at the friendly snake who appeared to be more than willing to help her.

Ransa's skin color was similar to the soft brown of Kaileen's eyes. Her eyes, however, were much different than her own, yellow with a large, dark circle in the center. They were friendly eyes.

Kaileen watched Ransa, fascinated, as her thin forked tongue occasionally flicked out of her mouth before quickly disappearing back where it came from.

"Why do you do that?" Kaileen asked with interest. She didn't seem to realize she was staring.

"Do what?" Ransa questioned, unsure of what she had done.

"The thing that keeps coming out of your mouth," Kaileen replied. "What happened to it? It looks like it's broken or cut. Did you hurt yourself?"

Ransa laughed with amusement. "It's my tongue, and no it's not broken or anything. That's just how it is, naturally. It helps me to smell things. I guess you could think if it as if my nose is in my mouth."

Kaileen chuckled and thought about how much she liked this odd creature who was so very different than her own people.

"Come on. Let's go meet my family," Ransa invited as she began slithering towards the cluster of rocks leading to her home.

After a brief hesitation, Kaileen followed, still somewhat uncertain about where the snake was leading her. She was afraid it could all be a lie and understood there was a possibility that the snake may lead her into a trap. She didn't know why Ransa would do such a thing unless she was looking for a meal and was leading her to a larger group of snakes to help with the kill, but she didn't think so. Even though those other creatures came and killed everyone without any kind of reason, she felt some kind of strange connection with this single, slithering reptile.

After having gone through some of the most difficult times of her life, Kaileen was nearly to the point where she didn't care anymore. She had lost her family, her friends, her home, her entire life. What more could be taken from her now? Death would be a welcomed respite from the pain which threatened every waking moment, nearly overwhelming her shattered heart.

They entered Ransa's home and Kaileen slowly settled into a new routine. At first she spent quite a bit of time to herself, but she eventually became accustomed to living with Ransa and her family. At first she was quiet and shy with the group of snakes but over time, she became one of the family. They watched this wonderful, gentle creature bloom like a long dormant flower as they lovingly and patiently helped her begin putting her life back together.

Before long, she felt as though she had been with them forever.

Time moved on, though, as it often does, and one day, Ransa

returned from a hunting trip with the fresh carcass of a large cave rat. She brought it into their home and hastily pulled Kaileen aside.

"What is it?" Kaileen asked with a curious smile. Her welcoming expression quickly faded, however, when she saw the serious look on her friend's face.

"There were creatures downstream," Ransa answered in a rapid, stressed voice.

"Okay," said Kaileen as she sat down on a rock. "Creatures, downstream, in the cave… what a concept!" Although her own voice was teasing, her eyes were stern and her smile seemed almost painted on her face. Something about these unfamiliar creatures had completely stressed out her friend.

"I'm serious, Kai!" Ransa said, a little irritated with Kaileen for trying to joke when she was being totally serious. "These creatures were different than any I've ever seen! I think they were female, from the way they talked, but Kai," Ransa hesitated and dropped her tone into an almost inaudible whisper, "They had LIGHT sticks!"

Kaileen's smile immediately disappeared from her face and her eyes filled with the old, familiar sadness. Her gentle reptilian friend and her family had been so wonderful to her, opening their home and welcoming her without any hesitation. Kaileen had always feared this day would eventually find her.

"Light sticks?" Kaileen asked in a trembling voice.

Ransa nodded as her orphaned friend suddenly jumped to her feet, her eyes darting around the room.

"Do you think they were looking for me? If they are, I have to go away," Kaileen said hastily as tears began filling her eyes. "I couldn't stand to see another family murdered in front of my eyes, especially if it's because I'm the one those evil creatures are looking for!" She struggled to maintain some sort of control over her emotions as memories of the past filled her heart with a burning ache.

"Kai, we don't know if it's even you they are looking for, so just hold on a minute and let's think about this," Ransa said as she slithered over to her friend and rubbed against the dark, cool skin of Kaileen's leg. "Besides, they weren't dressed the way you

215

described the creatures from before. These creatures were just… different."

She looked up with hopeful eyes and offered her friend a reassuring smile.

Kaileen didn't want Ransa to know how much this bit of news worried her and she returned Ransa's smile as she tried her best to hide her distress.

"So, what should we do?"

"I think we should just sit tight right where we are," Ransa answered. "The cave rat I caught today will feed us for a few days and our home is fairly well hidden." Ransa paused as she tried to convey her thoughts into words. "You're part of the family, Kai, and I'm sure the other family members would agree that we don't want you to leave. We've all suffered sadness and heartache during our lives in this cave, and we've all become stronger because of it."

Kaileen offered an agreeable nod as a single tear slowly traced a wet path down her face. She loved this new family of hers and couldn't bear to see them get hurt.

"Please stay with us," Ransa continued as her own eyes got misty.

"But what if…?" Kaileen began, but Ransa interrupted her.

"We don't know if these WERE those creatures, Kai. It's worth it to me to take the chance, but I really don't think they were the same creatures."

Kaileen looked down at Ransa. The little snake with the big heart and bigger personality was staring at her with stern expression. After considering Ransa's words, Kaileen knew she was beaten.

"Okay, but we must talk to the others and everyone must promise me that whenever they go outside of our home, they will be more careful than they've ever been before." She scowled at the snake when Ransa seemed to just brush off her words. "I mean it, Ransa. If they won't agree, I will leave. Immediately."

Realizing how serious Kaileen was about this, the two friends immediately called a family meeting. Not surprisingly, everyone agreed without hesitation that they wanted Kaileen to stay. They also gave their word that they would be very careful.

That night, they went to bed, each satisfied with their agreement and happy they were still a complete family.

The next day, however, they heard the voices just outside their home…

TWENTY-EIGHT

"Look!" Diam said excitedly as she pointed at the sunlight as it pierced the nearby darkness like a knife.

"Wooo hoooo!!!" she shouted joyously. "We found it, guys!"

"Diam! Shhhh!" Tonia scolded her. "The creatures who live here may not want us here!"

Micah drew his sword just in case there was trouble. He definitely wished Nicho could be here with them though, because he was finding out rather quickly that he didn't enjoy being in charge of things. It failed to occur to him, however, that if Nicho were with them, they wouldn't be in the situation they found themselves in.

Inside the snake cavern, Ransa slithered over to the entrance and stretched her neck out until it was almost touching the smooth surface of a nearby rock. Within seconds, Kaileen silently joined her and together they listened to the muffled, broken voices coming from outside of their home. They held their breath and looked at each other with wide, frightened eyes, neither one recognizing the voices they heard.

"What do we do?"

Although her friend was speaking in an almost inaudible whisper, Ransa could hear the fear in her voice, loud and clear.

"I'm going to go out and see what they're doing," the snake said.

Her sight was very good in the dark, like Kaileen's, but she was smaller than the kalevala and would be able to maneuver around the rocks more easily – at least she hoped.

Without waiting for her friend to answer, Ransa peeked through the gray, musty sheet of moss covering the entrance to her home. A short distance away, on the other side of the tunnel, she could see rays of light flickering behind a large rock next to the water. Rings of light fell across the dirt and stones covering the ground between the stream and her home. She listened quietly – if she wasn't mistaken, this was where these voices were coming from.

Putting herself into stealth mode, she slipped from behind the moss and slithered down the smooth rock slope. The dim light provided by the intruders illuminated her way but wasn't necessary – she knew this part of the cave better than anyone else, including her own siblings. Ransa quickly positioned herself behind a large rock, hoping that if their visitors began to move, she would be able to blend in with the earth colors of the tunnel and avoid detection. She continued listening quietly and soon overheard something that demanded her complete, undivided attention.

They were looking for the Wiltoa.

That was her! She totally did not understand why they would be looking for her and her family. Did they somehow know that Kaileen was staying with them in their home? She remained deathly still as she continued to eavesdrop on their conversation.

"Okay, so what do we do now?" Diam asked quietly, settling down after her initial excitement of thinking they had finally found the right cavern. "Should we just call out for them?"

"I don't know what we should do," Micah whispered. "We don't know if they're friendly or if they're like that sneaky Muscala."

Muscala!

Ransa trembled as she heard the giant snake's name. She had heard many stories about him, more than she cared to count. Everyone knew about the angry, devious, giant snake that slithered ominously through the tunnels not far from here. The stories described an evil reptile who was not easily frightened and who would do almost anything to get what he wanted.

"Let's just sit here a few moments and rest. If we sit long enough, maybe a splendid idea will come to us in a few minutes!"

TWENTY-NINE

A s they sat trying to figure out what to do about their situation, Tonia suddenly felt the hairs on the back of her neck standing straight up. The accompanying, unsettling feeling crept over her like a hairy spider, prickling at her with every one of its eight spindly legs, each step across her skin endless. She stood up and looked around the area and although she didn't see anything strange, she just couldn't shake the odd feeling that had come over her out of nowhere.

It took her several seconds, but she suddenly realized it almost felt as though they were being watched.

"Hello?" she called out. She held her torch out in front of her as she began making her way around the large rock, moving towards the center of the tunnel.

"What is it, Tonia?" Micah asked, sensing something he couldn't quite put his finger on. He stood up and moved closer to her, his sword still drawn.

"I don't know," she whispered back as Diam joined them.

"Hello?" Tonia called out again.

Prick, prick, prick – the feeling was still there but she just couldn't figure out what was causing it. Strangely enough, it seemed to intensify as she reached the center of the cavern.

"Sssss."

A soft hissing noise suddenly seemed to fill the air around them. Had Muscala followed them even though he swore he couldn't fit through the narrow tunnel? There was no way he could have gotten through there – unless, of course, he lied about knowing how to get here. Tonia wouldn't put it past the sneaky reptile, not for as little as a minute or as long as a million moon cycles.

"Ssssss." The noise they heard was soft and not very threatening, but seemed to fill the air around them. What was making that sound?

Tonia and Diam drew their weapons and they all stood still, looking around the room. They all heard the noise, but still could not see anything.

"We are looking for a family of cave snakes called 'Wiltoa'," Micah offered, unsure of what or whom he was talking to.

"Hello?" Diam called out quietly.

"Sssssss," they heard again.

Diam saw it first, over near the rock close to where they had been sitting. It was a small snake that partially blended into the rocky background. It barely moved, alone in the shadows as it quietly watched them.

"There!" she whispered to the others.

"Hi," Tonia greeted the snake quietly. "My name is Tonia, and this is my brother and my friend. We need to find the Wiltoa, cave snakes that are supposed to be living in this part of the cave. At least we think it's this part of the cave, but we could be lost so we might be wrong…"

Diam nudged her friend in the ribs, prompting her to get on with it.

Tonia nodded and continued.

"Sorry. Do you know where we can find them?"

Ransa silently watched this odd, female creature, tasting the air with her narrow, forked tongue, unsure of what to do. She recognized this one and the other female as those she had seen the day before when she was out hunting for food. She peered at them through the darkness, her eyes moving from one to the other as she weighed her options. None of these creatures were dressed like the evil beings Kaileen had described, but if it wasn't them, then who were they?

After a long moment, Ransa decided to take a chance and try talking to them. She could at least find out what they were doing in the cave, and why they were looking for the Wiltoa.

222

"What are you doing in here?"

Ransa remembered what Kaileen had told her about the weapons the evil creatures had carried. These creatures before her appeared to have weapons too, but they just didn't seem to be as evil as the other ones from Kaileen's past.

"We're looking for the Wiltoa and it's very important that we find them," Tonia said softly as she sat down on a rock.

"Why?" Ransa asked with caution as she considered her routes of escape. She just didn't know what was about to transpire but wanted to be prepared in case it wasn't good.

Tonia watched as the snake's focus darted around the room. Her voice was quiet and calm when she spoke.

"We need to find them… they have some information that we need."

Ransa watched her cautiously. "I can tell you I know where you can find these snakes, but first I must know why you need to talk to them," she challenged. "What is it that is so important to you?"

Tonia lowered her sword in hopes of convincing the slithering shape that they meant no harm.

"Look, we came across a large snake in another part of the tunnel. He told us to look for other snakes called Wiltoa. They can tell us where we can find another creature…"

Diam, seeing that Tonia was beginning to get upset, took over where Tonia left off.

"The other creature's name is Kaileen. If we don't find this creature and get the information we need, their brother will die. We have to rescue him so we can find our way out of here."

They all watched as Ransa thought over what she just heard. After another long moment, she finally spoke.

"My name is Ransa," she said, "and I am a Wiltoa."

They looked at the snake with complete surprise. It had not occurred to them that this creature might be one of the ones they were looking for. The most they were hoping for was that the snake might be able to at least point them in the right direction.

Tonia sat down on the dusty floor.

"Ransa," she said, sadness appearing in her dark eyes. "We need your help. My brother is being held against his will in a dark hole in one of the tunnels upstream. The giant snake who lives there will not free him unless we help him with a quest." She stopped and looked at the snake.

"Do you know where we can find a creature called 'Kaileen'?" she asked quietly, her voice filled with desperation.

The three children were caught off guard when suddenly they heard a noise behind them. Micah whirled around in time to see a creature walking upright, heading directly toward them. He held out his sword and the creature stopped, looking at them, one at a time.

"I am Kaileen," the creature said. Her voice was flat and without emotion.

As Micah whirled around to confront Kaileen, Tonia jumped to her feet as she unsheathed her own weapon and held it out in front of her. She glanced over at Diam and was relieved to find that her friend had done the same thing.

In the torchlight they could see that Kaileen was smaller than anyone in their group. She had dark, gentle eyes, but they knew better than to assume that the character of the creature matched the character of the creature's eyes. If only they knew the tragedy this creature had suffered, perhaps they would not have judged her so unjustly. After getting a good look at her, they could definitely see the resemblance to the many skeletons they had found in the other cavern.

Kaileen did not carry a weapon but stood before them, empty-handed and motionless.

The trio of friends stood where they were for a moment, sizing up each other and the situation. Slowly, Tonia lowered her sword again. She took a deep breath before she spoke.

"Kaileen, we desperately need your help. There is a snake…"

"Yes… Muscala. I know the name," Kaileen said firmly. "What of him?"

"He believes that you have possession of a jewel, a very special amulet, and he has sent us on a quest to find both you and the amulet. Once we do, we are to find the gem and return it to him." Tonia paused. "If we don't do as he asks, my brother will die."

Kaileen looked at them quietly before she shook her head.

"I know of no amulet."

224

The three explorers listened to Kaileen's reply in disbelief. They sat for a long time, letting her words register in each of their minds.

She didn't have the amulet. Without it, Muscala would not release Nicho and their brother would surely die in the snake's dark home. When the reality of this hit, Tonia's eyes began filling with tears.

"You're sure you don't have it?" Micah asked.

The young boy looked at Tonia, then Diam, before his eyes dropped to the cavern floor. He shook his head in silent shock. He could not believe this was happening. After getting utterly lost in the cave yet managing to actually find the creature Muscala sent them to find… he just could not imagine going back to the large snake empty-handed.

"Living here, in the darkness of the cave, is the only life I have ever known," Kaileen explained. "What use would a gem, a piece of jewelry, have for me? I have a rock collection, but I know of no amulets or gems."

Her last words caught Tonia's attention as she was wiping the tears away from her eyes.

"You have a rock collection?" she asked the creature quietly.

"Yes," Kaileen answered. "My people, my family, and my friends, were slaughtered in cold blood many moons ago. My rock collection and the clothes I wore are the only things I have from that horrible day."

"But you have a rock collection," Tonia said with a puzzled look on her face, almost as if she was telling Kaileen something that the kalevala didn't already know.

When Kaileen nodded, Tonia asked, "Can we see it?"

Kaileen looked at her for a moment, still unsure of whether or not to trust this creature and her friends. They were unwanted in this part of the cave, but they did not appear to have any violent intentions. They still had their weapons out, but she did not feel like she was in any immediate danger.

They all watched the kalevala as she suddenly lowered her hands to her lower abdomen. The whole time they were talking to her, they failed to notice that she had some type of pouch secured there. She dug deep within the pouch for a few seconds before she began walking towards Tonia. As she did, she held her closed hand out in front of her, palm down.

"This is my rock collection," Kaileen said with a smile.

Tonia held her hand out and Kaileen dropped seven rocks of various size and color into it. They felt cool as they landed in her hand. Tonia held her torch closer to the rocks in order to get a better look at them, and as the torchlight fell on the mysterious rocks, Tonia gasped.

Micah and Diam had taken a step closer to Tonia to see what Kaileen was giving her. When they heard her surprised reaction, they all suddenly realized that one of the stones obviously stood out from the others.

The odd piece of hardened earth was dark in color, but in the bright torchlight they could see that the dark color was actually a deep red. They could also see that the stone was encased by a bright, shiny gold trim. Although the border had some scratches, it was most certainly made from gold more superior than any of them had ever seen. After being tossed around in the stream, the stone surprisingly had only a few minor scratches in it – all of which did nothing to detract from the beauty of the trinket.

Tonia looked from the stone to Kaileen, and then looked at Micah and Diam.

"I think this is it," she said quietly. Her voice quivered as she held her hand out so Micah and Diam could get a closer look at the mysterious object. Although she didn't expect it, she wasn't surprised when Micah reached out to take it from her.

As soon as his fingers touched it, the stone lit up with an instantaneous deep, red aura that filled the room. He proceeded to pick it up and hold it gently in his hand.

Kaileen took a hasty step back and crouched down, fearful of the glowing red light.

Ransa had quietly slithered over to be closer to Kaileen. As the stone began to glow, Ransa hissed in surprise.

Within seconds, they could all hear a low humming noise emanating from Micah's opened palm.

"Wow," Diam gasped as her eyes moved from Tonia to Micah. "It's beautiful!"

Tonia nodded at Micah.

"That must be it," she said but after a few seconds of silence, her smile of satisfaction shifted until it had curved into a frown. "This is an amulet, but it's glowing just like the stones did, and like them, it only glows for you, Micah. But this isn't like the other stones."

"What other stones?" Ransa asked from the dimly lit shadows next to Kaileen, her voice trembling with uncertainty. "What other stones are you talking about?"

Tonia's sight was fixed on the glowing, red stone in her brother's hand. Its fiery glow held her mesmerized as she remembered those times when they used to sit in front of the village campfire. Then, too, she would sit, almost trance-like, watching the red and orange embers as they flickered in the dark night. With difficulty, she broke her gaze away from the glowing stone and turned towards Ransa.

"We found a few other stones here in the cave, and they all reacted the same way as this one did when Micah held them. But also like this one, they would not react that way when anyone else held them." She paused, turning to look at her brother. "For some reason, the stones would only glow like this for him."

"Sssssss," Ransa hissed quietly, deep in thought. After a moment, she asked, "What colors were these other stones?"

Diam looked at Ransa, then answered, "Blue, green, purple and yellow."

Ransa looked surprised before turning her dark, serious eyes on Diam. "Are you sure?"

"Yes," Diam and Tonia said in unison. Next to them, Micah closed his hand over the stone, dulling the fiery red glow that had filled the cavern.

"Why do you ask?" Diam asked.

Ransa gazed at them for a moment, unsure of how much she should divulge. What she knew was only what she had heard when she was younger, when she overheard her parents talking once about magical stones, gentle dragons, and wizards…

"When I was just a snakelet, I heard stories about magical stones," she began.

"What about them?" Micah asked. Although he had closed his hand, small rays of the glowing, red light slipped through the cracks between his fingers and the low, humming sound could still be heard. Now, however, instead of sounding like it was coming from only near Micah, it almost sounded like it was everywhere in the room.

Ransa looked at Kaileen who was staring at her with a curious fascination. After all the time she had spent with the snake family, Kaileen had never heard any of them talking about magical stones.

Ransa smiled at Kaileen before offering an explanation.

"This is something we had not yet had the chance to talk to you about."

Kaileen nodded in silent understanding as Ransa continued.

"My parents as well as some of the elder Wiltoa used to talk of magical stones which had been scattered throughout the cave long ago. The stones had magical powers and were well sought after. My parents never saw these stones, you understand. This was only what they had heard, passed down many moons from snake to snake."

Ransa looked at Tonia and Diam, then at Micah.

"It was said that only a special creature could use these stones, and when that special creature held them, the stones would shine like the sun on a cloudless day, or the moon on a cloudless night. This creature, whatever it was, would be able to hold these stones all at once and summon a portal," she whispered.

"A portal? To where?" Diam asked with excitement, although her eyes remained doubtful. Could Micah be the special creature Ransa was referring to?

The snake remained silent for several seconds as her focus moved from one stranger to the next. She didn't understand why, but she felt she could trust these creatures. It did not matter that she had never seen anything like them before and might never see anything like them again. All that mattered was that right here, right now, she felt deep down that she could trust them.

"A portal that would go to another world?" Diam whispered again.

"To a world of dragons," Tonia whispered in return.

"You've got to be kidding me," Micah said. His raised a disbelieving eyebrow as his stare of doubt moved from Ransa, to

Kaileen, to Diam, and lastly, to Tonia. "She's kidding, right?" he asked his sister.

Tonia shrugged, feeling as doubtful as he was, unsure and filled with disbelief.

"You're telling us these stones will create a portal that could take us to another world?" Tonia asked Ransa. "A world of *dragons?*"

"Yes," Ransa answered. "This is what has been passed down to us, for many generations." She paused then added, "I have never seen any portal, but creatures such as I am tend to believe our elders."

Micah opened his hand. The familiar humming continued, and the room quickly filled once again with the soft, warm, red glow being created by the amulet.

"There's more you must know," Ransa continued. "The stories explain how these stones must be held at the same time in order for them to work their magic, and they will only create the portal in a certain part of the cave."

"What do you mean, 'in a certain part of the cave'?" Diam asked. "What part of the cave would we have to be in?"

"I'm not certain about its location," Ransa said quietly with a shake of her small, round head, "but the elders also talked about a place known as 'Still Water' – this is the place, I believe, where you must go."

"Still Water?" Micah asked. "The place we would need to take these stones is called 'Still Water' but you don't have any idea where we can find it?"

His eyes blazed with doubt as he turned to look at Tonia and Diam. After a long pause, he bowed his head, shaking it from left to right. "This is just great." Exasperation was more than evident in his voice.

"I wonder if Still Water is the place we went by. You know – the place in the tunnel where the water was motionless and we couldn't figure out where it was coming from?" Diam suggested, questioning her own logic. "Unfortunately, if we hadn't gotten lost like we did, we would know how to get back there."

Tonia said excitedly, "Yeah, that must be it!" but her sudden burst of excitement was quickly followed by a long sigh.

"Then again, if we didn't get lost, Nicho wouldn't be in the hole and we never would have known anything about the Wiltoa, Kaileen, the amulet, or Still Water," Micah added.

Tonia propped her elbow on her leg, closed her fist and rested the side of her head on it, deep in thought. She closed her eyes and tried to remember details about their adventure over the past two days. After a long moment, she finally spoke again.

"I think Still Water is on the other side of the one large cavern, but of course, I don't remember where that cavern is."

"Wait!" Diam said as she rested a hand on her friend's arm. "We've got these colored stones that glow for Micah. Now we have the amulet Muscala is looking for that we have to return to him in order to save Nicho. Maybe we can return the amulet to Muscala first and get Nicho, and then we can see if we can find this Still Water place and create the portal with the other stones?"

"No," Ransa said with a firm shake of her head.

"No? What do you mean 'no'?" Micah asked. "What's wrong with her idea?"

"If you want to open the portal to the world of dragons you must have the colors of the rainbow – ALL of them. If any one of them is missing, it will not work," the snake explained.

"But how many colors of the rainbow are there?" Diam asked.

"From the stories I heard as a snakelet, there are five primary colors. Red, yellow, green, blue and purple," Ransa said. "If you do not have all of them, the portal will simply not appear."

"This is just great," Tonia said as her shoulders slumped with defeat. "One of my lifelong dreams is to see a dragon, and just when it seems I might actually, unbelievably, have the chance to fulfill my most desired dream, it suddenly begins to look more and more like it will never happen."

"Kind of like hanging a piece of chickenbird meat in front of your nose, just out of reach, huh?" Micah tone was humorous but his face remained serious. He turned to look at Ransa, then Kaileen. "We must return the amulet to Muscala. You know that, right?"

Ransa nodded as she looked at fellow cave mate. She understood what they needed to do, but ultimately, it was Kaileen's decision. It was her amulet – her precious 'rock'.

"Kaileen," Tonia said pleadingly as she turned her complete attention to the gem's owner. "Without the amulet, my brother will die. I know you understand what this means, how scary it is and how much it hurts. Please, please help us? Help us to avoid another senseless death in this cave!"

Kaileen had been looking down at the ground as she listened to the conversation. She slowly lifted her gaze to look into the soft brown eyes of the girl who was now kneeling before her. She stared into the girl's misty eyes as they stared back at her, full of life, questions and love for her brother.

Kaileen did understand. She understood that she would never be able to go back to the past. She could never return to that day long ago, she could never stop the vicious slaughter that had happened in the safety of her home. She also understood that maybe, just maybe she could help these young creatures. She had an opportunity to help them so their brother did not have to perish as hers had.

"Take the amulet," she said softly, her own moist eyes moving from Tonia to Micah. "Take it to the evil serpent and save your brother."

Tonia could not believe her ears. Kaileen was giving them the amulet! Tonia raised a hand to her mouth stifle a cry of happiness, unable to believe the odd, dark creature before her was actually willing to help. Tears streamed down her cheeks and all she could do was smile at Kaileen. The kalevala watched her curiously and, when she smiled back, Tonia leaned forward and gave her a hug.

"Thank you," she whispered softly. "Thank you for helping us."

Kaileen hugged her back gently, and then released her before taking a step back.

"How can we ever repay you?" Tonia asked as she wiped her tears off her cheeks with the back of her hand. "I don't know what we might have that you could use in here, but if there's anything you can think of, we will gladly give it to you in return for your selfless decision."

"There is one thing," Kaileen said softly. She hesitated as she looked up at Ransa.

"I want to go with you, back to where this snake, Muscala, is holding your brother. I would see this creature, see if he knows anything about the other creatures that invaded my home," she stated solemnly.

Ransa stared at her friend, her eyes filled with surprised. "What?"

Kaileen offered her friend a nod that was filled with hope for her friend's understanding.

"Ransa, I love you and your family, with all of my heart, for taking me in when I had nowhere else to go. You gave me food, you gave me shelter, but more importantly, you gave me love. You also gave me time to heal. Because of you and your family, I have learned what it is to love life again."

She paused for a moment and looked back down at the floor as she tried to organize her words before speaking. When she looked up again, her own eyes were pooling with tears. She remained where she was but slowly raised her arms from her sides, palms facing upward, as if she was about to be handed a very large object.

"But for all the food and love you have given me, there is still a painfully large emptiness trapped within my heart, within my soul. It has always been there, a deep-seated need, coursing throughout my entire being – a need unlike any other. It's an incredible desire to find those who took my family away from me."

She paused for a moment, her sad eyes suddenly turning angry.

"I must know why this amulet is so important! I must find my way to this sorcerer and ask him what gave him the right, the nerve, to order troops across the countryside in search of a small, red rock? I need to ask him why it was so easy for him to order creatures killed, all for a measly colored piece of hardened, lifeless stone!"

As she fell silent, a sob escaped from between her sealed lips and she crumpled to her knees, helpless against the sadness and anger, which overtook her like a storm.

Ransa slithered quickly to her grieving friend, rubbing her narrow yet quite muscular neck along the kalevala's lowered head as she tried to soothe her. Tonia didn't hesitate and stepped closer to the kalevala, kneeling in the dirt beside her. She wrapped her arms around her again, tighter than she had before.

"I'm so sorry," Tonia whispered to Kaileen, feeling her pain and sorrow as the kalevala shook with emotion. "I am so, so sorry."

Within seconds, Diam was next to them, encasing the group with her arms as well. After tucking the amulet in his pants pocket, Micah's resolve crumbled and he also joined them. The group remained huddled this way for an indeterminable amount of time, each of them feeling the intense grief consuming this gentle creature. After a moment, Kaileen finally quieted and raised her head to look at the others. Her weak attempt at a smile slowly moved across her tear-streaked face.

"Thank you," she said with a sniffle. "I guess I had a little bit of something bottled up inside, didn't I?"

"It sounded like it," Tonia agreed as she offered the kalevala another reassuring, gentle hug. The others backed away, giving Kaileen space as she shifted and stood back up. Her dark eyes, although still filled with sadness, were quite serious. Her gaze moved from one to the other before she finally spoke.

"Please understand that I must go with you."

A heavy silence fell across the group as they stared at her with uncertainty.

"I know you don't like the idea, but this is something I must do – regardless of whether or not you approve," Kaileen stated firmly as she gazed across the dimly lit cavern at her new friends. Micah interrupted her when he raised a hand to get her attention.

"I think you must understand something as well," Micah said sternly. "We are deadly serious when we tell you Muscala is a dangerous creature. Each of us has seen and experienced this with our own eyes."

"I know," Kaileen said with an understanding nod.

"Once we get back to Muscala and give him the amulet, he will release Nicho. As soon as he does this, we will be moving on, looking for another exit to the cave," Diam chimed in.

"Yes, I know," the kalevala repeated. "I would like to accompany this snake when he returns the amulet to this sorcerer. I would know who he is!" Her final words were spiked with seriousness while her eyes remained bright with determination.

"What if he won't take you with him?" Diam asked. "Have you thought of that?"

They didn't know the evil snake very well, but they all had a feeling Muscala would not be very interested in company of any kind going with him to take his place at Lotor's side. Unless, of course, the purpose of a travel partner was to provide Muscala with a meal during his excursions. In which case, knowing the snake as they did by now, the accompanying creature would probably BE his meals during his travels.

"Then I will follow him," Kaileen said with confidence.

"Kaileen," Tonia said, "listen to us! You do not understand what kind of angry, evil creature Muscala is! He is a sneaky, deadly, hungry snake! He would just as soon eat you as take you with him!"

"I think you should stay here, with Ransa and her family," Diam suggested. "They love you. They are your family now."

"If I stay, then the amulet stays," Kaileen said firmly. Her gaze did not waver as it shifted from Diam to Micah before finally settling on Tonia.

The boy stared at the dark skinned creature, frustrated because she appeared unwilling to cooperate. He decided to try one more time.

"Kaileen, you cannot change the past, no matter how hard you try. Your family and friends are gone, and you can do nothing, NOTHING, to change it! You must move on, like the sun moves across the sky."

His words were gentle as he spoke, and he took a step closer to her so he could look directly into her dark, anguished eyes.

"Live out the remainder of your life here, with those who so obviously love you. If you come with us, there is no way of knowing what will happen to you, just as we do not know what will happen to us. At this point, the only thing we know is we must go back to Muscala to get Nicho. Once this has been done, we will most certainly move on."

"Please, Kaileen," Tonia pleaded quietly, "please stay here."

Kaileen shook her head, her eyes sad yet bright with an undying determination.

"If I stay, the amulet stays," she repeated.

Tonia, Diam and Micah looked at each other. They knew there would be no changing Kaileen's mind. Tonia rested a warm, understanding hand on Kaileen's arm and nodded.

"Okay," Micah said, "if that's the way you want it. Before we can go, though, you must give me your word on a few things."

"I am listening," Kaileen said. Beside her, Ransa hissed her disagreement did not speak her thoughts.

"When we travel, you stay in between us. I'll take the lead, and one of the girls will take up the rear. You will stay in the middle, where it is safer."

Kaileen nodded and waited for him to continue.

"Also, when we get to the cavern where Muscala lives, you stay back, in the shadows, until we have my brother out of the hole. Once he's out, we will be moving on. If you decide to stay with Muscala, your fate is in your own hands." Micah paused for only a second when he asked, "Agreed?"

"Yes," Kaileen answered.

"I'm going, too," Ransa said from the shadows behind Kaileen.

"Oh, come on!" Micah said in an irritated tone. "You've got to be kidding me! First the turtles tagged along and now we have to bring the two of you?"

Ransa hissed at Micah, anger flashing in her eyes.

"You cannot expect me to stand by and see this creature I've grown to love as a sister just walk away from me, possibly to never see her again! I will accompany you as you go back to Muscala, and hopefully he will show us all a way out of the cave. If I can find a way out of this place, I can return here, get my family, and we can move on to a better life, outside of the dust and darkness that is such a large part of our existence."

Micah listened to the snake and shook his head in disbelief, then proceeded to toss the girls a questioning glare. Not surprisingly, Tonia nodded her affirmation. Micah sighed. He knew it was useless to argue with them, especially when he was so outnumbered.

"Okay, let's get moving." His tone was direct and slightly defeated.

They gathered their things and prepared to head back to

Muscala's home. Kaileen had everything she wanted, which consisted of her bag of rocks and the clothes she was wearing. Ransa would come back after talking to the giant snake, so she was not concerned with bringing anything else. She was, after all, a cave snake... what would she really need to bring? She did, however, return to her family for a few moments to let them know what she was doing and to tell them she would be back shortly. After promising to return, she joined the others, and they began making their way back to Muscala.

Micah resumed his position in the lead, Tonia walked in the middle, and Diam took up the rear, with Micah and Diam each holding a torch.

They walked for a few moments in silence, until Diam asked, "So, what's the plan when we get back to Muscala?"

Micah turned and glanced back at her before he answered sharply, "To get Nicho back." He immediately saw the pained expression on her face caused by his curtness and he looked away briefly, sighed and turned back to her, this time apologetically.

"I'm sorry."

He stopped and turned, resting a hand on her arm.

"I shouldn't snap at you. I'm just stressed about what we'll find when we get back."

Diam nodded her understanding.

"It's okay."

Micah took a deep breath then said, "Other than getting Nicho back, I'm not sure what we should do. Just make sure you're prepared for anything," he said in a much calmer voice.

They reached the stream and as they entered it, Tonia addressed Ransa and Kaileen.

"Do you want us to carry you?"

Ransa looked at Kaileen and shook her head. "I'm fine." Kaileen smiled and added, "Me, too."

Tonia nodded and they continued on their way, each quietly wondering what would happen once they reached the giant snake and knowing they would do whatever it took to save Nicho.

THIRTY

Soon they were very close to Muscala's lair. Just before they entered the cavern, Micah turned to address the small group following him, eyeing first Kaileen then Ransa.

"I want you both to stay here," he whispered to them sternly. "Stay out of sight and out of the way. I don't want to have to worry about you, too. I'll have enough on my mind just trying to get Nicho out of this place."

"We will," Ransa whispered back.

"Okay," Kaileen also whispered, giving a slight nod.

The Wiltoa and the kalevala waited in the dark tunnel as the other three headed back into the ominous dwelling of the fearsome Muscala. Micah carried the amulet in his pocket with the other stones. They approached the dark hole in the cavern floor and Micah beckoned the reptile.

"Muscala, we're back!"

"Micah? Tonia?" Nicho called out at the sound of his brother's voice.

Their hearts all filled with relief – Nicho was still alive! None of them had mentioned anything about their lack of trust in the giant snake, but it was definitely a thought that ran through all of their minds at some point during this long, never-ending day.

"Nicho?" Tonia called out to her brother as she shuffled quickly over to the dark hole. She dropped down onto her stomach and immediately extended her head over the edge. She had to hold back her long hair to keep it from blocking her view. "Are you okay?"

As soon as her face cleared the torch-lit space at the top of the hole, Tonia heard an odd, unfamiliar sound in the depths below. Just as she was about to ask Nicho if he needed anything, Muscala rose up from the darkness and appeared directly in front of her without warning.

His dark, wide, forked-tongue was flicking wildly, slicing through the air very close to Tonia's face. The snake's thin mouth widened as he looked at her with a fiendish expression on his face. Her dangling, chestnut-colored hair began moving back and forth in response to the gentle, albeit unappealingly scented, breath of the giant reptile.

"Ahhh, you have returned so sssoon! Does thisss mean you have good newsss for me?"

Tonia squealed in surprise and rolled backwards, nearly rolling into Diam who stood nearby. She hadn't anticipated that the snake would appear directly in front of her the way it had and the almost overwhelming stench of its ancient, unappealing breath chilled her deep inside.

Muscala laughed with glee. It was an evil laugh, indeed.

"Oh, ho, ho! You almost gave me sssuch a fright!" he said heartily as he tossed a sarcastic smile at the new arrivals. "You really shouldn't do such things, you know! Bad thingsss could happen to…" he paused, "…less fortunate creaturesss who still reside in the depths below me, especially if I were to fall from a distance such as this!"

He paused to revel in his wit before he nodded with satisfaction and continued.

"My body, being made of mossstly muscle, could very easssily cause pain and discomfort to other creaturesss if I were to land on them from such a height!"

Diam stood close to Tonia, in between their two hidden friends and the snake's abode, and rolled her eyes in exasperation. Her sword was drawn but held down at her side, just in case Muscala decided to be sneaky. She couldn't wait to get Nicho out of the hole and be on their way, away from this snake. He was the most arrogant creature she had ever met in her life!

Tonia recovered from her scare and stood up where she ended up when she rolled away from Muscala just a few moments before.

"Excuse me, but I would like to look down at my brother and see how he's doing. Do you mind?" Her voice was filled with sarcasm as she glared at the snake. She was getting tired of his games and it showed.

Muscala returned her gaze and found he was quite tempted to tease her, but then thought better of it. These creatures were definitely smaller than he was, but he was outnumbered by three to one. Well, four to one, if he was to consider the unwelcome boy in his home below. He considered her question as a different thought suddenly struck him.

Although they were ALL unwelcome, it was possible that this might be a good thing, especially if they had his amulet…

"Ssscertainly," Muscala replied innocently as he moved out of the way for Tonia to get by. She immediately returned to the edge of the hole and looked down at her brother, completely ignoring the snake.

"Nicho, are you okay?"

Tonia's voice trembled slightly as she peered over the rocky ledge for a glimpse of her brother. She sighed with relief, thankful when her eyes quickly found him. He was still sitting at the bottom of the abyss, but had shifted his location slightly. Luckily his torch was still burning, providing him with a soft ring of light in the snake's dark home.

Nicho looked up at Tonia with hope in his eyes. "Yes, I'm okay. It will be good to get out of here for sure." He paused and took a deep breath, relieved to see his sister. "Not that my host hasn't been kind and courteous!" he shouted, knowing Muscala would hear him. In fact, he hoped more than anything that the snake would hear the sarcasm in his voice.

Muscala paused for a moment, closing his eyes as if trying to ignore Nicho. He tilted his head and turned without acknowledging Nicho's words and focused on Micah.

"Ssso," Muscala began as he slowly inched his way closer to the younger of the two boys, "did you complete your quessst as I asssked?"

Micah glared at him as he answered in a harsh, defiant tone. "Yes."

"Ahhhh, this isss wonderful newsss!" Muscala hissed, smiling brightly. "Now, where is my amulet? I mussst see it!"

Micah's lack of response caused Muscala to prod further, "Well?"

They could all tell that the snake was getting impatient, and inside, they were all silently glad. Maybe they could dish out a little discomfort his way, instead of vice versa.

"Well? Well? Where isss my amulet?" Muscala said anxiously as his voice escalated from soft, gentle words into a loud, bellowing shout. "I mussst see my amulet!"

"In due time," Micah said calmly as Tonia stood up, brushed off and joined him at his side. "First, release our brother."

"No," Muscala quickly replied. "Firssst the amulet, then the boy."

"No," Micah and Tonia challenged the snake at the same time.

"Release Nicho, then we will see about your precious rock," Diam said as she moved to stand beside her friends.

The snake glowered at them, unsure if he should challenge their surprising disrespect towards a creature of his power and stature. He could just kill the boy, but then he would risk being over-powered by the other three. He knew it would do him no good to get the amulet and make his way back to Lotor, only to die from injuries from the potential battle which would certainly occur if he harmed their brother.

Muscala glared at them with angry hesitation, his focus moving from the boy to the girls. After a long moment of consideration, he nodded. "Very well, then. I will releassse your brother. You give me your word that you will hand over my amulet?"

Although he doubted these lesser creatures could dupe him, the thought of relinquishing his upper hand in the matter made him uncomfortable.

"Release Nicho," Micah said firmly, "and the amulet will be yours."

Kaileen and Ransa watched motionless from the shadows of the tunnel, still unseen and unheard by the snake.

Muscala hesitated only briefly before quickly disappearing into the semi-darkness, down to where Nicho stood, waiting patiently.

The older boy had been listening quietly to what was going on above him and was ready to get out of his dark, dry prison. He could hear agitation in the snake's voice as it argued with Micah and Tonia and, although he wanted nothing more than to leave this place, he was proud of them for standing strong. From the way things sounded up above, Nicho was about to be set free, which both gladdened and relieved him. The snake's entire home gave him the creeps, but then again, their entire situation did.

As Muscala had requested, the few times the boy suspected the snake was away, Nicho had not ventured deeper into the underground tunnel. He had seen enough of the snake's home in his one little area as it was – he didn't need to see anymore.

Nicho was patiently waiting at the bottom of the abyss, hoping things would turn out positively for them all. He glanced up and saw nothing but darkness overhead, then realized it was Muscala, descending rapidly towards him. Within seconds the large reptile stopped just inches from Nicho's face.

"Climb on my back," the beast ordered.

Nicho sensed the urgency in its demeanor and nodded. "Muscala definitely wants his amulet," he thought. With a small smile, Nicho scrambled up onto the snake's back and quickly held onto its neck with one hand while he tightly grasped the lit torch in the other. As soon as Muscala felt the boy firmly grab onto his scaly neck, he ascended to where the others were waiting. As he did, Nicho could feel the large, well-toned muscles throughout the snake's body rippling and flexing. The snake was certainly very arrogant, but he was also undoubtedly quite powerful. They cleared the top of the abyss and Muscala stopped, allowing Nicho to climb off of his back.

As Nicho slid to the ground, Tonia was immediately at his side. She threw her arms around him and held him in a tight embrace. Micah and Diam followed suit, both smiling. They were relieved to see that he was indeed all right. Although he was a little tattered and dirty, Nicho was alive.

"ENOUGH!" the snake bellowed with angry impatience. "Enough already! You have your preciousss brother, now GIVE ME MY AMULET!"

Nicho, startled by the snake's reaction, drew his sword as he stood next to the others. They all looked at Muscala and could see his eyes flashing with a deep, unmistakable anger. Micah saw his brother's gesture but wasn't sure what they should do. Should they try to fight the snake so they could keep this special stone he still carried in his pocket? Or should they just give the stone up and go on their way?

His questioning gaze glanced past Tonia until he spotted Kaileen. She stood in the shadows in the tunnel, her hands clasped before her, turning over and over within each other. She had suffered enough.

Without any further hesitation, Micah decided they should fight. He raised his sword up to chest level as he glared at the angry snake.

"The amulet is no more," he said to the snake, his voice filled with renewed confidence. "There was no creature, no amulet, nothing. We originally entered this cave peacefully, only passing through, and we will exit it the same way." As he finished his sentence, the others in the group also drew their swords and stood defensively side by side. They were obviously prepared to fight for their freedom, and their lives, if necessary.

"What?" the snake asked in amazed disbelief. "Are you admitting that you tricked me?"

His voice dripped with anger and his eyes flashed hungrily.

"You tricked me into releasssing thisss menial creature you call your brother? Tricked me by telling me, lying to me, saying you had my amulet, and you would give it to me if I releasssed him?"

His eyes, always red and probing, now flashed like burning cherries as he began rocking back and forth a few feet away. The anger boiled in him like water in a pot over an open, blazing fire.

"HOW DARE YOU!" he bellowed. His voice echoed for endless seconds off the many walls of the cave. The infuriated serpent began slithering towards them, malicious intent emanating off of him with a thick, invisible aura. Oh, they would pay!

Micah, Nicho, Diam and Tonia were frightened, but stood their ground defensively.

242

"What good would it do you to kill us?" Micah asked the snake. "If you kill us, you will have no idea what we found on the quest you challenged us with. You will know nothing of what is beyond the narrow tunnel that you can no longer fit through. But," he paused, not only to keep the snake's interest, but also to get his own thoughts together, "if you decide to let us live… well now, what might *that* mean for you?"

Micah's mind was spinning with many thoughts, with different ways to get through to this arrogant snake. At first he thought they might be in real trouble, but as his mind continued to race, he suddenly had the answer!

The snake was very conceited, believing he was the greatest creature in this cave, probably believing he was the greatest creature who ever lived! Micah knew the only way they would be able to get out of this cave alive would be to use this knowledge against the snake.

Muscala stopped, a puzzled look clouding his once intensely angry eyes. What was this young brat mumbling about now? He began his rocking motion as he had done earlier as he waited for more information – left to right, left to right.

Tonia suddenly understood what Micah was trying to do and decided to help him out a bit.

"Muscala, I think we may have a proposition for you," she began.

Micah looked at her, trying his best to hide his surprise. What was she doing?

"If you give us your word that you will allow us to go on our way, *we* will tell *you* what we found on the other side of the narrow stream."

Muscala watched her quietly as she paused, giving him time to consider her offer. Although he was a bit confused, Micah smiled to himself, proud of his little sister. She could be quite an asset – when she wanted to be, of course.

Muscala appeared interested in what Tonia was saying. He stared at her cautiously for several seconds before he spoke.

"Go on."

"If you would rather kill us and risk never knowing what we found, what we saw, then be certain that we will not die without

243

a fight."

The others watched the reptile, the seriousness of her statement written across all of their faces. They would fight if necessary but would rather end this peacefully.

Muscala remained where he was, still rocking back and forth, considering her words in silence. He had always been a curious snake, and his curiosity got the better of him. Without any further hesitation, he began slithering slowly towards them. When he was only a few feet again, he stopped and stared at them.

"Tell me what you know, and perhapsss I will spare your livesss," he said with an angry, confident hiss as he struggled to get the upper hand in the situation.

"No," Micah answered firmly. "Give us your word that you will spare our lives and we will tell you what we know."

"Hisssssssssss," he said angrily. They could see his growing anger again flashing brightly in his eyes. "I AM MUSCALA! YOU HAVE NO RIGHT TO TREAT ME THISSS WAY!"

The children felt the ground rumble in reaction to the snake's booming voice, and before the distant echoes died away into silence, Muscala suddenly turned and disappeared down into the darkness of the abyss.

A long, uncomfortable silence followed.

The others remained where they were, puzzled by the snake's reaction and uncertain about their next move.

"He's whacked," Diam whispered quietly, and Tonia chuckled as she nodded. She looked back towards the tunnel and tried to see Ransa and Kaileen, but they remained out of sight.

"Good," she thought. If she couldn't see them, hopefully Muscala wouldn't either.

"Well, what should we do?" Micah whispered to Nicho. After a pause, he added, "By the way, how are you doing?"

Nicho frowned at his brother and punched him playfully in the arm. "I think we should try to get out of here… and I'm fine, thanks for your concern," he added in a sarcastic tone.

Micah smiled at Nicho's reaction and glanced over at the girls. They nodded, also ready to move on. Tonia raised an index finger at Micah, gesturing for him to hang on, and made her way over to the tunnel to see where Ransa and Kaileen were. She found them, hiding quite well in the shadows around the corner.

"We're going to try to get out of here," she said to them quietly. "Do either of you know where this Still Water place is?"

"I've only heard of it, but don't know where it is," Ransa answered sadly. Kaileen simply shook her head no.

Tonia nodded her understanding then quietly spoke to them again, her eyes serious.

"I really think you both should come with us. Muscala is very angry now, and I don't think it's a good idea for either of you to stay here and try to reason with him or ask questions." She paused as she shook her head. Although the larger snake had disappeared without a trace, her heart was still racing with trepidation. "He's a very, very dangerous snake."

As Ransa and Kaileen listened to her and considered their options, Tonia added, "He's already told us he will basically eat anything, especially if and when he's hungry. Come with us and help us find Still Water. We need to find our way back out of this cave, if possible, and you need a better life. Please, come with us…"

The others were watching Tonia as she spoke quietly to Kaileen and Ransa. They were so focused on Tonia's invitation that none of them noticed the large shadow approaching them from the nearby shadows.

"Well, well, well… What are we looking at?" Muscala hissed, as Micah, Nicho and Diam immediately turned, swords held in front of them.

"Hmmmm… do we have company?" Muscala asked them sarcastically.

He had slithered to the side of the cavern, and from his new location was able to clearly see Ransa and Kaileen. Tonia stood in front of them, her sword also drawn.

"Hmmmm, it seemsss as though maybe you *did* find sssomething on your travelsss through the narrow stream, didn't you?" He looked directly at Ransa and Kaileen. "Do you have sssomething to give me?"

They all stared at the snake in bewildered silence, hearts thumping, each of them wondering what to say. It was Micah who was the first to speak up.

"They have nothing for you, Muscala."

The snake turned quickly and glared at the young boy.

"Let *them* anssswer my question!" His voice boomed around them again and his eyes flashed with an almost uncontainable anger.

Ransa looked at Kaileen and nodded.

"The boy is correct. We have nothing for you."

Muscala turned his glare from the boy to the smaller snake. He stared at her in silence for a moment, unsure of whether or not she spoke the truth, before he turned his attention to the kalevala.

"And you? Do you know if you have anything for me?"

She eyed him angrily as memories of her past flooded into her mind like a raging river. For a split second they saw her eyes widen with anger, then her own voice echoed through the tunnels around them.

"Let's see if you have something to tell me, shall we?"

She glared at the snake as she continued, her unexpected outburst surprising everyone in the room.

"Do you know what happened to my people? Who slaughtered them in cold blood? Can you answer MY question?"

Although she stood before the snake with out a weapon, Kaileen's angry voice was fueled with renewed confidence. Too many strong emotions had been bottled up inside her like an explosive gas for far too long. Everyone around her sensed this and knew they could do nothing to stop it.

"Your people?" Muscala asked in confusion. A small smile began playing across his face as his eyes brightened with a sudden understanding. "Ahhhhh, you mussst be Kaileen!"

"Yes," Kaileen answered as the smile on the snake's face widened. "I am Kaileen, possibly the last of my people; I am all that remains of a kind, gentle people who died for no good reason."

She shook as she fell silent, tears of pain streaking wavering lines down her face. She stared at Muscala as she continued.

"Do you know why they were killed? Do you know where I can find the one who is responsible for this senseless act?"

"No, I…" Muscala started.

"**I MUST KNOW**!" Kaileen interrupted him before he could

finish, her eyes bright with anger. "You must tell me what you know!"

Muscala looked at her, surprised for a second time by her outburst. He was not used to being on the receiving end of this kind of anger. He began slowly rocking back and forth again, considering her demand.

Micah, Tonia, Diam and Nicho watched this, swords still ready, uncertain of their proper place in the ongoing conversation. They didn't know the giant snake well enough to read his thoughts, but they would be willing to bet a pia seed to a shell that they were likely not very good ones.

Ransa was also unsure about how to handle their situation. All she could do was watch as Tonia tried calming Kaileen.

"Kaileen, it's okay," the girl said. "We can take you with us. We'll take you out of this cave and help you start a new life."

"NO!" Kaileen shouted with a sob as her eyes pooled with tears. "I will not be able to live a new life until I know where to find the one that ordered my people killed! I must find him and confront him, and if I have my way, I will repay him by killing him myself! Without mercy! Without hesitation! Without feeling as he cries out, begging for his worthless life!"

With this statement, Muscala stopped rocking, a new anger flashing from somewhere deep within his eyes. He was determined that he would protect Lotor, with his own life if necessary. He would not allow any harm to come to the powerful sorcerer and was confident that, once he returned the amulet to Lotor, all would be well.

He slowly began slithering towards Kaileen, veering wide, away from the ones with the weapons. He knew what he must do – he must put an end to this miserable creature's life. Then, she and her kind would be no more! He understood without any doubt that he was just the creature to take care of this.

Nicho and Micah took a step to the right, trying to read the snake's intentions, wanting to stop him before he could get near Kaileen. Another creature also saw what was happening and was determined to protect the kalevala in any way possible.

Ransa began slithering hastily away from Kaileen and before anyone knew what was happening, she had turned and headed straight towards the giant snake. She would not let him hurt this creature that was more like a sister to her than she had ever dreamed possible.

"Nooooo!" Ransa shouted at the giant reptile. She sprang from the ground and was soon flying through the air, discharging her sleeping venom in mid leap.

"You will not hurt my sister!"

As the smaller snake flew through the air, a few short bursts of venom sprayed from her mouth in a fine mist, hitting the intended target. Ransa landed on the dusty tunnel floor with a soft thud in between Muscala and Kaileen.

Muscala turned towards the smaller creature in response to her outburst. He found himself quite taken by surprise as the liquid spray began to sting his eyes. The sour scent burned his tongue and scent glands, and instantly his vision began to blur. He saw this snake, the much smaller version of himself, begin swimming in and out of focus before his very eyes.

"What have you done?" he hissed angrily. He had not been expecting much of anything from this tiny snake as it waited next to his intended victim. It took him a moment, but he soon realized what had happened.

As Muscala shook his head from side to side in an effort to rid himself of the sleeping venom, the others watched in disbelief as Ransa tried to spray him again. This time, however, the only thing that ejected from her was a light mist that quickly turned to nothing but air. Although she was smaller than this monstrous snake before her, Ransa fervently hoped she was large enough for her venom to make a difference.

All she could now was wait.

After writhing around the tunnel entrance for several long, painful seconds, the pain and discomfort finally lessened enough so Muscala could continue his advancement. He glared at Kaileen but was pleased to discover that, after all his jerking and slithering around from being sprayed, he was now only a few feet away from his intended prey.

Unbeknownst to Ransa, the venom she had sprayed Muscala with *was*, in fact, working its magic on him. The only thing she knew as she watched him approach her friend was that she had to do everything in her power to protect Kaileen. Her cold blood raced with an almost overwhelming sense of protective love, and she reacted without a second thought.

In an instant, Ransa reared back and lunged at Muscala, yelling, "I won't let you hurt her!"

Kaileen immediately knew what her friend had in mind and cried out an immediate protest.

"Ransa, nooooo!"

But it was too late.

Ransa was suddenly flying through the air, mouth wide, teeth glaring in the torchlight. She hit Muscala in the neck, face first, her small, razor-sharp teeth penetrating his leathery snakeskin.

Muscala's vision, affected by Ransa's venom, was still blurry. He heard Kaileen's shout, then could make out some sort of hazy, undefined object coming straight at him. The large serpent realized too late that it was Ransa flying toward him. In the next instant, he felt a stinging pain in his neck as her teeth pierced his skin.

At the same time, his mind began to feel foggy, and he realized with shocked surprise that the sleeping venom from this small snake was possibly going to put him to out.

"Aaargh," he shrieked as he began rapidly thrashing left, then right, struggling to throw this meddlesome creature off of his muscular neck. As soon as he did, he would forget the kalevala for a moment and crush this troublesome snake between his jaws. He would make sure, once and for all, that she would not bother him again.

Ransa's eyes were clamped shut and she held on to Muscala's neck with jaws of steel.

Tonia and Diam yelled out, trying to get the giant snake's attention. They needed to get him to stop thrashing long enough for one of them to grab Ransa and pull her off. They didn't dare go near the writhing bodies with their weapons drawn for fear of hurting their friend. Muscala's thrashing continued as the smaller snake continued biting the larger one, holding on with her teeth with every ounce of strength that remained in her tiny body.

"Get off... of... me!" Muscala yelled groggily. Although he was still moving too fast for the girls to catch him, his side to side thrashing did appear to be weakening.

"Get off... of me!" he repeated. With a growl and a sudden burst of renewed energy, Muscala whipped his upper neck wildly to the right.

Until now, Ransa had maintained her firm hold on Muscala, her teeth still clamped down on his neck in a death grip. She continued trying to spray him with her sleeping venom, even though her reserves felt as though they were empty.

When Muscala first yelled at her to get off, Ransa sensed the urgency in his voice. At the same time, she could feel more venom pulsating from her glands as a thin line of spray again misted the snake's neck and entered the fresh wounds that were created by her incessant biting.

The sour odor extended outward, filling the air. In his panic, Muscala began breathing heavier, unknowingly taking in more of the toxin from the air around him.

Ransa was prepared for neither the larger snake's strength nor his stamina. Unfortunately, due to her smaller size, it did not take long for her adrenaline rush to dissipate. With the second outburst from the giant snake, Ransa lost her hold on his neck. Before she knew it, she was suddenly flying through the air again, but this time it was not by choice. She struck the far wall of the tunnel with a loud thud before crumpling to the ground, motionless.

"Ransa!" Kaileen screeched as she ran to the injured snake's side.

"Arrrgh," Muscala grumbled again, much weaker than before. Realizing his rider was no longer on his back, the snake turned and tried to look at the shadows on the far side of the cave. His vision had become very blurry now and he couldn't make out much of anything. Instead, he began his rocking motion again, but unlike earlier, he now rocked erratically, seemingly unable to keep his balance.

The girls had huddled around the smaller snake and the boys stood guard just a few feet away. Muscala rocked from side to side for a long moment before he suddenly fell over on his side. The dust from the cavern floor billowed away from his now motionless body when it landed. For a few seconds they could hear him mumbling, "My... amulet... give me... my..."

Before long, this was followed by a period of odd, welcomed silence. The larger snake's movements had ceased and his eyes were now closed – he appeared to be sleeping.

Nicho approached the giant snake cautiously. Except for his sides moving in time with his breathing, Muscala was motionless. To relieve his anxiety, Nicho poked the snake roughly with his sword, but not hard enough to break through the skin. There was no response.

Kaileen was crying at Ransa's side. "Ransa? Please! Ransa!"

The smaller snake lay motionless on the cavern floor in a crumpled, shattered heap with her eyes closed.

"Ransa?" Kaileen cried, sobbing as she gently shook her injured friend.

This time, Ransa opened her eyes as she struggled to look up at Kaileen. When she did, her entire body suddenly tensed as her eyes clenched shut. Her reptilian face was set in a grimace of pain.

"Ransa!" Kaileen cried out. She wanted to help her, to take the pain away, yet was helpless to do so.

As quickly as the small snake's body tensed up, it suddenly relaxed. Her eyes opened briefly again, this time for the last time.

"Kai..." Ransa began as she tried to smile through her pain. "You... you... go on... get... out... cave!"

Kaileen shook her head vigorously before she replied.

"No. No, I can't. Not without you. I won't leave without you!"

Ransa painfully shook her shook her head no, then tried to speak again.

"You go... love... you..."

With that, Ransa's body tensed again, her eyes closed, and her body slowly relaxed for the final time. As Kaileen began crying, cradling Ransa's lifeless body in her arms, Tonia suddenly felt the now familiar buzzing in her head.

"Celio, is that you?" She thought to the smaller turtle, wondering what more could happen to them now.

"What?" Celio thought back to her questioningly.

"Is that you buzzing in my head?" she asked out loud, while the others looked at her, slightly confused.

"No," he answered.

Suddenly they heard a soft fluttering in the air somewhere above their heads.

"What in the world?" Tonia thought fleetingly. She glanced at Kaileen as the kalevala continued to hold Ransa, but the grieving creature seemed oblivious to everything happening around them.

After having sheathed their swords with the knowledge that the giant snake was asleep, the boys quickly drew their weapons again. They peered into the shadows above their heads, unsure of what they might find there. In the flickering torchlight they began to make out a small, dark, creature flying erratically over their heads, quickly darting here and there as it tried to get their attention.

As she watched it, Tonia continued to feel the buzzing sensation in her head. Before she knew it, specific thoughts began to fill her mind, like the sun breaking out from behind a fast-moving cloud. An odd, completely unfamiliar voice followed these thoughts and suddenly exploded in her head.

"The snake will wake soon! We must leave now! Now! We must leave now or we will die! Now! Now!"

Tonia shook her head in confusion.

"What?"

"Quickly! You must follow! We must leave! You must follow! Now! Now! Hurry!" The creature flying around their heads slowed down a bit, allowing them to identify it.

It was a bat.

"Are you the bat we found earlier in the cave?" Tonia asked it.

"Yes! Yes! We must leave before the snake awakens!" the bat shouted in Tonia's head. As it continued darting around the room, they suddenly heard a low groan from where Muscala lay on the tunnel floor.

"He wakes!" the bat continued shouting in Tonia's head. "We go now! Hurry! Now! He wakes!"

"The bat wants us to follow it," Tonia explained as Micah and Diam watched her quietly.

"Now she was talking to a bat?" they both thought, but neither voiced their words.

252

Sensing an urgency in the situation, Tonia began trying to pull Kaileen to her feet.

"Come on, Kaileen. She's gone. We have to go now."

"No," Kaileen said. "I must take her back to our family." The kalevala pulled out of Tonia's grasp as the groan came again from Muscala. It was slightly louder this time.

Unfortunately, the giant snake had collapsed in the middle of the tunnel, blocking both their way back to the stream and the path back to Ransa and Kaileen's home.

"But our family," Kaileen began, as a louder groan came from the snake. He was definitely waking up.

"Kaileen, we need to go NOW!" Micah shouted at the kalevala as Nicho began helping Tonia get Kaileen to her feet.

"Leave her," Nicho told Kaileen, referring to the snake's lifeless body. "Leave her or we'll all end up like her!"

"I don't care," Kaileen said, seemingly giving up hope. "My sister…"

"Listen to me!" Nicho shouted as he grabbed Kaileen roughly by her narrow, bony shoulders. The bat continued to dart around above their heads, buzzing frantic thoughts into Tonia's mind. From the dark tunnel a few feet away they heard groaning again, this time more audible.

"My… amulet…" the snake mumbled.

Nicho forced Kaileen to look into his eyes.

"Look at me!" he demanded.

Tears still trickling down her cheeks, the kalevala did as he asked.

"Don't you want to go on? Don't you want to see if there are any more of your kind? Don't you want to see if you can find this creature that killed your family? Your friends?" Nicho asked. He knew the words he spoke would sting her heart, but he needed to say something that would get the kalevala moving. If not, they'd be in a heap of trouble!

Kaileen nodded silently.

"If you want this then **get up now**! Ransa is dead! There's nothing you can do! You must think of yourself! Fulfill her dying wish. Do you remember what it was?" he asked.

Kaileen looked at him blankly as the bat continued slowly

circling them. Nicho's grip on her shoulders softened a little.

"She said you must go on and leave the cave," he said.

After giving her a few seconds to let this sink in, he then said the single thing he hoped would help her make the right decision.

"Are you going to disrespect her by not honoring her dying wish?" he asked quietly as he stared into her dark, anguished eyes.

Kaileen shook her head as she looked down at Ransa's lifeless body, still held firmly in her arms.

"No," she whispered as fresh tears filled her eyes.

"Nicho? We need to go!" Micah said. His trembling voice was filled with worry.

Nicho nodded then looked towards the tunnel where Muscala had been sleeping. In the shadows, they could see he was just beginning to move.

"We go! We go! We go nowwww!" the bat screamed inside Tonia's head again.

"Guys, we need to go… now!" Tonia said nervously.

"Let's go," Nicho said, gently pulling Kaileen to her feet.

Before she stood up, Kaileen let Ransa's broken body slip carefully back down to the tunnel floor. Then, after one final look at her friend, Kaileen willingly followed Nicho.

The bat, seeing they were starting to follow it, began leading them in the direction opposite where the snake was. This time they ran towards the tunnel on the other side of the abyss. Behind them, they could hear the snake as it tried to slither after them.

"Come back! Give me my… amulet!" he yelled groggily, without much force.

They took care as they followed the bat around the abyss, and just when they thought they were beyond hearing the snake as he continued waking up, they heard him yell somewhere in the distance behind them.

"Aaarrrgh! Give me my amulet!"

The bat began flying faster as it led them through tunnel after tunnel. They had to walk very quickly, almost run, in order to keep up with it. Kaileen was positioned in the middle of the group, with the girls in the lead and the boys at the end. The two glowing torches lit their way.

Tonia found herself wondering how long Kaileen could keep moving at the current pace. She was still obviously very upset. It wasn't like the kalevala had many choices about where she would go or what she would do.

For a few minutes, they wove through various tunnels as only silence followed them, and before they knew it, they suddenly found themselves in a large cavern that looked familiar. It didn't take them long to realize they were in the cavern of many tunnels.

"Where are you taking us?" Diam asked.

The bat, hearing her question, but not stopping for a second as it continued leading them, replied mentally to Tonia, "Far away, away from the snake."

Tonia repeated this to Diam.

Once they entered the large cavern, they veered towards the right. As they came to the end of the cavern, they had to choose which tunnel to go into. The bat quickly led them to one on the left. As they entered the tunnel, Nicho looked behind them. He did not see Muscala yet, but he could definitely hear the angry reptile as he regained both his strength and his voice. The snake was still shouting, more and more angrily with each breath, calling for the return of his precious amulet.

They followed the flying mammal into the tunnel as it led them through the shadows like a professionally trained guide. It darted ahead of them from tunnel to tunnel with little effort, the glow from the torches obviously unnecessary for it to find its way. Tonia imagined that this nimble creature must have been flying through these tunnels since the beginning of time.

Suddenly, without warning, the bat stopped.

Tonia and Diam caught it in time, stopping also, but Kaileen, Micah, and Nicho continued going. Before they knew it, they were all bumping together like a triple-decker sandwich.

"Hey!" Diam called out. She stumbled as she was bumped from behind, which caused her to run into Tonia.

"Oops," said Nicho. "Sorry. I didn't realize you'd stopped."

After Diam bumped into Tonia, nearly knocking her over, Tonia regained her balance and peered into the darkness as she tried to locate the bat.

"What's wrong?" she asked the flying creature as she spotted it.

The bat was now flying in low circles just a few feet ahead of them. As the others regained their balance, which put a little bit of space between them, Diam's whispered voice broke the silence.

"Look!"

The others looked where Diam was pointing and gasped in disbelief.

The bat had led them through tunnel after tunnel until they didn't know which direction they were going or if they had been there before. The maze of catacombs had become nothing more than a blur of darkness to them and, although no one said it, they all feared it would take a miracle for them to escape the web of shadows they found themselves completely entangled in.

As their eyes examined the small room around them, they could not believe what they were seeing.

Could it be this easy?

Directly in front of them, shimmering like a flawless, shiny stone in the torchlight, was Still Water.

THIRTY-ONE

Everyone stared in disbelief at the motionless body of water that glimmered magically before them.

Diam's focus rolled upward as she searched for their guide. She quickly spotted it, circling in the upper area of the cavern, directly over the water.

"How did you know?" she asked out loud as she watched it go around and around.

The bat, obviously settling down now, circled slowly a few more times before it finally landed on a rock on the opposite side of the water. It looked at them curiously before focusing intently on Tonia for a few seconds.

"It says it's been watching us, following us for quite some time, since we rescued it from the spider's web. It had a feeling we were not just passing through. It also suspected that there was more to our being here," Tonia explained.

She turned and glanced at the kalevala, wondering how she was holding up. Since leaving Ransa behind, Kaileen had been very quiet, almost as if in a trance.

Suddenly they heard Muscala's ravings once again, this time from not so far away.

"Give me my amulet!" the evil beast yelled, his menacing tone echoing through the tunnels from somewhere behind them. "When I find you, I will eat you! I will eat all of you, and I will enjoy every last, torturous moment of it!"

Thirty-Two

"Where did you go, you thieving, little pestsss?" Muscala roared angrily.

"It sounds like he's feeling much better," Tonia whispered sarcastically.

"And is much closer," Diam added.

"Micah, hurry! The stones," Nicho said nervously as he remembered how Muscala had laughed at them and their weapons earlier. Another thing to keep in mind, he thought, was how much angrier Muscala was now than before. If he caught up with them, someone was bound to get hurt or killed.

Micah began rummaging in his pockets, digging for the stones. As soon as his fingers touched one, his pocket began to glow as a soft, blue aura began peeking through the fabric on his hip. Within a few seconds, they all began to hear a soft, low humming sound.

"I'll find you and kill you!" Muscala called out, closer still. "I'll rip your bodiesss limb from limb! Piece by piece, until I find my amulet!"

As Micah withdrew the blue stone from his pocket and transferred it to his other hand, the room filled with a peaceful, glow the color of the sky, which consumed the light from the torches. Kaileen gasped, her eyes transfixed on the blue light.

"Wow," she breathed quietly. "It's beautiful!"

Micah dug deeper into his pocket, finding another stone. Again his hip area began to glow, but this time it was the color of blood. As he pulled the object from his pocket, the humming sound increased. When he put the most recent stone with the blue one in his hand, the aura filling the room changed to a soft, purple color.

"Hurry! Hurry!" the bat shrieked in Tonia's head. "He hears it! The humming! He's coming! Now! Go Now! Nowwwwww!"

Tonia's eyes widened and she touched his arm. Her voice was quiet but filled with an undeniable urgency.

"Hurry Micah. He's closer now."

By the stern tone of Tonia's voice, there was no need for her to specify who 'he' was.

One last time, Micah dug into his pocket, finding the remaining three stones. He quickly wrapped his fingers around them and his pocket exploded with a colorful mixture of yellow, green and purple. He hastily withdrew the remaining stones and the humming sound in the cavern became so loud that the entire room seemed to vibrate around them. The intensity of the reverberations in the air was evident in the water as well, seen by the various ripples skirting across the top of the liquid.

He held the red and blue stones in one hand, the purple, yellow and green stones in the other, obviously nervous about putting them all together in one hand. As he looked at the others for guidance, they heard Muscala's voice bellow through the tunnels again. He was much closer now.

"I can hear you! I can *smell* you! I **will** find you!"

"Micah, hurry," Nicho whispered with a frown, sensing the questioning look in his brother's eyes. It was too late for doubts now.

Nicho gave Micah a reassuring nod as Diam agreed, "Yes, hurry!"

Without any further hesitation, Micah gently transferred all of the stones into one hand. As they clustered together with barely audible, gentle clicks, the humming noise became almost unbearable. The entire cave seemed to vibrate with its intensity.

Everyone watched as the vibrations turned the gentle ripples across the surface of the water into a jumbled, burbling mess that was surprisingly synchronized with the humming noise which now completely surrounded them.

As they stared at the water which had come to life before

their eyes, an array of colors began to swirl across its surface – first red, then orange, yellow, green, blue and purple. The colors curled beautifully in front of their eyes as they watched in silent amazement. After a few seconds, the rainbow of color suddenly disappeared, silence filled the cavern and the water became black and motionless once more.

Somewhere behind them they heard Muscala as he continued yelling for them, frighteningly close now.

"What do we do now?" Diam asked, when the darkened water blinked with a flash of bright light then began filling with color once again. This time was different than the last, however, and they stared in awe as the colors all blended together in a brilliant combination of red, yellow, orange, green, blue, and purple.

"The colors of the rainbow," Tonia whispered in disbelief.

"It was just like Ransa said," Kaileen whispered as the tears in her eyes flowed freely. Tonia glanced over at the kalevala and realized she was smiling.

The colors suddenly became very bright, forcing them to cover their eyes. Then, just as quickly, the light faded back to a soft, soothing glow.

"Now! Now!" the bat screamed at Tonia, still in her head.

Tonia turned to look at the rock where they had last seen the bat, her eyes filled with confusion.

"Now, what?" she asked out loud.

The others looked at her as the bat leaped into the air from its rock. Realizing she wasn't talking to them, they also turned to look at their small, furry guide.

"Follow! Follow me! Now!" the bat screeched in her head.

Without another word or a glance back, the flying creature dove into the rainbow pool without any signs of hesitation. As it dove into the colorful pool, the rest of the group noticed that the colors did not ripple and water did not splash. The bat had just simply… disappeared.

"Wait!" Tonia shouted, but it was too late. The bat was gone without a trace.

"It said we should follow it," Tonia told the others.

"Yes," Kaileen agreed. "We must go. Go like the bat did… like Ransa wanted."

"Are you sure?" Tonia asked, her stomach in knots. "We don't know where the bat went! We don't know where it will take us!"

"We don't have a choice, Tonia," Nicho said. "If we stay here, Muscala will kill us for sure." He paused as he glanced at Micah, then turned to Diam. "Do either of you think we have a choice?"

From only a few hundred feet away, they heard Muscala as he rapidly bridged the gap between them.

"Aahhhh, yessss! I can *smell* you! I can sssee your light!" he triumphantly taunted them.

"No," Micah said. "Diam, Tonia, Kaileen, go!"

When Tonia looked at him with nervous, doubtful eyes he shouted, "GO!"

Diam grabbed Tonia's hand as Tonia grabbed Kaileen's. The kalevala did not try to pull away. Quickly Tonia counted, "One, two, three!"

In unison, the girls all stepped into the rainbow and silently disappeared.

Nicho looked at Micah.

"Go," Micah said. "If I go first, the portal will disappear."

Nicho looked at Micah with uncertainty. He wanted to argue, to protect his brother at all costs, but he knew there was nothing he could say, or do, to change Micah's mind. Micah was the one who held the magic in his hands.

"I'll find you," the younger boy said encouragingly.

Nicho nodded and, after giving Micah a quick hug, he followed the girls into the rainbow pool and silently disappeared.

Less than a second later, Micah suddenly heard noises behind him. He looked up in time to see Muscala as he entered the small cavern, breathing heavily and staring at the glow in the pool as if in a trance.

"What are you doing?" the giant snake hissed in a demanding, angry voice as its blood-colored eyes panned across the room, darting from Micah to the bright colors in the center of the floor.

"Where are the othersss?"

"Safe," Micah said. "Away from you!"

Muscala hissed at him, suddenly noticing the Dragon's Blood amulet glowing brightly along the side of Micah's opened palm, blending in perfectly with the rest of the shimmering stones.

"My amulet!" Muscala hissed with satisfaction. The reptile's smile widened as he stared at the luminous red stone. Hungry for success, revenge and a delectable treat, he began inching his way towards the boy who had turned his world upside-down.

"Pardon me," Micah said loudly, shattering the spell.

His concentration broken, Muscala stopped and glared at him.

"You were a most gracious host," Micah said with obvious sarcasm in his voice, "but our wonderful stay has come to an end."

As Muscala's eyes filled with anger and hatred, Micah added, "I'm sorry but I must go now."

Before Muscala could comprehend the meaning of his words, Micah bowed at the reptile and joined the others. Without a glance back, he stepped forward and disappeared into the rainbow.

About The Author

MJAllaire grew up in South Florida. After graduating high school, she joined the Navy and ended up in Pearl Harbor, Hawaii, where she met and married a submariner. Three children and ten years later, they moved to Connecticut.

She always had a love of reading and wanted her children to feel the same way. Her oldest son took an interest in dragons, but she had difficulty finding books for him so she decided to write one, keeping him in mind.

Newly divorced, raising three children and working a full-time job, she wanted to be a positive example for her children. She wanted them to know, above all, you can do anything you put your mind to.

For more information, please visit any or all of her websites below:

www.mjallaire.com
www.denicalisdragonchronicles.com
www.grizlegirlproductions.com
www.getkidstoread.org
www.booksbyteenauthors.com

Other books in this series are:

The Prisoner:
Denicalis Dragon Chronicles - Book Two

Dragon's Tear:
Denicalis Dragon Chronicles - Book Three

Dragon's Breath:
Denicalis Dragon Chronicles - Book Four

Please visit us at:
www.denicalisdragonchronicles.com
www.mjallaire.com